death in
reel time

also by brynn bonner

Paging the Dead

death in reel time

A FAMILY HISTORY MYSTERY

brynn bonner

GALLERY BOOKS

NEW YORK   LONDON   TORONTO   SYDNEY   NEW DELHI

G

A Division of Simon & Schuster, Inc.
1230 Avenue of the Americas
New York, NY 10020

First Gallery Books trade paperback edition March 2014

GALLERY BOOKS and colophon are registered trademarks of Simon & Schuster, Inc.

For information about special discounts for bulk purchases, please contact Simon & Schuster Special Sales at 1-866-506-1949 or business@simonandschuster.com.

The Simon & Schuster Speakers Bureau can bring authors to your live event. For more information or to book an event contact the Simon & Schuster Speakers Bureau at 1-866-248-3049 or visit our website at www.simonspeakers.com.

Manufactured in the United States of America

10 9 8 7 6 5 4 3 2 1

Library of Congress Cataloging-in-Publication Data is on file.

ISBN 978-1-4516-6187-3
ISBN 978-1-4516-6189-7 (ebook)

To Eleanor Harris Bonner, beloved and missed

acknowledgments

To my cohorts of the Weymouth 7: Margaret Maron, Sarah Shaber, Diane Chamberlain, Kathy Trocheck (aka Mary Kay Andrews), Katy Munger, and Alex Sokoloff, who provide brainstorming, camaraderie, encouragement, and some of the most ridiculous Balderdash definitions ever put forth.

To members of the Cary Writers' Group, for their input, especially Jo Ann Hoffman, beta reader extraordinaire.

To my agent, Cynthia Manson, and to Gallery editor Micki Nuding.

To my family, for their unwavering support.

And to all the past amateur genealogists in our family lines, thanks for marking the trail.

death in reel time

one

I FELT RIDICULOUS.

This was no way for a full-grown professional woman to present herself. I moved the gift bow someone had stuck on my forehead over to my temple, where I hoped it might make me look like an exotic island woman wearing a flower behind one ear. I sighed as I caught sight of myself in the mirror. It was a wasted hope.

"My mother used to tell me I was the greatest gift she ever got," I groused, "but even she didn't expect me to come gift-wrapped."

"Sophreena Angelica McClure, you need to get over yourself," my business partner and second mama, Esme Sabatier, scolded, adjusting the ribbon that ran across her ample chest like a beauty contestant's sash. "I am all about my dignity but you don't hear me complaining, do you? Anyway, we're not the gift; it's our genealogical services these wonderful friends are giving Olivia. This is just the presentation. Get into the spirit of the thing, girly."

Easy for Esme to say. She's a statuesque woman-of-a-certain-age with exotic features and a warm latte complexion. I'm shorter than Esme—much shorter. And small. My narrow body doesn't allow for frills. So while Esme looked festive, I looked like an exhausted child who'd confused her directions at the Maypole dance and gotten hopelessly entangled in the streamers.

"Esme's right, Sophreena," Marydale Thompson said, fluffing the multiple ribbons festooning my upper torso. "I know this is silly, but just go along with it, please? Olivia's wanted to trace her family history for as long as I've known her, and do *not* ask me how many long years that's been. She and your mother and me were friends since all you kids were little bitty things. Let's make this a special surprise for her, okay?"

I made an attitude adjustment and stretched a smile across my face.

Marydale Thompson had promised my dying mother she'd look after me, a vow she took seriously. She continues to hover over me even now that I'm in my thirties. And I'm grateful, most of the time anyway. Marydale's a person you want in your corner. When Olivia Clement had been diagnosed with breast cancer it was Marydale who organized a brigade to bring meals, drive her to treatments, and perform other acts of kindness. Now that the treatments were over and Olivia was on the road to recovery, her friends wanted to give her one more gift—me and Esme. Or our expertise, anyway.

Not to brag, but Esme and I run a primo genealogical service. We ferret out information other researchers could never unearth. Every once in a while we disinter long-buried family secrets in the process. Which can be a sticky wicket sometimes, especially since Esme and I have our own secret.

We're successful, in part, because we sometimes get help from the great beyond. Esme has the gift, or *maybe* it's the gift; maybe it's just heightened intuition. Could simply be Esme's own subconscious leaking through. Who knows? Even Esme isn't sure. But whatever you call it, it is maddeningly sporadic and the signs and messages she gets are often incomprehensible. Still, there are those stunning occasions when something spot-on comes through and we reveal a story no hours of poring over records in a dusty archive could ever have uncovered.

We guard this secret closely. In the genealogy world, where documentation and hard evidence are highly valued, this kind of folderol—getting information straight from the dead horse's mouth—is heresy. We'd be drummed out of the corps. Only our four closest friends—the four others in our genealogy club—know about Esme's special faculty. Marydale is one of those chosen few.

And so is Colette "Coco" Newsome, who at that moment opened the door from Olivia's living room a crack and stage-whispered, "Are y'all about ready? What's taking so long?"

Coco was dressed in her signature style: a long, gauzy skirt, a riotously colored tunic, and lots of jangling jewelry. Suddenly my ribbons and bows seemed positively staid.

"We're all set," Marydale said. "Are Beth and Daniel in there with Olivia?"

Coco snaked her hand through the doorway and beckoned impatiently. "Yes, yes, we're all here—waiting and waiting. Come on!"

Olivia was on the sofa with her two adult children. She looked expectant and more than a little perplexed at the sight of Esme and me in our strange accoutrement. Marydale made the presentation speech, then Esme and I were on.

I curtsied and Esme rolled her hand and bowed like a magician about to perform a trick.

"On behalf of all your friends," Marydale said, handing Olivia a card, "we give you the services of the best genealogists in the state—or perhaps the whole country—Ms. Sophreena McClure and her able assistant, Ms. Esme Sabatier. They're going to help you trace your family history and all of us in the club will pitch in, too."

Olivia's face lit up. Even her hair, which post-chemo had come back curly and white as lamb's wool, seemed to be illuminated.

"Isn't this great, Mom?" Beth asked. "You've wanted to do this for years."

"And it gets me off the hook," Daniel said. "I've done some fumbling around on the Internet but I had no idea what I was doing and figuring out who's who and how they're all kin makes my eyeballs do that cartoon thing where they circle in opposite directions."

"Not so fast, Daniel," Olivia said, patting him on the leg. "This will be a family project. I'll use it as a handy excuse to spend more time with you and Beth."

Anyone acquainted with this family would know that was no hardship. Beth and Daniel adored their mother and had been devoted to her throughout her health crisis. Beth had taken an extended leave of absence from her job as assistant principal at Morningside High School to be with her mother throughout her treatments. And Daniel, who was an attorney in nearby Chapel Hill, popped over daily to help out.

I'd known Beth and Daniel most of my life. They were older than I and we weren't close, but were friends the way the children of parents' friends often are. Like cousins, I'm told, though I have little personal experience with that relationship since my parents were both only children.

I'd idolized Beth when we were growing up. She was a class act. Beautiful in a refined way and, on top of that, super-smart and good at everything she tried. In high school she'd been that rare breed, a popular girl who was well regarded across the spectrum, not just with the in-crowd. The jocks, outsiders, Goths, and nerds all had liked her, too.

And Daniel? Be still my heart. The boy every girl had a crush on but didn't dare bring home to meet the parents. He had an edge, though he hadn't earned one. Not that I knew of anyway, but he had an air of imminent danger about him, veneered over, just barely, with an easygoing charm.

Olivia scooted to the edge of the sofa. "I'm going to get all blubbery. Tell me what I need to do to get started before I disgrace myself."

"First thing is to find out what you know," I said. "So that's what we'll do today. And Esme and I will want to go through all your family memorabilia to see what information we can glean."

"Oh dear," Olivia said. "I don't have much here. There are boxes of stuff in my uncle and aunt's old house out in Crawford. They were the last of the generation. They left everything to me. But Aunt Celestine passed on just before I was diagnosed and I haven't had a chance to go out there and sort through everything."

"Surprise again," Daniel said, walking over to pull away the bedsheet that had concealed boxes stacked behind the sofa. "Beth and I drove out to Aunt Celestine's house last week and gathered up everything we thought might be useful." He tapped the top of a disintegrating cardboard box, which was so the opposite of archival it made me cringe. "Oh, and by the way, I brought back Uncle Riley's gun collection, too. I figured they didn't need to be out there in that empty house. But not to worry, I know how you feel about guns. They're locked up out in your studio."

"And you'll never guess what else," Beth said. "Daniel contacted the pastor at the church that sponsored your missionary grandparents and asked if they had any information about them and . . ." She gestured toward Daniel to pick up the story.

"And the pastor's wife was pretty psyched to hear from me. Seems the old reverend's wife had been saving some boxes of your grandparents' things for years and she'd made the new wife promise not to throw them out in case someone came looking for them someday." He swept a hand to encompass more boxes in equally alarming condition. "And we did! And here they are!"

Marydale rose and said, "Good, then. I'll leave y'all to it. I need to get back to the shop." She snapped her fingers and her two Westies, Sprocket and Gadget, scampered over to get their leashes clipped on.

"I gotta go, too," Coco said. "Pottery's not gonna fire itself. Call us, Sophreena, and give us our assignments. You know the ancient-history club is on standby."

I smiled and nodded. Winston's shrew of an ex-wife, Patsy, had given us that sobriquet when Winston had gone digging into an area of his family history that she'd just as soon he'd kept hidden. Contrarians that we all are, we adopted it as a badge of honor. I'd already worked up a plan, dividing the family lines so we could get Olivia a good start on the project, and after I talked with Olivia I'd tweak the lists and drop by Marydale's shop to deliver hers and Coco's.

Marydale's papercraft shop, Keepsake Corner, is located right in the heart of downtown Morningside, about a mile from Olivia's house. It's my happy place. I go there often to get my fix of artisan papers and heritage scrapbooking supplies. It's right next door to the Morningside Craft Co-op, where Coco sells her pottery wares. Marydale and Coco had opted to walk over on this glorious North Carolina fall day. I was envious.

Esme and I shed our gift-wrapping and pulled up chairs to begin our initial interview. Normally at this point in the process Esme would have begged off, claiming pressing business elsewhere. She doesn't much care for the one-on-one with clients, but Olivia was an exception. She and Esme belonged to the same church and Olivia had been among the first to make Esme feel welcome when she'd moved here six years ago to join me in my genealogy services business.

Not that I'd been looking to take on a partner. I was just starting out and didn't have enough clients to support my own self. I met Esme down in Louisiana on my first big job, and though I found her a little scary in the beginning, I came to like her. A few months after the job was over she contacted me and told me we were to be partners in the business. She announced it as a fait accompli, and though I'm normally a cautious and analytical person, I agreed immediately. I still haven't figured out why I did that, but I've learned over the years that getting messages from the great beyond isn't Esme's only gift. She can also hoodoo people into agreeing to things before they even know what's happening. Especially me.

After Marydale and Coco were gone we talked logistics for a bit and decided that for the next session we'd set up shop in Olivia's dining room, since working at home was easier for her. Her recovery was going well and she was getting her strength back, but her stamina was lagging.

"We'll get you started on your heritage scrapbooks," I said, "but to streamline the process Esme and I will take a few of the boxes of artifacts home with us each day. We'll organize the material and put it into proper containers. Our task for today is a preliminary interview, and the first question we always ask is if there's any *particular* thing you want to know about your family history."

"Absolutely," Olivia replied immediately. "I want to know about my father. He ran off before I was born and I know very little about him. He was a forbidden subject in my family. What I eventually pieced together was that he ran off to avoid being drafted into World War Two. It brought terrible shame on the family. I'd like to know what became of him."

"Okay, tell me everything you know about your family," I said, grabbing a yellow legal pad and pen from my bag.

"Starting with what?" Olivia asked. "I don't know where to jump in."

"Just tell it however it comes to you," I said. "We'll help you sort it all out and make sense of it later."

I had my pen at the ready, but just then a loud *crack* split the air. I lost my grip on my pen, my legal pad, and my wits. Esme and I both startled and ducked down, clutching the arms of our chairs.

"Tony's home," Olivia announced breezily, craning to look out the front window.

"Sorry," Beth said, bending down to look at us, her face at a tilt. "His motorcycle needs some engine work. It backfires at the most inopportune times. That's Tony Barrett. He's one of my former students from Morningside High."

Esme and I both sucked in a breath as we sat up straight. I pushed my glasses up on my nose and adjusted my jacket, freeing the button from where it had caught on the chair cushion. This had not been my day for decorum.

"Tony's become a filmmaker," Beth went on, "and he's come back to make a documentary about Morningside. He's been staying in Mom's basement."

A moment later a young man I gauged to be in his early twenties stood framed in the living room doorway, his motorcycle helmet cradled under one arm. He had the brooding good looks of a brat-pack movie actor. His dark hair fell casually over one eye and he scooped it back and gave us all a white-toothed grin.

"Were you surprised?" he asked Olivia.

"You knew about this, too?" she asked.

"Yeah, it's cool." He walked over to Esme and me and put out his hand. "I'm Tony, and I know who you two are."

"Are we famous or infamous?" Esme asked dryly, shaking the proffered hand.

"Fame and glory all the way," Tony said, reaching across to give my hand its turn. "Listen, I know we just met and you don't know me," he said, "but I wanted to ask if I could elbow in on this project. A buddy of mine is doing these family history scrapbook videos and it's been a great gig for him to support his other work. I'd love to have one for my portfolio and I was thinking maybe I could do one for Olivia. It could be my gift to thank her for letting me roost here for a while."

I considered. "I suppose," I said, looking over at Esme, who stuck out her lower lip and wiggled her head to and fro before nodding her assent.

"Great," he said. "When are you gonna start?"

"We were just about to begin the initial interview," I said, retrieving my pen and pad from the floor.

"Can I grab my camera?" he asked, jerking a thumb over his shoulder.

I turned to Olivia. "Are you okay with this?"

"Sure, why not?" she said. "Though if I'd known I was going to have all this excitement today I would have primped a little more this morning." She smoothed the front of her red T-shirt and patted at her hair.

After Tony left the room I worried that I'd agreed too soon to his involvement. Video scrapbooking was a new trend, one I'd wanted to explore, but I wondered how the presence of the camera might affect the interviews and how much it might slow down the process. Esme must have been having the same second thoughts as she whispered out of the side of her mouth, "Just so he knows, he works on our schedule, not the other way round."

I was pleasantly surprised when Tony came back a moment later with only a small camera mounted on a slim tripod. I'd been anticipating an intrusive shoulder-mounted camera and an array of hot lights. He set up quickly in an out-of-the-way spot by the window and asked us to pretend he wasn't there.

Though I suspected that might be easier said than done, after a few minutes I forgot about the camera and it seemed Olivia did, too, though she was still struggling to find a way into her story.

"Let's try this," I said. "Start off with 'I was born in . . .'"

She nodded. "I was born in Crawford, North Carolina—that's about seventy miles from here—in January 1944. My mother's name was Irene Damaris Lockwood Hargett. People called her Renny. She was born August 17, 1924, and she died in 1981. I never knew her parents, my grandparents. Their names were Thomas Lockwood and Victoria Lockwood. I don't know middle names and I don't know my grandmother's birth name, nor any dates for them. They were foreign missionaries and they died in a ferry accident somewhere overseas just after I was born. They never set eyes on me.

"My father, the black sheep of his family, was named John Lamont Hargett. I think most people called him Johnny. He ran off before I was born, so he never saw me, either. His parents died young, too, so I didn't have any actual grandparents in my life. But my father's older brother, Riley Hargett, was like a grandfather to me. He and his wife, Celestine, lived right next door to Mama and me. They never had children of their own and they doted on me. I loved them dearly. Riley died in 1985 and Celestine passed a little over a year ago, at the golden age of ninety-seven. She lived alone in her own house until her dying day. That's about all I know."

"So if my math is right, your parents were very young when you were born," I said.

"My mother was nineteen," Olivia said. "Not too unusual for those times, I guess, but she'd be considered too young today. These days the gals are waiting longer to start their families, sometimes too long." I caught a sidelong glance in Beth's direction before Olivia went on. "I don't know my father's age. I really know very little about him. It was like the whole family just tried to erase him after he showed himself a coward."

There was a noise in the front hall and we all turned in unison as Beth's husband, Blaine, appeared in the doorway, looking preoccupied. "I figured I'd find you here," he said to Beth.

"Yes, we're giving Mom her present," Beth said, her voice bright.

"Oh yeah, happy birthday, Olivia," Blaine said absently.

"Not my birthday," Olivia said with a weak smile, "but thanks, Blaine."

Most townspeople would say Beth was lucky to have snagged the most eligible bachelor in these parts. Blaine Branch was the scion of a rich family and was handsome to boot. And as the owner of a large sporting goods store called The Sporting Life, he was a pretty big cheese in the Morningside business community. Still, I thought Blaine had gotten the better end of the bargain.

He'd given the rest of us only a cursory nod when he came in, and he went on conducting his business with Beth as if we weren't there, which earned him a checkmark for bad form in my tally book.

"Remember, Alan's coming in tonight. I promised we'd have a nice supper for him. Could you make one of your good dishes and make sure the guest room's all squared away?"

"I will," Beth said, turning back to her mother. "You remember Alan Corrigan, our college friend? He was Blaine's fraternity brother. He's coming for a visit."

"Oh, yes, Alan," Olivia said, managing to pack a lot of ambiguity into those three little words.

"We're just wrapping it up here," Beth assured Blaine. "I think Mom's about due for a rest. Tony and I have an interview set up with Charlie Martin in about an hour. I'll be home after we finish that."

"Charlie Martin?" Blaine said, searching his mental database. "That old geezer you hired to put the flowers in our front beds?"

"Charlie Martin," Olivia jumped in. "The older gentleman who is one of the few remaining World War Two vets around and who is a whiz of a fix-it man and a talented gardener. Plus, he's a very nice fellow."

"Sure," Blaine said, tipping his head back to accept Olivia's subtle reprimand, then turning to Tony. "I thought you said this film thing would only involve Beth a few hours a week. This is starting to eat up a big chunk of time."

Tony shrugged. "She's great with people. They open up to her." He tilted his head, letting his hair fall over his forehead, and fed Blaine a look that could only be described as defiant.

Blaine dismissed him with a scowl and turned back to Beth. "Just make sure dinner's done on time. Why don't you fix that shrimp-and-grits thing you do? Alan likes that."

"Sure," Beth said. "I could do that." Her smile never faded, but by the way her body tensed I could tell she wasn't happy.

I'm no chef, but Esme's a foodie and I saw her eyebrows raise slightly, so I knew what he was asking was probably not a whip-it-up-quick dish. I was surprised at how different Beth seemed around her husband. The calm, confident woman of five minutes ago had now devolved into a rabbity girl.

"I'll help, Beth," Daniel said. "I'll shop while you and Tony are filming with Charlie."

I noted that Daniel pointedly avoided looking at Blaine.

"Good, then," Blaine said, checking his watch. "I gotta get back to work. You all have fun with your"—he hesitated, then gave a vague wave of his hand—"whatever it is you're doing here." He gave a general nod to match the one he'd given us in greeting and Beth got up to walk him out. From where I was sitting I could see past the hallway to the front door. I watched as they said their good-byes. Blaine took Beth's upper arm and pulled her to him for a kiss. After she closed the door behind him she stood for a moment rubbing her arms as if to warm herself. I wondered if the crisp fall day had turned nippy. She looked up and our eyes met. She smiled and dropped her eyes. I felt heat creeping into my face. I'd been caught being a voyeur. I quickly looked away and got back to business.

"We're yours for the next two weeks," I said to Olivia, "then we have a job down in Wilmington and we'll be away for maybe as long as a month. Esme and I will take three or four of these boxes with us for tonight and archive them for our next session, whenever you'd like that to be."

"Could you come again tomorrow?" Olivia asked. "Maybe late morning?"

We agreed on 11 a.m. and Olivia went upstairs to rest. Beth made a cup of tea to take up to her while Esme and I shuffled through the boxes to decide which ones to take on this trip. Tony had gone off to round up his gear for the afternoon's filming and Daniel sat at a corner desk scribbling a grocery list for Beth's dinner party. I sighed. Daniel's immediate offer to step in and help his sister in a pinch had made me wish, not for the first time, that I had a brother.

When Beth came back she apologized for the hubbub. "We'll make sure there aren't so many interruptions next time, I promise."

She'd barely gotten the last word out of her mouth when we heard a car door slam outside. Beth looked out the window and mumbled something under her breath. "I'm so sorry, excuse me," she said, already heading for the door.

We watched as she practically ran down the sidewalk to intercept a man getting out of a sporty car. I don't know modern cars much. Ask me about old autos like Packards, Edsels, '57 Chevys and I can rattle off makes and models. It's a skill set I developed while analyzing old family photos. But anything past the fin era and I'm clueless. But I could tell this one looked expensive.

At first Esme and I tried to look busy and pretend we weren't watching, but soon we were standing there with Daniel, blatantly staring out the window. When the man turned toward the house I saw it was Peyton Branch, Blaine's younger brother. He and Beth were by the car and Peyton was gesticulating wildly, his face red. Beth was trying to calm him down, but with little effect.

"Those damn Branches," Daniel said, his fists clenched at his sides. "Blaine wants to throw his own sister to the wolves and Peyton's here bullying mine."

Peyton was a history teacher and an assistant coach at our alma mater, Morningside High. He and I had gone through school together, he being a grade ahead of me, and we'd been friends during our undergraduate years in Chapel Hill. He wasn't as handsome as Blaine and he wasn't such a smooth operator, but I'd always found him a congenial, down-to-earth guy. I'd never seen him like this. He definitely had a lather up about something.

"Should one of us go out there?" I asked.

"Not just yet," Daniel said with a sigh. "Beth will be ticked off if we don't let her handle whatever it is. She thinks she ought to be able to handle anything that comes her way."

The argument continued but Peyton appeared to simmer down as Beth made calming gestures, smoothing the air with her hands. Finally he got back into his car and drove away. Beth hung her head and pinched the bridge of her nose.

"You know how Mom's obsessed about finding out why her father ran off?" Daniel asked, his eyes fixed on his sister. "Well, there's way worse things than having a man disappear from a woman's life; sometimes the bad news is he stays."

two

ESME'S ON A SMOOTHIE KICK, SO MOST MORNINGS MY ALARM
clock is preempted by the whir of the blender. Not that I'm
complaining; the smoothies are delicious and way healthier
than the lumberjack breakfasts she used to serve up. Given
my small frame even one extra pound makes my clothes fit
funny.

I crawled out of bed and pulled on my work-at-home
uniform of jeans and T-shirt. Normally I try to dress profes-
sionally with clients, but Olivia didn't need convincing that
I'm good at what I do. She was my mother's friend and she
knows what motivates me to do quality work.

I brushed my teeth and tamed my hair back into a pony-
tail, the latter no easy task. I'd gotten my unruly auburn hair
from my father's mixed Celtic heritage. From my mother's
side I'd gotten my amber-brown eyes and slight build, though
the jury's still out on where on the globe these traits origi-
nated. The circumstances of my mother's adoption and her
ethnic identity remain shrouded in mystery despite all her

digging—and all mine. She'd wanted desperately to know where she came from and to find out about her people. Though she searched for her whole adult life, she never found much. I continue her quest, armed with lots more skill and training, and with Esme as my secret weapon. Yet answers elude me as well.

I slipped on my glasses and gazed out my bedroom window at our backyard. A gust of wind picked up a scattering of multicolored leaves. They lifted and swirled before skittering to the fence and joining up with a pile trying to smother the shrubs. I'd need to take some time this weekend to rake. Maybe I could get Jack to help.

Jack Ford is another member of our loosely organized genealogy club. He's also my best male pal. A part of me wishes we were more than that, a realization that has only lately come to me. But I haven't let on to him. I know what romantic complications can do to a friendship.

As if thinking about Jack had summoned him, I heard the distinctive growl of his diesel pickup pulling into the driveway. He's a landscape architect with a growing business, and did I mention he's really good-looking?

I headed down the stairs and reached the kitchen just as he did.

"Hey, you're up," he said. "I wasn't sure you would be, from the way you sounded on the phone last night."

"I'm upright and breathing room air, as nurses say, but I'm tired. We organized Olivia's family artifacts last night and I spent an hour or so on the Internet searching public records. Then we watched a movie, which put us to bed late. Whose idea was that movie anyway?" I asked Esme.

"Yours, and it wasn't worth the effort of keeping my eyelids up. No more subtitles." She handed me a glass of smoothie and lifted the blender jar in Jack's direction as an offering.

He put up a hand. "Thanks, but I had a man's breakfast, steel-cut oatmeal. Sticks to your ribs." He patted his midsection. Jack is short, for a guy anyway, though he's still a head taller than me. And in the interest of full reporting I should note he's well muscled.

"I'm on my way to work, but I've got a few mums left over from that job I did at the town hall," he said. "You want me to put them on your front porch?"

"Sure," I said. "I never turn down free flowers."

We heard a "knock, knock" call from the front hall, which was strictly perfunctory since Winston Lovett, the elder in our little tribe of genealogy buffs, was already inside. We have an open-door policy with our close friends, since our private rooms are upstairs and they're not likely to catch us in our skivvies.

Winston was carrying something that looked promising, wrapped in a piece of cheesecloth. "I baked this morning," he said as he came through the kitchen doorway. "Can y'all use a loaf of sourdough?"

"Sophreena never turns down free flowers and I never turn down free bread. Thank you, Winston," Esme said, nodding for him to set the loaf on the table. She held up the blender and raised her eyebrows.

Winston put out his hand in exactly the same way Jack had. "I'm good," he said. "Already had a big slab of the bread with jam."

Old habits die hard. Winston had gotten up before the roosters every morning for nearly thirty years to bake for Sugar Magnolias, the shop he'd owned in downtown

Morningside. Though he doesn't have to do it at ungodly hours anymore, he still gets the urge to bake, for which we are profoundly grateful—he shares generously.

"Was Olivia surprised when you gave her the present?" he asked.

"Yes, very," I said. "She's really excited about the whole thing. Which makes me want to do as much as we can to get her started, because you're never really done with your family history; there's always more to learn."

He held up a hand. "I know, as you've said many times, it's a process, not a project. I'm just happy my kids and grandkids have gotten into it; they'll keep it going long after I'm gone."

"With different technologies at their fingertips. In fact, we're stepping it up a little on this one." I told him about Beth's former student's plan to video our findings. "This'll be a good opportunity. We've had some requests for video scrapbooks in the past, but I haven't taken the time to learn the craft. Maybe Tony can teach us some stuff."

Esme harrumphed. "And maybe we can teach him a thing or two."

"What has he done to get you in such a snit?" I asked. "I like him."

"Nothing—yet," Esme said, puckering her lips, "but soon enough he'll do something that'll irritate me, I have no doubt."

"I remember that kid," Jack said. "He used to work at the one-hour photo lab at the drugstore when he was in high school. He was trouble looking for a place to happen back then."

"Beth has him staying with her mother, so she must think

he's okay," I said. "He's interviewing people all around town. Yesterday he and Beth were going out to talk to a World War Two vet named Charlie Martin."

"How is old Charlie?" Winston asked. "I haven't seen him in a while."

"You know him?" I asked.

"Sure I do," Winston said. "Everybody knows Charlie."

"I don't," I said. "And I thought I knew nearly everyone in Morningside, or at least knew of them."

Winston chuffed a laugh. "He's a bit of an eccentric. Ask our good friend Detective Denny about Charlie. He's had to roust him several times about carrying an old rusty pistol around with him. For protection, he says, like Morningside's Gotham City or something."

"I know him, too," Jack said. "He's a character. He's gotta be pushing ninety, though you'd never know it to watch him work a shovel or wield a hoe. He's self-taught, but the old dude knows more than I do about horticulture and he's a good handyman. He can fix about anything. He rides a bicycle around town that he's rigged up to pull a lawn cart behind. I'm not too surprised the name doesn't register. He keeps pretty much to himself."

"Well, apparently he's willing to talk with Tony and Beth," Esme said.

"Oh, Charlie would do 'bout anything for Beth Branch," Winston said. "She's sort of adopted him, I think. When she found out he was a World War Two vet she talked him into visiting some of the history classes to speak to the kids. Yep, he's a strange old bird, but he's interesting once you can get him talking."

"I like that," Esme said. "Some people are too quick to dismiss old folks. Like Beth's husband. He didn't seem to have any respect at all for Charlie Martin."

"Or anything, really," I said. "He was dismissive about the whole idea of the film. And he was pretty condescending about our project with Olivia, too. Maybe he's just an equal-opportunity thundercloud ready to rain on everybody's parade."

"Blaine can be that," Winston said with a sigh. "He's a little full of himself sometimes. But he comes from a good family and gives lots to the community. Donates uniforms to the Little Leaguers and all such as that."

"I'm not so sure that's his doing," Jack said. "His business partner, Bonnie Foster, lives in the condo next to mine. From what she's told me I think the community involvement is more her idea than his."

I knew Bonnie Foster, but only casually. We'd had a yoga class together, but since social chatting during meditation was frowned upon we hadn't interacted much. I did know that she was a lanky, athletic blonde with a deep, sultry voice, and I didn't especially like that she lived right next door to Jack.

"Blaine Branch may be citizen of the year for all I know," Esme said. "I'm just saying he's just not keen on Tony's project. Or ours. Probably because both take up Beth's time."

"He seemed distracted," I said. "Maybe that's all it was. A serious illness can put a lot of strain on a family."

"Ah, you're right," Esme said with a sigh. "How Beth and her husband get on is their business. As my mama used to say, you shouldn't go poking your nose into other people's family matters unless you're willing to get it punched. And what do I do? I go work with a genealogist who makes her living poking her nose in!"

As Beth had promised, the dining room at Olivia's house was set up for work when we arrived. The scrapbooking supplies Marydale had brought as part of the gift were stacked at the end of the table, the remaining boxes of memorabilia neatly corralled in the corner.

"Is this okay?" Beth asked.

"Perfect," I said. "How'd your shrimp and grits come out last night?"

"Delicious. And that's not bragging because it was all Daniel's doing. He loves to cook and he's so much better at it than I am. Speaking of which, he wants to have you all over for supper tomorrow as thanks for everything you've all done for Mom. He's already gotten yeses from Marydale, Coco, Winston, and Jack." She ticked them off on her fingers as she spoke. "I know it's last minute, but can you two make it?"

"Count us in," Esme said, without consulting me.

Olivia came down just then, eager to get straight to business. Tony had set a camera up in the corner of the room and given Beth instructions about where we were to all sit and how to start the recording. She clicked it on and we began.

"First off, credit where credit is due," I said. "The other members of the club are helping with the research and they'll each be taking a family line. But to get us started I did some preliminary research last night. And here's what I know so far from the public records available online: Your mother,

Irene Damaris Lockwood, married your father, John Lamont Hargett, in October of 1941. Your mother was seventeen and your father was nineteen."

"I wonder if her parents approved of the marriage. They would have had to sign for her with her being so young, wouldn't they?" Olivia asked.

"Well, you can't assume that," I said. "In some cases when a couple ran off and somehow managed to get someone to marry them without consent, the parents didn't want to cause a scandal by moving for an annulment or anything, since the woman would already be compromised." I chose the last word carefully.

"I see what you mean," Olivia mused. "I think Mama's parents must have been pretty starchy folks. They probably wouldn't have wanted to haul a ruined daughter back home to their congregation. Mama never talked a whole lot about them. I think she loved them, but she just didn't like to talk about them. I had the feeling there was some hurt between them some way or other. I know she was born in China and spent her early years there and I think those were happy times. She shared lots of stories about that time. But even then it was more about the places and other people she'd known than about her Ba-Ba and Ma-Ma, as she called them."

"We'll likely learn more about things as we go along," I said. "There were lots of letters in the boxes Esme and I went through last night. And your aunt Celestine kept a diary for years, did you know that?"

"Oh, yes. Her *book,* she called it. Every night after supper she'd do up the dishes and tidy the kitchen, then off she'd go to write in her book. I hate to admit this, even now, but I used to sneak around and try to find it, hoping to read her secrets. But apparently she had a very good hiding place. I never did find the darn thing."

"The *things*," I corrected. "We've found thirty-six notebooks so far. She started keeping a diary when she got married and kept at it pretty steadily, until shortly before she died. Lots to read through. Now, as for your father, he disappears from the public records in 1943. No account of him on census records, never held a driver's license or bought property. Nothing. It may be safe to assume he died shortly after he left your mother, though I wasn't able to find a death certificate, not yet anyway."

"I suspected as much," Olivia said. "Still, I'd like to know where and how he died."

"I'll keep digging," I said. "But if he was on the run he may not have had identification. He may have been a John Doe case. You need to prepare for the possibility that we'll never know what happened to him, but we'll certainly find out everything we can. Now, back a generation. Your grandparents on the Hargett side were John Corley Hargett and Gertrude Conner Hargett. They were farmers and apparently led a simple life. I have names, birth, marriage, and death dates."

"I remember Uncle Riley talking about them some," Olivia said, studying the names on the rudimentary family tree I'd created for her last night with my genealogy program. So far it was more like a family sapling.

"As for your uncle Riley, his full name was Riley Garson Hargett. He was born in 1915, so he was about seven years older than your father. He tried to enlist in the army in World War Two, but was rejected due to a heart murmur. He went to work at the post office in Crawford, filling the position of a mail carrier who'd been drafted. Riley worked at the PO for the next thirty years, until he retired."

I glanced up to see Tony passing by in the front hall. He stopped short and put his head around the archway. "Did I hear Crawford?" he asked.

"Yes," Olivia said. "That's where I was born and raised."

"I heard you say that yesterday," Tony said, stepping into the room. "I've got a film that was made in Crawford that you might be interested in."

"A film?" Olivia asked.

"Yeah, back during the thirties and forties, movie companies would go to small towns and film people going about their regular business. You know, like buying stuff in the hardware store, working in tobacco barns, or filling up their cars at the gas station. Or kids eating ice cream cones, riding bikes, or playing with their dogs. Everyday-life stuff. Then they'd splice it all together and give it a two-week run at the local movie house, charging a nickel to come see it. I've studied probably a hundred of these old films. It's where I got the idea for my homage to Morningside. The one from Crawford was made in the early forties. I could burn you a copy if you'd like."

"I'd love to see it," Olivia said. "Maybe I'll see people I know."

"I'll make two copies," Tony said, nodding to Esme and me. "Now I'm off to the art co-op to film your friend Coco throwing pottery." He hesitated. "Man, I hope she meant on the wheel and not at me." He gave us a grin before hustling out the door.

"He's too cute by half," Esme muttered.

We heard him exchange hellos with someone on the front porch and a moment later Daniel came in, carrying a bag that smelled like lunch. "Did I miss the party?" he asked.

"Just about," Beth said, "but we can give you a quick recap."

"I can't stay long. I'm meeting a client at a commercial space on River Road. He's only in town for the day and wants to see the place. Building's butt-ugly and an eyesore to the community. I'm embarrassed to be representing anybody who'd buy it, but what are ya gonna do? Us poor slubs gotta make a living, right?"

"You're a successful attorney, Daniel. I hardly think you qualify as a poor slub," Beth said.

"Yeah, yeah," he said, drawing up a chair. "Can I eat while we talk? I'll share."

"Sure, honey," Olivia said. "But I don't like you eating junk. Let me fix you something."

"Mom, it's not junk. It's an all-organic veggie wrap with goat cheese and fresh herbs. Friend of mine has a food truck that serves up all farm-direct, healthful stuff."

"Esme and I ate before we came over," I said, taking in the aroma. "I'm regretting that now. You'll have to tell me where I can flag down this truck."

"Um-hm," Esme said, reaching over to steal a nibble that broke off as he cut the wrap into medallions. "This fella can come park his rig right in our driveway. And while we're on the subject of food," she said, reaching over to grab a napkin from Daniel's bag, "you all need to know that once we start the scrapbooks there will be a strict no-food-or-drink policy in here. Everybody got that?" She looked around the table, swiping at her fingers.

"Aye, aye, captain," Daniel said, snapping a salute.

Esme smiled, but I knew she was dead serious. Once the scrapbooking started, pity the poor fool who tried to bring so much as a cup of coffee into the room, even if it was Olivia, the client, in her own house.

We worked for another hour, interviewing Olivia in more depth to mine tidbits of information she might not have known she possessed. We asked about school affiliations, churches, family friends, houses, automobiles, and community events. Sometimes Olivia seemed startled when a memory would pop up in response to our prompts.

After a while we could see her energy flagging, and when Daniel gathered up his food wrappers we took that as our cue to wind it up for the day. Just then Beth's cell phone rang and she snatched it off the table as if expecting an urgent call.

"Of course I remembered," she said, heading into the kitchen for privacy. "Yes, I'll be there soon," we heard her say, her voice placating. After she left the room her words were muffled but the tension in her voice was clear.

Olivia gave a worried glance toward the kitchen and Daniel balled up his lunch trash into a ball so tight I thought the wrappers might molecularly bond. Esme and I busied ourselves with packing up our things and pretended not to notice.

Beth came back in a moment later. "Mom, let me make you a snack before you go up to rest. I need to go do a quick errand in about an hour."

"Is it something I can do for you on my way back to the office?" Daniel asked.

"No, thanks, Daniel. I told Blaine I'd take his car in for servicing. I have a list of things I need to talk to the mechanic about. I'll have to do it."

"Or maybe Blaine could take in his own car," Daniel said.

"Oh, Daniel, don't start," Beth said, giving Esme and me a tight smile.

"How will you get home?" Daniel persisted. "You're not going to sit there and wait the rest of the afternoon."

"No, no," Beth said. "I'll put my bike on the rack and ride it home. I wanted to get in a ride today anyway. This gives me a good excuse to do it."

Daniel glanced his mother's way and pinched off whatever he wanted to say. "Sounds good," he said. "You're inspiring me. Maybe I'll go for a run after work." He shot the ball of wrapper toward the wastebasket and fist-pumped when he hit the target. "I'll see you later, Mom," he said, leaning down to busk her on the cheek. "See, this is what happens when you bring in the pros." He tilted his head toward Esme and me and smiled, but his eyes kept flicking back to his sister.

After Daniel left, Esme and I looked through the boxes again, deciding which to take with us this trip.

"Sophreena, would you and Esme stay for coffee?" Beth asked.

I was absorbed in the contents of the box and opened my mouth to decline, but Esme nudged me and I looked up. Beth had her back to her mother and the look on her face was almost pleading. Clearly she had an agenda.

"Love to," I said, "if it's not too much trouble."

We had a nice chat over coffee and some truly superior banana bread—Daniel's talents again, we were told. We even managed to work in a few more questions for Olivia while we were at it. When she went up to rest Beth checked to make sure her mother was out of earshot before she turned back to us.

"Thanks for staying," she said, her voice low. "I wanted the chance to talk to you. I can't imagine what you must think of us."

"We're not thinking anything, Beth," I lied.

"Then there's something wrong with your tension receptors, Sophreena," she said with a rueful laugh. "Listen, you know us. It's not always like this. This has been a hard year. We had a horrible scare with Mom's health. Blaine didn't like the idea of me taking the year off, so that's created problems. Then there's an issue with Daniel. He's decided he hates being a lawyer. All that school and all that work, and now he hates it. He's discovered this real passion for food. He wants to open a restaurant. He's trying to get backers and he asked Blaine and me to come in on it. Blaine flatly refused, so there are some hard feelings on that score."

"Well," I said, "since you're being so frank here, do you mind me asking what that little kerfuffle with Peyton yesterday was all about?"

Beth puckered her lips. "I know it's no secret in this town that the Branch family is practically at war. Sterling and Madeline are wonderful parents and they are not about to turn their backs on their only daughter. They've not only allowed Madison to come back home to live, but they've welcomed her as a prodigal daughter. She's Blaine's sister and he loves her, in his own way. But he thinks she's taking advantage. She hurt her parents very badly with the way she left and he can't forgive her for it. But Sterling and Madeline have forgiven her and they're doing everything they can to help get her back on her feet. I mean, that's what loving parents do, right? But Blaine is dead set against them giving her a penny, or even taking her in. Peyton sides with Madison and their parents and I'm caught in the middle."

"Not a good place to be," Esme said.

"You have no idea," Beth said softly. "Anyway, Mom doesn't know much about any of this and we're trying our best to keep stressful things away from her. But you're going to be around us a lot as we're working together on this project and I didn't want you to think we're this dysfunctional all the time."

"Family matters," Esme said.

"Pardon?" Beth said.

"Family matters can be complicated," Esme said with a sigh.

"Oh, I thought you were reminding me of how *much* family matters," Beth said, the wan smile back again.

"That, too," Esme said, patting her knee.

three

THE TEMPTATION TO BLOW OFF GENEALOGY WORK FOR THE AF-
ternoon was strong. Leaves needed raking, books needed
reading, bikes needed riding. But Esme and I both wanted to
give Olivia all the time we could before we left for the Wilmington job, so we pushed on.

Sometimes our clients want only a bare-bones pedigree
chart with names, dates, and maybe the occupations of their
ancestors and their country of origin. Or they want a coat of
arms they can hang on the wall in the den. Those are easy-
peasy jobs we can knock out in a day or two. Olivia's project
wasn't one of those.

She was looking for a deeper, richer family narrative. She
wanted the story of her people. And for that you have to dig
and shuffle through a lot of stuff. Often clients get completely overwhelmed by the task of taming all the photos,
heirlooms, and other artifacts a family accumulates over generations into some kind of logical order so that patterns and
identities start to emerge. That's where I come in.

I get to strut my stuff on these jobs since I absolutely rock when it comes to organizing, at least in my professional persona. In my personal life, not so much. Hence the need for frequent safaris into the deepest reaches of the house, hunting for my keys or a mislaid hairbrush or iPod.

But sorting clients' family artifacts is something Esme and I have down to a system. I was going through the boxes, examining each item for dates, placing each into a protective sleeve and then snapping it into a three-ring binder in its proper chronological position. Simultaneously, I was constructing an index database that included a description of each item and the noted or estimated date, so we could build on the information in a methodical, cumulative progression.

For amateurs the impulse is to start looking through things and get drawn into the contents of a letter or ponder over the identity of someone in a photo, only to suddenly realize an hour has passed and there's been no progress in organizing. With our method there's no sidetracking.

Theoretically.

The boxes we'd brought home from Olivia's on this trip included two containing Olivia's maternal grandparents' belongings and one with Celestine's personal diaries from the year Olivia's parents were married. I worked through the books trying hard to record the dates without succumbing to reading the actual text.

I failed.

Once I caught the word *bride* I was hopeless against the compunction to read on. I figured if I was going astray I should take Esme along with me, so I read the passage aloud to her:

Diary of Celestine Duffy Hargett

September 7, 1941

We met Johnny's new bride, Irene, today. Johnny calls her Renny and she says she'd like us to call her that, too. She is a beautiful child. And that is what she is; she is a child. So is Johnny for that matter. I wonder if she knows what she has got herself into. Johnny is my husband's only brother, and I love him, I truly do. But I can't make out what kind of husband he'll turn out to be. I expect not a very good one. I blame his mama since she doted on him right much and allowed him to skate by on near 'bout everything. Now he's grown tall, but not so much grown up. Maybe it's 'cause he's such a good-looking boy, but he has a very high opinion of himself and is bad to get aggrieved and pout or act out when he doesn't get his way about every little thing. I fear there will be some rough road ahead for these two young ones.

And doesn't that all make me sound like an old granny woman? I'm not but five years older than Johnny myself, but I dare say I've a better head on my shoulders in the first place and I've done a whole lot of growing up since me and Riley married, nearly six years ago now. Seems hard to believe it's been that long, and yet again hard to believe it's ONLY been that long. Seems to me I've always been with Riley Hargett. If not here in this place then somewhere up there in heaven where our souls got matched up long ages ago.

Renny is a t-nincy thing. Puts me in mind of a little sparrow. And seems like she's got the sweetest disposition you could imagine. Right off she hugged my neck and told me how glad she was we were to be sisters since she never had a sister. I never had one either so I told her I was just as glad as her. And I am.

I'll own up to some unfair judgment on my part. I was half expecting she'd be snooty. She is a town girl and her parents are both educated people who've traveled to lots of far-off places. I've heard they are none too happy about their daughter running off and marrying the likes of Johnny Hargett, who even his family that loves him will allow is a wild boy with not much prospects. Her folks were missionaries in China, which is where Renny was born, and they wanted her to go to college and become a learned lady, which will surely not happen now. This must be a heartbreak to them as Renny is their only child, at least their only one left with them in this world. I hear they once had a son, but he died when he was real little. I believe I recollect hearing it was of some disease he got from wherever foreign place they were serving as missionaries at the time. I imagine that would be the hardest thing a person could be called on to endure. I consider myself a faithful woman and I try to live a good example every day of my life but I don't know if I could ever answer the call to spread the Word if it meant putting my child in danger. If I had a child, I mean. Riley and me have long ago accepted that being mama and papa is not in the cards for us. Now that is a true heartbreak.

I still cannot believe those two ran off and got married without a whisper to a living soul. But with all that's going on in this old world I suppose folks are grabbing at happiness while they can. Who knows what tomorrow holds. That terrible war overseas seems like it's going to soon overtake the whole world. Every morning I wake up to the clear blue Carolina sky and the peaceful countryside around our little place and I can scarcely think of danger or strife. But Riley says it's coming. He says President Roosevelt will have no choice but to lead us into that big war soon. I hope with all my heart Riley is wrong since if the call to service comes I know he'll be first in line to answer. I'd be proud but scared half to death every minute he was gone away from me. I cannot bear to think on it.

Good night, dear diary. I will write more tomorrow.

Esme let out a sigh. "Not exactly a ringing endorsement of Johnny Hargett, is it? I hope Olivia means it about wanting to know about her father. People always say they want the truth, but sometimes what they're really hoping is we'll find something that proves it was all a big misunderstanding. That Uncle Edgar wasn't really a horse thief; he was borrowing the pony for some emergency. Or that Aunt Gertrude didn't really steal her best friend's husband; she was just there to comfort him *after* the split."

"I think Olivia's going into this with her eyes open," I said, lifting the jeweler's loupe from where it dangled from a chain around my neck. I put it to my eye to try to decipher the cancellation stamp on an envelope. "But I'll talk with her about it to make sure we're all on the same page."

Esme, wearing a paper mask to ward off the dust, was going through the box of Olivia's grandparents' things that

Daniel had retrieved from the pastor's wife. She took an envelope from the box and stared at it, then pulled the mask from her face. "This is a letter from Renny to her parents around that same time. Now that you've opened the door my curiosity's got the best of me. I'm gonna have to read it."

I wasn't in any position to protest, since I was the one who'd violated our protocol in the first place. "Go ahead," I said, "but read it out loud."

Esme slid the pages out onto a clean bath mat we use to absorb the dust. She unfolded the thin paper and gently pulled the pages apart, smoothing out each sheet in turn and studying it. "Okay, this is a letter from Renny to her parents. It's dated October 16, 1941."

Dearest Ba-Ba and Ma-Ma,

I know you are still angry with me and that makes me very sad. I am sorry it has taken me so long to write to you. First I had to get my courage up and then I realized I had no writing tablet so I had to wait until Johnny went into town to get me one. As you know paper is precious these days and having a whole tablet is a luxury.

I hope that you will someday find it in your hearts to forgive me for leaving to marry without your permission. If I'd had a sliver of hope you would have someday given me your blessing I would have waited, but I knew that day would never come, not for me to be with Johnny. You both had your hearts and minds set against him from the start. So I will say that I am so very sorry for disappointing you, but I am not sorry to be Johnny's wife.

I wish you would understand that all the talk of war and the horrors of what is going on overseas makes a person stop and think about putting good things off for a someday that may never come. I am hoping you will write back to me, Ba-Ba, and give me comfort and assure me that God will protect our country and that this will all pass and life will be peaceful and right again, and that you and Ma-Ma will love me still as you always have.

I am blessed to be welcomed into the Hargett family. Johnny's brother, Riley, and his wife, Celestine, live next door to us. Their house is close by, just a few steps across the yard. Riley is Johnny's older brother and together they own this farm their parents left them. It is beautiful here. Our houses are on a hill and we can see the valley below dressed out in autumn glory.

They rented out most of the farmland this year and the men who planted it are well into the harvest. Riley worked it alone for the past two years but the place is too much for him to handle with just the mules and he hasn't the money to buy a tractor even if he could get one with things like that so scarce right now. He's working for now at the livestock barn taking care of the mules coming up for auction.

As for Johnny, he never had it in his mind to be a farmer. He wants a job where he can use his mind. He's very smart, which you'll both come to believe when you get to know him. He really is a swell fellow and he's good with figures. He's going to try to get on with the Savings and Loan or maybe at the Tobacco Exchange.

Riley and Celestine have been so good to me since I came here. They are caring, faithful people anyone would be glad to count as family. Celestine is teaching me to knit but I am a poor student. I get the yarn all tangled and drop stitches then I must ravel everything out and start all over again. Celestine is patient with my fumbling fingers.

She's also showing me how to put up the vegetables from the big fall garden she and Riley tend and the fruit from the orchard behind our houses. She belongs to the Home Extension Club and she knows all about the proper way to do these things. We are putting by every-thing we can as many are saying there will be shortages even worse than now if we go into the war.

Celestine has complimented me on my cooking, Ma-Ma, and I told her the credit goes to you for having taught me since I was a very little girl, starting with how to cook rice when we were in China.

I hope that you will come for a visit soon so you can meet them and get to know Johnny better. Until then please know that whether you believe me or not I remain your devoted and loving daughter.

Renny

"Well, that answers one question," Esme said, sliding the letter and envelope into a flat paper bag to await the scanner. "Renny's parents surely did *not* give their permission for the marriage."

"And considering he ran off on her a short time later, when she was pregnant no less, looks like they were better judges of character than Renny. Sounds like she was a sheltered girl with stars in her eyes," I said.

"And she paid dearly for every twinkle," Esme said.

"I think what Olivia would really like to know is how her mother felt about her father and all that went on before he left them. That's certainly what I'd want to know if I were in her shoes. Too bad Renny wasn't willing to talk with her about it."

"It is," Esme agreed. "My mother talked ceaselessly about my father. I don't have clear memories of him, since I was only four when he passed. But my mother helped me know him. Hardly a day passed without her mentioning a food he liked, or a piece of music he was fond of or how my laugh sounded like his. She didn't make him a saint, though. She'd fuss, too, telling me how I left all the kitchen cabinet doors standing wide open just like he used to do, which drove her crazy."

"Speaking of things that drive a person crazy," I said, "why did you accept Daniel's invitation for both of us yesterday, without even a by-your-leave to me?"

Esme was unbowed. "You said yes in your head. I can't help it if I sometimes overhear your thoughts. You think loud. And anyhow you can thank me later. Daniel's made a few dishes for Olivia to bring to the church potlucks and once folks get wind which one is his they'll elbow little old ladies out of the way to get to it. He's good. And it's a nice way to show his appreciation. I knew you wouldn't deny him that. And I knew you'd want to go because the others are all coming, including Jack."

While Olivia was ill, Jack had brought his landscaping crew over every week to mow her lawn and trim the hedges.

These were chores Olivia had taken care of herself right up until the time she was diagnosed. She'd tamed the yard into submission with a push mower and manual garden tools. She'd been a healthy, strong woman and years of constructing the whimsical, kinetic metal sculptures she welded had given her better-than-average upper-body strength. It had been hard for her to accept that she couldn't manage the upkeep of her house, even temporarily.

Winston had pitched in with household chores for Olivia. And, of course, kept her supplied with fresh baked goodies. Esme and I had secretly hoped a romance might blossom between the two of them. Winston had been alone for a year, ever since his shrew of a wife, Patsy, had gone off to visit her sister for two weeks then on day fourteen announced she wasn't coming back. True confession: The last part hadn't seemed all that tragic to the rest of us. For years we'd wondered how a wonderful man like Winston ever got hooked up with that old crabapple in the first place. But they'd been together a long time and Winston was sad, more for the sake of his kids and grandkids, I suspected. Patsy had turned her back on all of them.

As for Olivia, she'd been widowed twice over. Bethany's father, Quentin Saunders, had been in Vietnam. He survived that hell, but it haunted him. Afterward he became deeply involved in the movement to bring home comrades being held as POWs, and in an anvil-heavy irony he'd been killed in an accident aboard ship when he was returning to Vietnam as a delegate on a negotiating team. He'd gone in peace, not as a warrior, but the war had claimed him all the same.

My parents had been close to Olivia and Quentin and I'd heard them talk about how devastated Olivia had been. Beth had been conceived just before he left on the mission, so she'd never known her biological father, either. But unlike her own mother, Olivia made certain her daughter knew the man her father had been.

After Quentin died, Olivia had moved in with his parents and put all her energies into raising Beth. Her in-laws, Silas and Regina, loved her like a daughter. They were concerned about her, submerged as she was in her grief. They tried to get her out into the world to open up new possibilities for her. In fact, it had been Silas who'd introduced her to George Clement, a counselor at the VA center where he volunteered. He invited George to dinner in a flagrant attempt at match-making. It worked—eventually. George and Olivia became friends, and a long while later, more than friends. The wedding was held in the backyard at the Saunderses' home, with Beth as flower girl and Silas and Regina as witnesses.

George was a good stepfather and a year later Daniel joined the family. Shortly after that both Silas and Regina passed away, leaving the house and all their worldly posses-sions to Olivia and George.

The Clement family lived happily together in the house for a little over a decade, before George succumbed to a respiratory ailment, leaving Olivia a two-time widow. Maybe she'd decided not to risk the pain of loss again.

In any case, Olivia and Winston had remained friends only. But sometimes that's even better than a romance. At least that's what I tell myself when I'm with Jack.

four

We'd arranged to be at Olivia's house an hour before the designated dinner hour on Saturday to do some more interviewing with Olivia before the others arrived. But when we got there she was nowhere to be found. Tony was in the family room, his laptop and a couple of external hard drives set up on the coffee table.

"I just got in, but I think she's up resting," he said, his eyes darting quickly toward the stairs then back to the computer screen. He'd been holding his cup-sized earphones away from his ears, probably hoping for a short interruption, but when we didn't leave he slipped them down to his neck and clicked the keyboard to stop whatever he was doing. "She had a bad night last night I think," he said. "I heard her moving around at like three in the morning."

"Okay, we won't disturb her," I said. "We'll go in and pack up all the stuff off the dining room table. I assume we'll need it for dinner."

"No worries," Tony said. "Me and Daniel took care of the dinner venue this morning." He pointed toward the screened porch that ran the entire length of the back of the house. "We're all set up out there and we've got heaters if it gets chilly. Go look. It's like something from one of those hipster retro blogs. Daniel's got the touch for this stuff."

Esme and I peeked out and both of us let out an involuntary *ooh*. Olivia's house was not fancy and she'd never had the money for much updating, though it was warm and inviting in a lived-in kind of way. But the old house worked in total harmony with Daniel's décor. He'd traced multiple strands of tiny white lights along the vaulted ceiling of the porch. A long table was appointed with a maroon tablecloth; an ivory runner traced the length, with candles in vintage glass canning jars placed at intervals. Olivia's mismatched chairs had been draped in slipcovers. Ivory linen napkins telescoped out of wineglasses and each place setting of china was different from all the others.

"Beautiful," Esme pronounced, walking out onto the porch. "Look, here's my place." There was a place card done in a nice calligraphy. Not as good as mine, but good. I searched for my place, which was set with blue and white china with a windmill design and a blue wineglass and water tumbler. Esme's was white porcelain with a black and gold band, her glassware amber.

"He does have the touch," I said. "Hope the food is as good as the décor."

We went back inside, where Tony had resumed his work. We tried to tiptoe through unobtrusively but he pulled the headphones down to his neck.

"Pretty cool, eh?" he said.

"Magical," I said. "What's this you're working on?" I

pointed toward the computer screen, on which an elderly man was frozen in place, his head back as if he were giving an idea some serious consideration. I recognized him, but only vaguely.

"Marking the rough footage of one of the interviews with Charlie Martin," Tony said. "Wanna watch?"

"You sure we wouldn't be bothering you?"

"No, it's okay. I'm just making notes of where to cut," he said, pointing to a list of time marker notations. He picked up a little gizmo and attached it to the computer's port. "I'll put this splitter on so you can get the audio, but I won't be able to hear you very well." He pulled the earphones back up but held them away from his ears. "So don't think I'm being rude if you say something and I don't answer."

I motioned for him to go ahead and he let the padded earpieces fall into place. Esme was muttering again. Clearly, he hadn't won her over quite yet.

Charlie Martin was a grizzled old guy. His hair was cropped close to his scalp and he had a short, unkempt beard and wiry eyebrows that stuck out in all directions, probing the air like little antennae.

I could see what Tony meant about Beth being good with people. She teased Charlie without being condescending or disrespectful. And when he wasn't forthcoming she coaxed him along, saying things like "Oh, Charlie, would you tell Tony what you told me before about . . ." This seemed to rev Charlie's motor when he was about to go into a stall, and so the interview moved right along.

He talked freely about his time riding the rails when he was a young man, sleeping in hobo camps and working here and there for food. But when Beth started on questions about the war, he turned somber. And when she asked about the men he served with he went totally silent and looked down at his hands. After a few beats he looked into the camera, his face set hard, and snarled, "Turn that thing off."

The screen went blank and then the picture blinked back on again. Beth switched tracks and asked Charlie questions about gardening and plants for a couple of minutes and then made another attempt at eliciting wartime stories. He hesitated, then looked into the camera and slowly shook his head.

When I looked at Esme, she had a hand spread across her forehead, a pained expression on her face. I reached behind Tony to touch her shoulder. "You okay?"

She cleared her throat and patted my hand, but she didn't turn to look at me. "Lots of ghosts from that dark time," she said, her eyes squeezed shut. "Lots of haunted souls."

We all looked up as Olivia came into the room from the screened porch. Her face was red and her clothes were stained with dirt and spotted with perspiration.

"I thought you were upstairs resting," Tony said, snatching the headphones off. "Where in the world have you been?" He got up and guided Olivia toward a chair and she collapsed into it.

"I am so sorry, Esme and Sophreena," she said, panting as she wiped her forehead on her sweatshirt sleeve. "It was such a beautiful day I decided to rest in the lawn chair out in the yard. And then I was feeling so good I decided I'd try walking down to the lake. I used to do that several times a day and never gave it a thought. I made it down fine and

I thought *so far, so good*. But I had to rest a while before I could make the walk uphill. It was wet and slippery from last night's rain and I couldn't seem to keep my feet under me good. I should have taken my phone. I'd have called you to drive your motorcycle down and get me, Tony."

"Yeah, wouldn't Beth just love that? Me putting you on the back of my bike? But I could have done the fireman carry," he said, doing a pantomime.

He was trying to get a laugh from Olivia and she obliged. When she excused herself to take a shower, Esme and I left Tony to his editing and went to the dining room to lay out the notes to get Olivia started on her heritage scrapbooks.

I glanced at my watch as we sorted through the selection of background papers Marydale had brought over. "Maybe we're going to be dining fashionably late," I said. "It's after five and Daniel's not even here to begin the cooking."

"I'm told he's very picky about his ingredients. He likes fresh and local," Esme said. "Winston said he was going right to the farm to get some things."

Olivia came in looking refreshed and quite spiffy in a rust-colored pantsuit. But she was moving stiffly. I had a hunch she had suffered more than a little slipping and sliding in her trek up the hill. We tried to work for a bit but she was distracted and couldn't concentrate on the questions, which was just as well, since the others started arriving a few minutes later. We'd just settled in the living room when Daniel came rushing in from the kitchen.

He welcomed us and did a quick survey of the room. "Mom, where's Beth? I was counting on her to do hostess duty while I cook."

"She's not here yet," Olivia said. "But I think I'm capable of acting as hostess, especially considering this is my house." She started to rise, but Daniel put a hand on her shoulder.

"Of course you're capable, Mom," he said. "The point is this is supposed to be a treat for you, too."

Olivia frowned. "What in the world happened to your arm?" she asked, tracing a long, nasty scrape along his forearm.

"Little farm mishap," he said. "Two of the goats conspired to push a gate open. I was in the wrong place at the wrong time. It's nothing. I'll go find Tony and press him into service until Beth gets here. He'll have some appetizers out to y'all in a jiffy. Dinner will be served in about an hour. Hope you're all hungry."

We chatted companionably, but I noticed Olivia didn't seem herself. On closer inspection I could see she had her own assortment of small injuries, souvenirs from her afternoon's misadventure. She'd broken fingernails, scrubbed up her knuckles, and had a blooming bruise on her ankle that was only visible when the hem of her pants hiked slightly. Daniel hadn't noticed. I wondered if Olivia would report the incident to Daniel or Beth later, and debated whether I should rat her out if she didn't. I leaned toward her and asked if she was okay.

"I'm fine," she assured me, grasping my hand. "I'm a little concerned about where Beth is, though. It's not like her to be so late. And without calling."

"Would you like me to go call her?" I asked.

"Yes, please, would you do that? I'll enjoy myself more if I know what's holding her up."

I stepped out to the kitchen, where Daniel was in his element. He was moving with efficient speed and directing Tony to do the same. I held up my phone. "Your mom is worried about Beth and wants me to call, but I don't have her number."

He nodded toward a list on a bulletin board hung by an old-fashioned wall phone. I called both Beth's home number and her cell and got voice mail each time. "Maybe she's somewhere with Blaine," I said. "Will he be joining us, too?"

"Blaine wasn't invited," Daniel said, his voice flat. "But I'm getting a little worried myself. This is *not* like her."

"Want me to go over to her house and see if she's there?" Tony asked.

"Yeah, that'd be great," Daniel said, "but take the appetizers out first, please."

Tony held the tray high, fancy-waiter style, and I followed in his wake, half convinced the enticing aromas wafting from the tray might actually be able to lift me right off my feet like in the cartoons.

I slipped in next to Olivia and whispered to her that I hadn't been able to reach Beth, but that Tony was going over to check on her.

She smiled and nodded, moving a stack of magazines from the coffee table so Tony could put the tray down. Daniel followed a moment later with a huge tray laden with three pitchers, tumblers filled with ice, and some stemware.

"Jack, would you play bartender so I can get back to the kitchen?" he asked, then pointed to each pitcher in turn. "There's ginger iced tea, raspberry lemonade, and sangria. Please, enjoy."

When he had gone I picked up a little cocktail plate. I tried to be dainty but by the time I was done I'd piled one of everything onto it. There were stuffed mushrooms, some kind of tiny tart, figs stuffed with goat cheese, and several things I couldn't identify but was eager to try.

We heard Tony's motorcycle start up and I winced involuntarily, awaiting the backfire, but I heard him pull out onto the street and purr away with no startling bang this time. We laughed and talked for a while longer, then Daniel came to check that we had everything we needed. I considered telling him I'd like every appetizer he had left in the kitchen put into a doggy bag for me to eat later, but I resisted.

Tony was gone for quite some time and when he returned I didn't hear his motorcycle in time to prepare myself. The backfire almost made me dump my plate of goodies into my lap. Tony made quite a striking picture standing in the doorway in his black motorcycle jacket. He carried his helmet by the strap in one hand and pushed his hair back with the other. "No answer at the door," he reported. "But her car's there and I think I heard the shower running inside. She'll probably be along soon." The helmet slipped from his grasp and rolled over to the baseboard. I saw him grimace as he reached for it and noticed that the fingers on his right hand were horribly swollen. Had they been that way earlier? I didn't have time to ask.

Daniel clapped his hands together and announced, "I think we'll have to go ahead without her or else dinner's going to be ruined."

Olivia seemed about to protest, but after a moment's hesitation she managed a wobbly smile. "Yes, I'm sure she'll

understand. Something must have come up. Oh, and I forgot, they're with one car; maybe Blaine had the car, maybe
that's why she's late. Anyway, she can join us whenever she
gets here."

We'd made it through the salad course and still Beth
hadn't arrived. I was annoyed with her since I was a little
worried now, too, and I couldn't concentrate every cell in
my body on enjoying the food, which even my untrained
palate found extraordinary. Daniel and Tony started bringing
in the main course of salmon topped with a chopped salsa-
type stuff, tiny herbed potatoes the size of jelly beans, and
asparagus with some kind of yummy yellow sauce. We were
halfway through dinner when Beth appeared in the porch
doorway, her hair wet and her clothing slightly rumpled. She
was pale but there was high color in her cheeks and her eyes
glinted.

"I am so sorry," she said, looking up and down the table
as if she weren't entirely sure where she was. "I was," she
said, then there was a moment of silence as if she was trying
to remember something. "I just let the time get away from
me," she said finally. She slipped into her seat, then seemed
startled by a thought. "Oh, Daniel, I'm so sorry. Can I help?"

"Everything's under control," he said, giving her a tepid
smile. "Tony stepped in. Glad you could make it."

"Good, that's good," she said, settling back in place and
unfolding her napkin. She had her head down and her movements were strangely slow and measured. Esme and I exchanged looks. Something wasn't right.

The conversation resumed and Daniel went to the
kitchen to get Beth's plate. As he put it in front of her he

bent down to whisper in her ear. She squeezed her eyes shut and nodded. I assumed he was asking her if she was okay. I also assumed she was lying through her teeth when she indicated she was.

In contrast to the rest of us, who did everything but pick up our plates and lick them, Beth pecked at her food, frowning occasionally as if she'd tasted something odd. I wondered if she'd actually been the one who hadn't wanted to invest in Daniel's restaurant because she didn't like his food. If that was the case, she had buckshot for taste buds.

We lingered for a while over dinner and Beth excused herself from the table twice. She seemed unsteady on her feet and I saw Olivia's worried gaze follow as she left the room each time.

Daniel invited us to retire to the living room for dessert and coffee—key lime pie and a chocolate almond torte, which made me sorely regret not planning ahead and saving room for both.

The doorbell rang as we were filing in. Olivia was already seated and Daniel and Tony were both carrying trays, so Esme went to answer the door.

I heard her voice take on a particular lilt and I detoured to the front hall.

"Couldn't stay away, could you?" Esme said to the visitor. "You were invited as my plus-one, you know, and you said you couldn't make it. You missed a fine, fine dinner, but you can still join us for dessert."

The door opened wider and I saw Detective Denton Carlson of the Morningside Police Department standing on the front porch. Denny is a very large African-American man and one of the few around who could be a match for Esme, in size and in many other ways as well. They'd been dating for more than a year now, though she still refused to call it that. According to her they were just "passing time" together. Esme's an independent woman, sometimes to a fault.

"Hey," I called. "I thought you were on duty tonight."

"I am," he said with a sigh. "Sorry, Esme, I'm not here to see you, though I'm always *happy* at the sight of you." He gave her a half smile. "Is Bethany Branch here?"

"Yes, she's in here," I said, jerking a thumb back over my shoulder.

"I need to see her," Denny said, stepping across the threshold, his big body filling the doorway. "It's official business, I'm sad to say."

He walked purposefully to the archway into the living room, Esme and I trailing behind him. Everyone looked up, smiling, and then the smiles faded, one by one, as they took in the look on his face.

He nodded a general greeting, scanning the room until his eyes lit on Beth and locked. "Beth, could I have a word with you in private?" he asked.

She looked back at him and seemed to have trouble bringing him into focus.

"Why would you want to do that?" she asked.

"Bad news, I'm afraid," he said. "I really need to speak with you."

She didn't move and didn't seem to comprehend what she'd been asked to do.

I could see he was deciding whether to push further to

get her alone. Finally he walked over and pulled a chair in front of her. He sat, his knees almost touching hers, and took her hand.

"It's your husband, Beth. There's been an incident. I'm so sorry to have to tell you this, but Blaine's dead."

five

A SHOCKED SILENCE FELL OVER THE ROOM AND FOR THE FIRST
time I realized what people mean when they say it was as if
time stood still. Beth stared at Denny, an eerie, perplexed
smile on her face.

"No, he's not dead," she said. "It's not that. Not that at all.
I did yard work today; there were so many leaves to rake. The
shade is lovely in the summer, but then you have all those
leaves." She put out a hand, palm open. "I've got blisters
even though I wore work gloves the whole time."

"Beth," Denny said, cupping her shoulder with his hand.
"Beth, I'm sorry, but Blaine is dead. There's no mistake. We
found him in the lake about a half hour ago."

Olivia let out a sound that was somewhere between a
squawk and a gasp and moved quickly to Beth's side. Winston stood to let Daniel get to her as well, but Beth shrugged
off her mother's embrace and wiggled out to stand near the
window, fists clenched at her sides. "That's not right," she
insisted. "It wasn't that hard, only who would think two trees

could make that many leaves. Really? I just get so tired. I can't go on like this. I can't be the one who—"

Suddenly she stopped babbling and it was as if her core had melted. She crumpled to the floor before anyone had a chance to catch her. Out cold.

Olivia, Marydale, and Coco immediately formed a triage team, scurrying to get cool cloths and smelling salts. They seemed to know what they were doing. The guys looked on helplessly and I asked if I should call 911. Olivia shook her head. "I think it's the shock. Let's give her a minute."

The rest of us stepped across the hall to the dining room while the women, Daniel, and Tony saw to Beth. Almost everyone had been stunned into a speechless stupor or else they were trying to be circumspect, but Esme was neither. She set right in on Denny, shooting questions rapid fire. What happened? Was it an accident? A car wreck? Where did it happen? Was he absolutely sure it was Blaine?

Denny held up a hand. "Look," he said, glancing around the group before his eyes came back to rest on Esme. "You know I trust you all not to run your mouths, but this is an active investigation and I've got to watch what I say. I'll tell you this much. It was not an accident, though it hasn't been ruled on yet. A kayaker came upon his body floating in the lake. Poor kid was shook up so bad he had to be sedated. Cause of death is not official, the coroner will make that call, but there's no question it was Blaine Branch; I saw the body myself. Jenny's at the lake securing the scene; she hates doing notifications." He took a breath that swelled his big body even bigger. "Can't say I care for it, either. Worst part of the job."

Jennifer Jeffers was Denny's partner. She's a bit of a prickly pear and for some reason she hadn't taken a shine to Esme or me. Neither of us had the warm fuzzies for her either, but she was good at her job.

Denny glanced toward the archway into the living room and all eyes followed. Beth was sitting up now, though she seemed almost catatonic. Daniel and Tony half carried her to the couch. Then Daniel came out to talk to Denny.

"Denton, you said an incident. What exactly do you mean by that? An accident or what?" he asked.

"I'm not free to say more right now, Daniel, I'm sorry," Denny said, slipping past him into the living room while the rest of us hovered in the hallway.

"Beth," Denny said, going down on one knee beside the couch, "I'm so sorry, but I need to ask you a few questions. When's the last time you saw Blaine?"

Beth frowned and looked to Denny as if she couldn't take in the words. "I woke up and he was gone," she said in wonderment.

"So this morning is the last time you saw him?" Denny asked.

"His car is in the shop," she said. "He did *not* take his car. He's around someplace. Alan took him somewhere. Alan told him it was finished, but Blaine won't accept it. Wait, no, that can't be right, Alan left already, didn't he? What day is this, I can't think." She frowned up at her mother. She shook her head as if to clear it but the effort made her wince and she became even more befuddled. "So many leaves," she said again with a heavy sigh. "I can't do it all. I told him, *I can't do this*. It wasn't a lie, not really. Maybe of onission." She frowned at the fractured phonics and tried again. "Of odission." She gritted her teeth. "Omission," she said, enunciating each syllable with labored attention. "Not dead, though. A surprise, and not like me at all. But not dead."

"Beth," Daniel said, his voice firm, "do not say another word." He turned to Denny. "She's invoking. She's in no shape to be talking to you until we know what this is all about."

Denny frowned. "Daniel, this isn't an interrogation, it's a notification."

"I don't care what you call it," Daniel said. "Until we know what's what, she's not saying another word. I'm her lawyer."

"Daniel, you're a real estate lawyer," Olivia said, her words quiet and gentle.

"I'm a *lawyer*," Daniel repeated. "And we're done talking. Beth is going to the emergency room to get checked out. Right now." He pulled his keys from his pocket and handed them to Tony. "Go get the car, would you?"

"I'm coming, too," Olivia said.

"Mom, why don't you stay here," Daniel said. "I'll call you."

"I'm coming, Daniel," Olivia said in a tone that brooked no argument.

"Do you think Beth's okay?" Tony asked, for perhaps the tenth time. He, Jack, Winston, Esme, and I were working to clear away the dinner table, put away food, and get the dishes washed and packed back into the boxes Daniel had used to bring them to Olivia's.

"I'm sure she's fine," Esme said, though she didn't sound sure and I wasn't, either. Beth definitely hadn't been herself from the moment she came in the door at Olivia's that evening and her reaction to the news that Blaine was dead was strangely disconnected.

Marydale and Coco had taken Olivia to the ER in Marydale's car so they could bring her home if need be. Marydale had promised to call the minute they knew anything. Apparently they didn't yet, as my phone had gone stubbornly mute.

Esme put the tablecloth into the washer and we finished tidying up the kitchen and packing up all the family history stuff to take back to our house. In the South when there's a death in the family the food pours in. It's what people do because it's something they *can* do. The dining room would be needed for its normal function over the next few days.

As I handed Tony a stack of scrapbooking supplies to put into a box I noticed the injured hand again. I asked him about it.

"Second time I've done that, you'd think I'd learn, right?" he said. "My kickstand jammed and I got my hand slammed trying to release it. It's nothing."

I saw his hands were shaking. "Tony, Beth's strong, you know," I said, confident in the truth of that statement, at least.

"I know, I know," he said. "I just don't like to see her like that. She's always got her act together. Always. But tonight? Even before that cop came she seemed all strung out or something."

"I don't know what to tell you," I said—another true thing. "We should hear something soon. Try not to worry. You're really fond of Beth, aren't you?"

"Fond? What do you mean by that? Like am I crushin' on her or something weird? Nuh-uh, not like that. I owe her, is all; I owe her big-time. I was headed into zombieland—just another one of the walking dead—when she first knew me back at Morningside High. Let's just say I was into a lot of stuff that didn't bode well for my future health and well-being. Hadn't been for her I'd be in jail, insane, or dead by now. She sure deserves better than—"

Just then my phone rang and I snatched it out of my pocket. Marydale, as always, was calm and collected, but there was concern in her voice. "It wasn't just shock. Beth has a concussion. It's serious but not life threatening. She can't remember what happened. All she remembers is waking up out in the yard and she barely remembers that. Apparently she must have fallen and hit her head on something when she was doing yard work. The docs are saying she may be addled for a while and probably won't remember much about this whole day by tomorrow. They've run tests and done scans and they don't think there will be any lasting damage but they're going to keep her overnight for observation. We're trying to convince Olivia to come home, and I think she's about ready to give in. She's totally exhausted. Daniel will stay here with Beth."

"How is Beth taking the news about Blaine now that it's had a chance to sink in?" I asked.

"I'm not sure it has sunk in," Marydale said. "She just keeps saying things that make no sense and insisting he isn't dead. I still can't get my mind around it myself and I don't have a concussion."

"I know what you mean. We cleaned up here, but is there anything else we can do?" I asked.

"I don't think so," Marydale said. "Denny's notified Blaine's family. Daniel talked to them on the phone and let them know what's going on with Beth. They'll probably be taking over the arrangements, under the circumstances. Frankly they'd probably have taken over regardless of the circumstances."

"Yeah, I understand Sterling Branch is a take-charge kind of guy," I said.

"He is," Marydale said with a sigh. "I don't mean that as a slam against the man. He's a good guy, and he and Madeline will be crushed by this loss. But Sterling has never been the sort to stand on the sidelines. And in this case that's good. Beth is in no shape to deal with anything right now. I just can't imagine how this happened, Sophreena. None of it makes any sense. I don't think we're getting the whole story from Beth."

"I don't think so, either," I said.

What I thought, but didn't say aloud, was that it was probably best we were spared the particulars.

six

OVER THE NEXT THREE DAYS WE GOT TO KNOW A LOT ABOUT Blaine Branch. His life and, of course, the circumstances of his death were examined at length in every form of media. Attendees at his funeral overfilled the church and spilled out onto the sidewalk. He was lauded for his charitable works, his service to the community, and his success as a businessman. He was eulogized in glowing terms by his fraternity brothers, friends, and members of the various boards on which he served.

I noticed that Peyton seemed to be keeping himself somewhat apart from his family. Several times I saw him staring at Beth, his eyes narrowed. I couldn't read anything into his expression, but it was unsettling.

Madison Branch seemed on the verge of a breakdown. Marydale sat beside her at the funeral, holding her hand. Marydale's daughter and Madison had been best friends growing up and Madison still regarded Marydale as she would a beloved aunt. Marydale had spent a lot of time with her since she'd come back. I knew Madison was in a fragile state and it was the worst-kept secret in Morningside that her return had caused a rift in the family. She'd been a wild child in her teen years, and at the age of twenty-six, when she should have outgrown her wild-oats stage, she ran off with a sandlot volleyball player, flipping her entire family the proverbial bird on her way out of town. Six months later he crept out of their hotel room somewhere in Portugal, leaving her with ten dollars in her purse and two thousand dollars in hotel bills. Sterling and Madeline had rescued her, brought her back home, and built her a little studio-sized house on their property. They'd been supporting her financially and in other ways for the past year while she tried to figure out how to get her life together. Blaine had been incensed. He believed in the bad karma/tough love school of relationships. He'd barely spoken to Madison during the past year and had continued to pressure his parents to cut her off.

At the funeral, in contrast to Madison's emotional un-spooling, Beth was stoic. Either Olivia or Madeline was by her side every minute making sure she didn't overtax. She appeared shell-shocked, registering little as people approached with condolences. True to Marydale's prediction, the Branch family had taken over all the arrangements for the funeral, consulting Beth only when necessary. Which was a good thing. Blaine's sudden death and her own injury left Beth barely functioning.

Some of the mourners probably came out of obligation to Sterling and Madeline Branch, while others were drawn by more prurient impulses, but many were there to support Beth. True details were slowly leaking out: that Blaine had been killed by a blow to the head, that the death was ruled a homicide, that Beth, too, had been injured on the day of Blaine's murder. In addition the rumor mill was grinding away. Blaine and Beth had been a prominent couple in Morningside and his murder was the stuff of TV crime docudrama. Even as his life was being lauded inside the church, it was being torn apart in shops and cafés. There was gossip that he was having an affair, that he was caught up in shady business dealings, that he was a secret gambler or drug addict. That neighbors had heard gunfire at his home on the day he died. None of it was supported by anything as cumbersome as facts. It seems that when the murder of an ordinary citizen occurs, people will search for any motive to assure themselves that if they simply stay away from whatever misstep or vice got that person killed, they can stay safe from harm.

Esme and I had continued to work on sorting and organizing Olivia's family artifacts so they could all be stored away in good order; we were expecting to continue with the project after the first of the year, when things had settled down. So I was surprised when, two days after the funeral, Olivia called.

"Are you and Esme still available to work on my family history?" she asked.

"Well, yes, we're here for another week. But we weren't sure you'd be up for it right now after all that's happened. It's okay if you'd rather wait."

"No, I want to keep going, if that's okay," Olivia said, then let out a whooshing breath that came through the phone line so clearly I could almost feel its warmth on my ear. "The thing is," she said, "we're desperate for something to distract us right now. Beth especially. I'm worried about her. If I'd known she'd take this so hard . . ." She went silent and I thought for a moment that we'd lost our connection.

"Olivia, you still there?"

"Yes, sorry. The thing is, Beth needs to keep her mind and her hands busy. Things are such a mess. This is not how she intended her life to go and she's just sort of checked out right now. I need to get her involved with something."

"If you think working on this will help, we'll be glad to do it, Olivia," I said, though I doubted there was much that could distract Beth right now. "When would you like us to come?"

"How about tomorrow morning? Beth is staying with me for now. Do you know she can't even stay at her own house? They're saying it's a potential crime scene. Which is ridiculous; Blaine wasn't even home that day. He always left the house early on Saturday mornings to check in at the store then go off to play golf or tennis or shoot at the range or whatever."

"I'm sorry, Olivia," I said. "I hadn't heard they'd taped off her house. I know it must be distressing, but they're just being thorough."

"I suppose," Olivia said. "But I have to tell you, though I've always been fond of Denton Carlson, I resent some of his questions and I don't like the way he's treating Beth."

"I know he's pushing her hard, but, Olivia, you know he just wants to find out who did this so Beth can begin to put it behind her," I said.

"I *do* know that," Olivia said with another big sigh. "But I don't have to like it. No matter that she's a grown woman,

Beth is still my baby and I wish I could protect her from every hurt in life. There's nothing as fierce as a mother's love."

"Just hang in there, Olivia," I said. "It'll all be okay."

I said it, but I wasn't totally convinced.

"We going back on the job?" Esme said after I hung up the phone. "So soon?"

"Yes, looks like it," I said.

"Celestine will be happy," Esme said. "She is mighty eager for us to get cooking on this family history."

"When did she make contact?"

"When I started packing up these boxes. I think she's enjoying having us read her diaries. She fancies herself an author now and she doesn't want us to stop."

"Well, I don't think fans will be lining up at midnight to snatch the latest release, but her diaries are interesting and I think Olivia and Beth will be enthralled. Maybe they will distract Beth, at least for a time. I wonder if she's remembered any more about that day," I mused as I looked out the window into our backyard. The leaves that had made charming, colorful wind devils last week were now amassed in a sodden, knee-deep pile. We'd definitely need to rake or they'd be so heavy they'd be nearly impossible to move. I thought of Beth babbling on about dealing with the leaves in her yard the night Denny came to tell her Blaine was dead.

"According to Denny," Esme said, "Beth remembers even less now than she did that night. The doctors predicted that might happen. She can't remember being at her mother's that morning, nor anything she did that afternoon, including doing yard work. She can't even remember coming to dinner at Olivia's that night or how she got there. The morning after, when Denny went to the hospital, she couldn't even remember that she'd seen him the night before and he had to break the news about Blaine to her all over again. Talk about the devil in the déjà vu!"

"I hear the department is getting pressure from Sterling Branch," I said.

"Yep, as if they needed more pressure. Every available officer in the Morningside Police Department is working the case. Jennifer Jeffers is lead detective on this one, and, much as it pains me to say it, since we're not exactly bosom buddies, I wish her great success."

"Does that take some of the pressure off Denny?"

"Not a jot or a tittle. The pressure on Denny all comes from that big heart of his, not from outside. Anyhow, you can't blame the Branches. They want to know what happened to their son."

"As any parent would," I said.

"Maybe not *any* parent," Esme said, holding up a letter she'd taken from an envelope a few minutes earlier. "This is to Renny from her daddy. I want to know did he forgive her, so I'm not waitin'. I'm gonna read it now. Do you want to hear or not?"

"Yes," I said with a sigh. "We've really fallen off the organizational system wagon, but I want to know, too. And anyway, we only have one more box to index so we'd be reading it soon anyway.

Esme unfolded the pages and smoothed them with her cotton-gloved hands. I could see Thomas Lockwood's straight-up-and-down handwriting marching across the page, uniform and precise.

"It's dated November 4, 1941, so he got back to her pretty quick. He says,"

Daughter,

We are glad to learn you are well and that you have good people to depend on there in Crawford. However, do not interpret those sentiments to mean that we in any way condone or approve of the disobedient path you have chosen. We remain sorely injured that you have willfully ignored our counsel and our expressed command that you disassociate yourself from that boy. You have dashed all our hopes and dreams that you would become an educated and accomplished woman in this world and one pleasing to God to achieve the world hereafter. We are fearful of what the future holds for you.

As for a visit, that most assuredly will not be possible. Not now, and perhaps not ever. You must give us time to mend and to prayerfully consider the proper course. And aside from our own feelings, there is the issue of timing. For we will soon meet with the mission board to find out what shall be our next posting.

We had hoped to have you safely settled at Women's College under the tutelage of Mrs. Babcock before accepting another foreign mission, but you have scuttled that plan with your impetuous and unwise decision to run away and make a secular partnership with that boy. I surely do not recognize it as a marriage as you made no promises to God in a proper church.

I have made inquiries about Riley and Celestine

Hargett. People who know them assure me they are good, simple people. I hope they will look after you.

Alas, I cannot send you false reassurances about the state of affairs in the world. The war clouds are gathering and we'd all best prepare ourselves. There is evil afoot, daughter, and we will be called upon to stand, stalwart and unflinching, for what is good and right.

And now I must close. Please know that what I have expressed in this missive comes from both your mother and me. Do not depend on your mother's soft heart to win you absolution for what you have done. We love you with an abiding love, but we cannot pretend that we are not gravely disappointed in you. But there is no turning back now so we can only hope and pray for the best for you and turn our efforts to our call to service.

Your father,

Thomas Lockwood

"Wow, crusty old coot, wasn't he?" I said.

"No wonder Renny didn't choose to share much with Olivia about her parents. There are only seven letters here from the parents to Renny. Five written by her father and two by her mother. They were all in the boxes from her aunt Celestine's house. So Renny kept them, but I doubt she shared them. I'm betting Olivia never even knew they existed."

"Could be," I allowed. "I can understand why Olivia's mother didn't want to talk about Johnny. But why wouldn't Celestine and Riley? He may have been a draft dodger, but he was still Riley's brother."

"Your idea of a draft dodger is different, Sophreena. Your

parents were Vietnam era. Lots of guys tried to avoid going to 'Nam. Young people saw that as an unjust war. It was an accepted decision to become a conscientious objector or to run off to Canada, at least among the young. In World War Two it wasn't like that. That was my mother's generation and she told me a lot of stories about how it was back then. People were behind the war effort. Victory gardens, Rosie the Riveter, paper and scrap metal drives, doing without and making do. And everybody, right down to the schoolkids, was expected to play a part. Refusing to go fight would have been a disgraceful, unforgivable thing to most people."

"Still," I said, "you'd think that would have faded a little with the passage of time. Olivia said she asked her aunt Celestine about her father just before she died. She was in her nineties, for heaven's sake. That stuff was all so far in the past what could it possibly matter now?"

"Oh, you'd be surprised," Esme said, shaking her head. "People will take so much baggage with them into the hereafter they need a pack mule for a spirit guide."

seven

WE'D JUST FINISHED GOING THROUGH THE LAST BOX OF OLIVIA'S artifacts when my cell rang.

"Kayaks or rowboat?" Jack asked, without preamble.

"Rowboat," I said. I knew he was finishing up a job today and I'd half expected a call proposing an outdoor activity at some point in the afternoon. I had hoped for leaf raking, but a turn around Misty Lake in a rowboat sounded much more appealing. Still, maybe I could have my cake and eat it, too.

"Could you load your gas-powered leaf blower in the truck?" I asked. "If Marydale were to bring Sprocket and Gadget over right now they'd disappear into the leaf mountain in our backyard."

"Sure thing," Jack said. "Be ready in fifteen."

This is why a friendship is better than a romance, I told myself as I clicked off. If Jack were my boyfriend, I'd have been vexed by the short notice and by his taking me for granted. But he wasn't my boyfriend; he was my amigo, my pal. And never mind that lately he was my pining heart. That was my problem and I was just going to have to deal with it. I wanted Jack Ford in my life until the end and I wasn't about to do anything to put our friendship in jeopardy or make things awkward between us. I'd tried to think of him as a brother but that definitely wasn't working. Forcing brotherly thoughts while admiring his blue eyes was *icking* me out.

Esme was planning to do the grocery shopping for the week. Having been brought up Catholic, I could have easily let myself feel guilty about running out on her, but she loved the grocery store; I hated it. She enjoyed browsing, comparing prices, and reading labels while I stared longingly out the store windows wishing I could escape the fluorescent glare and get out into the sunshine.

"Thank the Lord," she said when I told her I wouldn't be going with her. "Honestly, Sophreena, having you along is like taking a three-year-old shopping. You ask 'are we nearly done' every five minutes."

"I never do that!" I protested.

"In your head you do," Esme said. "Now you go paddle your way across the lake and I'll go sidle my way through the Harris Teeter and we'll both have a happy afternoon. Leastwise I will if Celestine will let me have a little peace."

"More messages from beyond the veil?" I asked.

"Same message, she's just amping it up. Hurry, hurry. Read faster. For such a gentle countrywoman she's turning into quite the diva."

The lake was smooth and untroubled and the October afternoon so warm Jack and I had both shed our sweatshirts before we even got the boat in the water. The craft was homely, scarred, and weather-beaten, but Jack refused to gussy it up. He maintained the hull, repairing and water-proofing as necessary, but otherwise tried to keep it looking the same. His father had built the boat with him when he was a boy and it helped him navigate more than waterways.

No motorized craft were allowed on the lake, but there were a few kayaks and wind sails out, and there'd be more when school let out for the day.

We lifted the boat off the back of the truck, me taking the land end, bracing myself and bending my knees to take the weight.

"No matter how many times we do this, it always amazes me you can lift your end," Jack said. "You're stronger than you look."

"I watched a lot of Mighty Mouse when I was a kid," I said.

Jack laughed as we put the boat down at water's edge. "Well, that explains a lot. But Mighty Mouse was a little before your time, wasn't he?"

"Yeah, but my dad had movie reels filled with cartoons. He had them transferred to videotape and we'd watch them together. I liked them better than the stuff being made when I was little. I mean *Teenage Mutant Ninja Turtles*? What was that about? What was your favorite cartoon?"

"Hate to admit it," Jack said, "but I worshipped *He-Man*. I was small for my age and he made me feel even more inadequate, but I figured if I could just get my hands on one of those swords I could kick ass."

The boat rocked as I climbed in and I had to grab at the sides to steady myself. Jack laughed and underscored the taunt by taking a wide-legged stance, shifting his weight from side to side, rocking the boat wildly while maintaining perfect balance. I wanted to put my foot up and kick him overboard, but I knew he had his phone and keys in his pocket. I'd have to plot a comeuppance for later.

We settled into an easy rhythm, oars synchronizing by virtue of both muscle memory and the Martian mind-meld Jack and I have going on. With the exception of the one, rather large secret I was keeping about my feelings for him, Jack and I were open with one another.

"Any news about the investigation?" he asked.

"Not that I've heard," I said. "I know the heat is definitely on."

"I figured that. How's Beth doing?"

I told him what Olivia had to say that morning and about how we were to pick up on her genealogy project.

"That'd be good," Jack said. "Keep 'em busy. I know Daniel's worried this whole thing will put a strain on his mother and slow down her recovery."

"I didn't realize you knew Daniel so well," I said.

"Yeah, I mean kind of. We were on a rec-league volleyball team together and I got to know him even better when I was doing Olivia's yard work. We've gone to a couple of basketball games together, did a Habitat for Humanity gig, stuff like that. I saw him late yesterday afternoon as he was leaving Bonnie Foster's house and I was just getting home. I think he's handling some business things for Beth."

"I don't know Bonnie well," I said, fishing for how well Jack might know her.

"We're friendly neighbors," Jack said, "but not like pals or anything. She's nice and scary smart. She grew up out in the mountains somewhere. She and Blaine were college friends. Reading between the lines I'd say he brought the financial backing to the business and she brought the day-to-day operations savvy."

"I'd expect she'll be able to keep the store, right? They probably had some kind of partner-survivor policy. Most business partners do that so they won't lose the business if anything happens to one of them."

"Yeah, I think so. Bonnie insisted they take out a policy to protect her when Blaine took up rock climbing a few years back. She said if he wanted to dangle off the side of the mountain and endanger himself that was his call, but he wasn't going to take the business down with him. She's got everything she owns invested in the place." Jack frowned as he studied something on the opposing shoreline.

I looked over to where a cluster of kayaks and paddleboats were circling. I saw a flutter of torn yellow tape on one of the dock posts and realized this was the spot where Blaine's body had been found. "Oh God, looky-loos," I muttered.

"Morbid curiosity," Jack said. "It's a human condition."

"You know, I always thought Blaine and Daniel got on pretty well," I said, "but the last time I saw them together it was Tension City."

"Back when we were playing volleyball Daniel would bring Blaine along sometimes and I know they played tennis together. But I think they'd kind of gotten crossways of one another over time."

I told him about Blaine's refusal to invest in Daniel's restaurant. "Maybe that's what soured things."

"Don't think so," Jack said, paddling extra strokes to align us with a bend in the shoreline. "Things were already mucked up with them before that happened."

"Daniel seems to have it in for Peyton, too," I said.

"Now that I don't get," Jack said. "Peyton's a good guy, and a great coach. The kids at Morningside High all think he walks on water. He's really good with them. Doesn't lose his temper like a lot of coaches do. He's an easygoing, mellow guy."

"You wouldn't say that if you'd seen him last week," I said. "He got into an argument with Beth and he was—well, whatever the opposite of mellow is."

"An argument with Beth? I can't even imagine that."

"Me neither, except Esme and I saw it with our own four eyes. I was mildly curious at the time but after all that's happened, I'd *really* like to know what it was about."

"Wait, you're not thinking it's anything to do with what happened to Blaine, are you?"

I shrugged. "Who knows? It was strange, and when something like this happens, anything out of the ordinary pricks up your ears."

Jack paddled alone, alternating the paddle from side to side, while I ate cheese and crackers and drank a bottle of water. When I was done, I took over and passed him the snack bag.

The sun, apparently jealous of the autumn leaves, was gathering in reflected glory and painting a swath of sky, the golden orb drifting slowly and gracefully toward the horizon. We'd need to turn soon or else we'd run out of daylight. And while moonlight boating could be lovely, it could also be creepy.

I thought of the young kayaker who'd come upon Blaine's body. As it happened he was one of Peyton Branch's football players. The poor kid had already been unhinged by finding a body and he'd completely freaked when he found out it was his coach's brother.

We were on the east side of Misty Lake, which is for regular folks. Bike and hiking paths snake along the shoreline and most of the small piers are shared by neighbors or owned and maintained by the town. Olivia's house was an exception. The house was situated at the end of the public space and had a long, steeply sloping yard that ran down to the lake, with a small private dock at the bottom. Olivia's house may have been modest, but her lot was as luxurious as any surrounding the mansions on the west side of the lake along Crescent Hill.

"That's funny," I said, as we came even with Olivia's dock. "She just told me a few days ago her boat was stowed up in the garage loft. Now it's tied up at the dock."

"Maybe she's ready to start taking it out again."

"Maybe," I said. There was no mistaking Olivia's boat. It was a flat-bottomed skiff like Jack's, but Olivia's was distinctive. She'd made two small kinetic sculptures and attached them on each side aft. As we disturbed the water with our oars the ripples went out and set the metal pieces chiming.

In healthier days Olivia had routinely used the boat to visit Beth, whose house was on an almost direct east-west line across the lake. It was quicker by far than driving around the lake, and Olivia enjoyed being on the water.

As we came closer I noticed flattened vegetation and slickened streaks of mud near the water's edge. My mind flashed back to Olivia's stained pants and muddy shoes on the afternoon she'd tested herself by walking down to the lake.

"I wonder if she took the boat out," I mused, not realizing I'd spoken aloud.

"When?" Jack asked.

"The day Blaine was killed."

"Maybe she did," Jack said with a shrug. "What does that matter?"

"Good question," I said, staring out across the lake to the group of looky-loos still circling Blaine's watery grave.

Denny was sitting at the kitchen table watching Esme cook. She'd decided a home-cooked meal was just the ticket for reducing his stress levels. Maybe, but the meal she was whipping up would do nothing good for his *cholesterol* levels. Pork chops, mashed potatoes with gravy, big slabs of Winston's sourdough bread with butter, broccoli smothered in hollandaise sauce, and, in a token nod to healthful eating, a small green salad. Plus, given Denny's notorious sweet tooth, I was sure there was a pie or cake cooling somewhere.

Denny's immense body seemed in danger of melting over the sides of the kitchen chair, he was in such a slump. He looked as if he hadn't slept in days.

"Anything new?" Jack asked.

Denny leaned on the table and drew his hand down hard over his face as if ironing out the bags under his eyes. "Not a whole lot," he said. "We're learning more on background about Blaine Branch's life, but none of it's been useful in finding who killed him. Not yet, anyway."

Over the last few months Denny had become an adjunct member of our club, though he hadn't been read in on everything. He wasn't working on his own family history—yet, though I think we've stirred the notion for him. And he didn't know about Esme's gift. But he'd learned to trust our discretion and he claimed talking things through with us was helpful, so I had no reservations about asking questions.

"What have you found?"

"Nothing damning," Denny said. "I think everybody knows Blaine had a wild streak when he was younger. He got into trouble in his college years, usually over stunts his idiot frat brothers put him up to. Some of those hijinks look very un-PC now and I'm sure he wouldn't have liked them bandied about after he'd become an upstanding citizen of the community, but none of it was too serious."

"Could it have been something as simple as a robbery?" Jack asked. "I mean, everybody around knew Blaine had money, and more than a few knew he had a habit of carrying a lot of cash on him just for show."

"You got that right," Denny said. "Blaine liked having a roll to flash. Not smart and totally unnecessary nowadays, when practically everywhere you go they take credit or debit cards. But no, for sure not robbery. His wallet was still in his pocket, plenty of cash in it, and he was wearing a pricey watch."

"Olivia told me you've cordoned off Beth's house," I said. "What's that about?"

"We don't know where it happened. We're trying to trace Blaine's movement on that day. And we found blood out in the yard at his and Beth's house. We're assuming it was Beth's from where she fell and hit her head, or whatever happened with her. Still," he said, turning a palm up, "we've gotta cover all the bases. There's something off about the place. And Beth won't be much help unless she gets her memory back. Jen was over there this afternoon with a crew going over the yard again. We're also looking at the fishing wharf behind The Sporting Life. That's near the spot where Potter's Creek feeds into the lake and the current is strong there; it could have carried a body out to where the kid found him."

"What makes you think he might have been killed there?" I asked.

"Slim evidence, really. But according to the timeline we've got so far that's the last place someone remembered seeing him that morning. We had the tech guys out there yesterday and they found trace amounts of blood on the wharf, too. But the store had a fishing gear clinic there last week and it hasn't rained since. Could be fish blood or maybe somebody got a barb in the finger or something. Anyhow, it's in the testing pipeline."

"But he was, for sure, at the store that day?" Jack asked. "I thought Bonnie said she didn't see him at all."

Denny nodded again. "Same thing with the store employees, but two people saw him in the parking lot. There's a door from the lot into a hallway that leads to his office, so could be he didn't check in with anybody, or never got a chance to. All I can say is that's the last sighting of him we've got. And this was from two different people who say he was there around eleven a.m."

"Do you know any more about how he was killed?" I asked.

"We know he was struck on the back of the head with something hard and flat, and we know he was hit with considerable force. So the how we know. Now all we're missing is the who, the why, and the where." He sighed and Esme set a glass of iced tea in front of him and patted his shoulder.

"It'll all come clear," she said. "But for now you need to give it a rest for a while. Sophreena, you and Jack want to join us for supper? There's plenty."

"Love to, Esme, looks great, but I've got a meeting with a client," Jack said.

I decided Esme and Denny deserved some privacy. "I ate already," I said, figuring cheese and crackers counted so it wasn't a lie. And I could always sneak in for midnight leftovers if there were any. "Jack's gonna help me with the leaves until he has to go to his meeting, then I'm gonna see what I can find out for Olivia."

"All right, then, you two have fun," Esme said.

I watched, astounded, as she served up Denny's heaping plate. "Bon appetit, y'all," I said. "And maybe a brisk walk after supper would be in order, else I might come back and find you both in a food coma."

"I suppose," Coco said. "Anyhow, I spoke with a very kind gentleman at the mission society and he'd be happy to get you some better scans of these two photos, for a small fee, of course. Those are just photocopies, one of her grandfather and one of her great-grandfather. Between you and me, I wouldn't hang either one of those up in the kitchen. They might curdle the milk."

"They do look a little stern, don't they?"

"You're too kind, Sophreena. They look like prophets of doom. The Easter Island statues have more vibrancy than these two."

She put both hands on the worktable, stiffened her arms, and flexed her back, letting out a little groan.

"Long day?" I asked.

Coco stood and worked her neck back and forth a few times. I half expected her to drop to the floor and assume a yoga position. She's been known to do that during our club meetings.

"Not so much long, just frustrating. Marydale asked me to give Madison Branch some pottery lessons. You know Marydale's doing her mother-hen thing with Madison, right?"

"I know she's concerned about her and wants to help."

"Yes, well, and I worked with her all afternoon. I think she could probably do pretty good clay work if she could get herself together to concentrate. The girl's a mess."

"She's not exactly a girl, Coco," I said. "She's almost my age."

"Oh, trust me, she's a girl," Coco insisted. "A very impulsive, very unstable girl. But Marydale loves her dearly, so I know there's got to be something to her. I'll try to get to know her and mentor her if I can."

eight

I FELT INVIGORATED AFTER AN HOUR OF LEAF WRANGLING out in the crisp fall air. After Jack left I went into the workroom, woke up my computer, and jotted down some strategies for a search. As my hands hovered over the keys I heard Coco's voice in the front hall. She chatted with Esme and Denny for a couple of minutes, then came into the workroom in her usual whirlwind fashion, clutching a sheaf of printouts.

"Hey, Sophreena," she said, "I hit a pretty productive vein with Olivia's maternal grandparents through their missionary society. Thought I'd get these to you early in case you want to get some of the original stuff from them. Three generations of missionaries, her grandparents the last. Lots of info on her grandfather, though not so much on her grandmother," Coco sniffed. "Even though from what I can tell she did just as much of the work as he did."

"Different times, Coco," I said, reaching for the printouts.

"You're a good egg, Coco," I said.

"I'm a fried egg," she said. "I'm going home to sink into a hot bath."

"Thanks for this," I said, motioning to the printouts. "Great work."

"I was taught by the best," she said as she picked up her bag and made for the door.

I searched through databases on the Internet for a while, trying to catch Olivia's father's trail, but Johnny Hargett had left few footprints after he slipped out of Crawford, North Carolina, leaving behind his very pregnant young wife.

All I'd managed to find was an arrest record for John L. Hargett on a drunk-and-disorderly charge in a town about thirty miles south of Crawford. The name Hargett was not uncommon, but the middle initial narrowed things down. If this was our Johnny he'd spent three days in the county jail, was released, and walked out into the sunlight and right off the end of the earth. Or so it would seem. I made a note to follow up. Maybe I could unearth the actual arrest record.

I spent another fruitless fifteen minutes searching, but none of my sources coughed up any information. I decided to go back to mining Olivia's family artifacts.

Celestine Hargett's collection of diaries was enough to make my genealogist's heart go pitter-pat. She wasn't a particularly inspired writer, but she'd taken her teacher's instruction in the Palmer Method earnestly and her hand-writing was consistent, easy to read, and tidy. And she was *dedicated*. She wrote in her journal daily, almost without fail. And even in those rare instances when she skipped a day or two she'd do a roundup summary of what had transpired in the gap when she made her next entry. She was open and confessional in the diary—up to a point. She was circumspect enough that she must not have entirely trusted her hiding place.

I located the diaries that covered the period between Johnny and Renny's marriage and the time he disappeared and brought them to the worktable. Then I went to the closet and grabbed a stack of the dot-matrix printer paper I hoard for constructing timelines. I stretched it out along the length of the worktable, reinforced the perforations with tape, and drew three lines down the length of the paper: one for Olivia's paternal family, one for her maternal family, and one for historical events to set the family into the context of their times. I ticked in all the birth, marriage, and death dates that we knew and a few major historical markers, then opened the first diary and began to read.

October 25, 1941

I am bone weary, but proud. I put up fifteen pints of applesauce and eight of apple butter today. They looked so pretty I couldn't help but stand there in the cellar and admire the way the light from the window hit the sides of the jars. Riley helped me gather the apples from the orchard yesterday and Renny helped with the peeling, though the child is really more hindrance than help. She peels one for every four or five of mine and takes off half the apple with her knife. Though that's better than taking off a finger, which I can see she could do real easy. I saved all her peels to boil up to

*make jelly if I can get the sugar. Else I'll strain it out
for juice. No sense wasting.*

*But still and all, I do love having her here. She is
good company and sweet as they come. She wants to
learn how to do things and is trying her best to please
Johnny, which is turning out to be no easy thing. As I
feared, he is sulky and short with her when she doesn't
do things the way he wants them done. The two of them
put me in mind of younguns dressing up in the big people's clothes and playing house, neither of them with the
first idea about cooking or cleaning or washing clothes
nor nothing. Sometimes it is comical to watch, but other
times it makes me sick to heart.*

I read through several more entries, learning more about
how many pints and quarts of things Celestine put by than I
really wanted to know. She sprinkled in a little gossip and a
few references to what was going on in Crawford. I scanned
until another passage caught my eye:

November 24, 1941

*Well, you'll never guess, but we are to be movie stars.
There is a man in town who is making a picture show
about all us folks who live in Crawford and he says he
will show it in the movie house when it is done and we
can come see ourselves. I wish we'd got more notice so
I could've made a new dress, but I'll have to make do
with one I've got because he'll just be taking the movies for the next two days. Everybody's all excited about
it and that's a right good thing since we've mostly just*

been scared and nerved up about the war here lately and not had too much cause to be lighthearted. Riley says we'll go into town both days and maybe we'll even get on there twice. He's going to wear his good suit and his nice Panama hat one day and his regular old work clothes on the other. I told him I will wear good dresses both days; I've got no wish to be up there on that big screen in an old housedress and apron. Renny is going to wear the dress she wore when her and Johnny married. It is store bought and is a little batiste dress with a fluttery skirt and lots of ruffles on the bodice and it fits her little figure to a T. And I know Johnny will go dressed to the nines. He's got a bit of the dandy in him.

So maybe Olivia *would* get to see people she knew in the Crawford movie. And maybe one person she never had a chance to know.

As promised, Tony had burned us each a copy of the movie, but with all that had happened we hadn't had a chance to watch it yet. I decided that should be the first thing on the agenda tomorrow. Maybe a movie would be the thing to distract Beth for a little while—if anything could.

nine

TONY SET THE CRAWFORD FILM UP FOR VIEWING ON OLIVIA'S
family room television. I'd prepared the night before by making copies of all the photos I could find from that time period
among Olivia's family artifacts. There were precious few. Olivia's people were not avid photo buffs.

There were six photos of Celestine and Riley Hargett from
that time period. They were black-and-white, scalloped-edged
prints that had faded with time but at least we'd know who we
were looking for in the movie. There was a studio portrait of
Renny, and several small amateur snapshots. In nearly all of
them she was smiling a tentative, shy smile, standing with her
feet together and her shoulders slightly hunched, looking like
a little girl making her First Communion.

Of Johnny Hargett there were only two likenesses from
the period: one studio portrait and one almost worthless
blurry snapshot.

I'd scanned nearly all of Olivia's photos since there were
so few of them. In contrast to her wealth of diaries and

letters, there was a dearth of images. Since this was essentially a pro bono job, Esme and I wouldn't be scanning all of the family artifacts. Olivia had a computer and scanner and we would encourage her to scan everything and show her how to organize the digital images. It is tedious, time-consuming work we only do for our full-service clients. Likewise the scrapbooks. We'd teach Olivia techniques and help her organize the flow, but she'd be putting together her own heritage scrapbooks, and, in my humble opinion, that's how it ought to be. Which unmasks me as a total hypocrite. Although it seems wrong to me to pay an outsider to do such a personal thing as recording family memories, I don't mind at all collecting the hefty fees we get from full-service clients to do just that. Why, sometimes I *tsk* all the way to the bank.

I dealt the photos out to Tony, Olivia, and Beth, though I wasn't sure Beth was in any condition to recognize her own self, much less relatives from another era. She was pale, her movements jerky, her hair unwashed, and her eyes dull and hollow. I'd never seen her like this before. 'Course, she'd never lost a husband before.

But she was struggling to put on her game face. I suspected it was more to ease Olivia's mind than because she had the remotest interest in family history at the present moment.

Olivia studied the stack of photos. She was happy to see the ones of her aunt and uncle looking young and vital, and she smiled sadly at the ones of her mother. When she came to the studio portrait of her father she frowned. "I've never seen this picture before. Is this him?"

"Yes, that's your father, Johnny Hargett. You've never seen this photo?"

"Never," Olivia said. "I'd remember. When I was little I used to ask what he looked like and I was told this"—she held up the blurry snapshot—"was the only picture we had."

"The studio shot was in one of the boxes from your aunt's house," Esme said. "It was inside an envelope."

"Why in the world would they have kept it from me?" Olivia asked, though I didn't think she was expecting an answer. She studied the photo more closely. "He was very handsome, wasn't he?"

"Yes, he was," I said. "I think Daniel looks a bit like him."

I filled Olivia in on what I'd found out about her father, which was not much, and all of it bad.

"Well, that tells me something, doesn't it?" she said, pursing her lips. "Maybe he ended up in prison, for a long time, I mean. Is there any way to check that?"

"I don't think that's the case, Olivia, at least not in this state. I'll keep looking, but in the meantime, I've got to tell you that your aunt Celestine's diaries are real treasures. She writes with so much detail about her daily life and about the people she knows. We've barely begun reading them, but after we watch the movie we'll fill you in on what we've learned so far."

"I can't wait to read them," Olivia said. "I've wondered about those things all my life. I don't suppose she's let out any deep, dark secrets."

I laughed. "Not unless you consider her recipe for pepper jam privileged information."

"We're all set," Tony said, clicking the remote.

"Should I make popcorn?" Beth asked, trying to bend her mouth into a smile, then wincing from the effort.

"I'm a Jujube gal myself," I said.

"No food or drink," Esme said sternly as she claimed a prize spot on the sofa.

"Don't expect a complicated plot," Tony said. "Don't expect any kind of plot. This is like you were talking about with the aunt's diaries, except it's a whole town's memoir. Lots of details but not a whole lot of context, and there's no audio."

A simple title, *Crawford, 1941*, lingered on the screen and I encouraged Olivia to do a running commentary on places and people she recognized while I jotted down observations that might warrant further research.

The title screen gave way to the march of the school-children. They'd lined up by class, younger kids first, and paraded across the camera's focus field. Little boys in overalls or baggy trousers and girls in thin cotton dresses, all genders holding hands with no self-consciousness and clearly intrigued by the camera. Each class was led by a woman, almost all of them sporting wire-rimmed glasses and most with wavy hair pulled back and bundled at the neck. Some had kind faces and smiled at the children; others could have stopped a train dead on the tracks with a disapproving look.

"Recognize anyone?" Beth asked her mother.

"Some of the faces look familiar," Olivia said with a frown, "but I can't put names to any of them."

As the older kids trooped by there was bravado and swagger. Then came scenes taken around the schoolyard. I was amused to see that high school never changes much. There were fleeting shy smiles from the nerdy kids clutching their stacks of books in those pre-backpack days. Then there were the jocks, their striped baseball caps cocked at jaunty angles, mugging it up and demonstrating their mighty swings as they tested the bats and tapped at the sandbag bases. Then the camera literally *caught* the outsider kids out behind the school building. A girl pulled a cigarette from her mouth and smirked at the camera while a boy looped an arm around her neck and pressed his cheek against hers.

"I don't believe it!" Olivia exclaimed.

"What?" I asked, my pen at the ready.

"That's Mrs. Porter. She was my fourth-grade teacher. The woman was the prissiest, meekest little thing you'd ever want to meet. I guess she wasn't always such a goody two-shoes."

"People change," Esme said with a laugh. "I sure wouldn't want you all getting hold of any high school movies of me."

We sat through a visit to the hardware store, where an eager young clerk standing by a chest-high refrigerator demonstrated some newfangled ice cube trays equipped with a handy release lever to a young woman who seemed mighty impressed. Men examined hammers with great earnestness, as if they were complex tools whose function was difficult to divine.

Then the camera operator moved to the streets, catching anyone who came by on the sidewalk.

"Popsicles were a major food group to these people," Tony said as a small girl walked by licking the last vestiges of sweetness from a stick. "Oh, and they love this one. It's in every single one of these old films."

A young man riding a bike came even with the camera operator and suddenly hoisted himself up and put his foot on the bicycle seat, his other leg held out behind him. He rode on by with a triumphant smile, then the action suddenly reversed and the rider went backward and came to a seated position on the bicycle.

"They'd run pouring lemonade backward into the pitcher, or somebody going off a diving board, then back up again. *Bloop*." Tony made a cupping motion with his hand. "I mean it's funny, but not all that funny."

"You had to be there, I guess," I said.

"Yeah," Tony said, "I suppose that was a high-tech yuck back then. When we were studying these we called them Triple P films—pranks, pets, and Popsicles."

"There's Uncle Riley," Olivia said excitedly, leaning toward the television. "Ah, look at him, so straight and tall and young."

"And Aunt Celestine," Beth said. "She was so pretty when she was young."

"She was beautiful when she was old, too," Olivia said. "Just more on the inside than the outside."

Esme leaned over close to me and murmured, "Uh-uh, Celestine did *not* like that comment."

The couple moved toward the camera and struck a pose, Riley with his arm around his wife's shoulders. They looked at one another and the affection between them was unmistakable.

"They were quite a team," Olivia said, obviously lost in her own thoughts. "Whatever life threw at them they faced together."

The camera panned slowly to catch another couple and we all gasped. There in sepia-toned live action stood

Johnny Hargett, his arm around the tiny waist of his new wife, Renny. She smiled shyly and looked up at him, but he was focused on the camera, his chest swelled, his grin cocky.

Renny reached up to adjust a little hat that shielded her eyes against the sun and Johnny grabbed her arm and pulled her in tighter against him. She smiled, but as the camera lingered she rubbed at her arm and her smile faded. Johnny took a watch from his vest pocket and swung it by the fob in an arc. When it came to rest in his palm, he pushed the latch to open the watch cover, looked at it, grinned at the camera, then returned the watch to his pocket.

Beth made a strangled noise, then got up from the couch, knocking a stack of magazines from the coffee table as she fled the room.

"Oh no, what was I thinking?" Olivia said. "She doesn't need to be watching happy couples right now."

"Should you go after her?" Tony asked, pushing the pause button.

"No," Olivia said with a heavy sigh. "Let her be. She'll let me know if she wants me. She needs to deal with this in her own way."

We watched the rest of the movie, with dogged determination now, the banter squelched. There were no more sightings of Olivia's kin, though she did recognize a few more townspeople.

We went in to get Olivia started on the scrapbooks and I kept expecting Beth to join us after she'd regained her composure. But an hour went by and no Beth. Finally Tony came in, shuffling his weight from foot to foot.

"I'm not sure what I should do," he said. "We're supposed to go film a segment with Charlie Martin this afternoon, but I think Beth must be sleeping or something."

"Let me go check, Tony," Olivia said, jumping at the excuse.

"I'd just cancel," Tony said to Esme and me after Olivia had left the room. "But if I don't get this done today it's going to set me behind by at least another week. I'm already off schedule because of, well, you know, everything that's happened."

"Do you have a deadline?" Esme asked.

"Self-imposed," Tony said, with an anxious glimpse toward the doorway. "I want to enter it into a couple of documentary festivals."

Olivia came back in and gave Tony a sorrowful look. "Tony, she's not feeling well. She said to tell you she knows she's letting you down and she feels terrible about it, but she just can't do it today."

"I could pinch-hit for her if you'd like me to," I said. "Not to toot my own horn, but I'm a pretty good interviewer."

"Oh good," Olivia said. "Yes, you go on with Tony and tell Charlie I've got some flower bulbs for him to put in for me when he gets a chance. 'Course, that's just an excuse to get him to come to supper. If I have a little job for him he'll come; otherwise he'd never get out to be with people. That's got to be lonely for him." She glanced toward the stairs again. "People aren't meant to be alone."

ten

AS WE WERE LEAVING THE HOUSE A WIND OFF THE LAKE PUT one of Olivia's kinetic lawn sculptures in play, spinning a top wheel that caused the metal bits suspended from it to strike a bottom plate shaped like a clamshell.

"Man, I love that thing," Tony said. "It's like wind chimes on steroids. And that sound is like nothing I've ever heard. It's not a *clang* and it's not a *bong*. You can't call it a peal or a toll. What *would* you call it?"

"An Oliviation!" Esme said.

"That's great," Tony said. "Mind if I use it?"

"You're welcome to it, but I'll expect a cut of your royalties," Esme said.

Tony laughed, but when Esme didn't smile back a worried look crossed his face.

"She's yanking your chain, Tony," I told him.

"You enjoyed that, didn't you?" he said to Esme, more an accusation than a question.

"Immensely," she admitted.

Tony stopped and hoisted his camera bag, adjusting the strap on his shoulder. He shielded his eyes against the late afternoon sun, and his eyes focused on the metal sculpture again. "You know," he said, glumly, "I was having a great time with this project until Blaine up and got himself killed. I set out to make a positive film about this great small town where everyone gets along and people look out for one another and then, *bam,* one of its citizens gets murdered. Doesn't really fit the theme. And even this," he said, pointing to Olivia's sculpture. "It's great, and I know how she loves it, but when I interviewed her about her sculptures yesterday it seemed to make her sad. I don't get it."

"She's worried about Beth," Esme said. "And she's probably wondering if she'll ever be able to do anything like this again."

"Oh man, I never thought of it like that," Tony said, slapping his forehead. "I shouldn't have asked her about it right now."

"I'm sure it's fine," I said. "These are things she faces every day. It may be even harder for Olivia than for most women in her situation. She was an incredibly strong woman, used to doing very active things."

"She's still strong," Esme said. "She exercised to keep herself in shape all during her treatments, much as she was able anyway. Woman can still lift and carry with the best of 'em. She's just got no staying power. That's what's got her frustrated. She knows she can't do this"—Esme motioned toward the *oliviating* sculpture—"until she can stay with it for more than a few minutes. But I believe she'll get back there. She's a determined woman."

Tony looked toward the driveway. "Uh-oh, I forgot. Beth

usually drives when she goes with me. I've only got my motorcycle, but I've got an extra helmet."

"No, sir, that won't do," Esme said, before I'd had a chance to answer.

I hadn't relished the idea of hanging on to Tony as I choked on car exhaust and the October wind tried to strip the skin from my face, but I put up a protest just so Esme didn't get the idea she could boss me around. Which, of course, she could and did on a regular basis.

We took my car, dropping Esme home along the way. Tony gave me the directions to Charlie Martin's place. It was what is known euphemistically in Morningside as a garden apartment, which meant it was tiny. I knew the place. The five units had been carved out of a fifties-era motor lodge. One of my college friends had stayed there for a summer while she worked in the pro shop at the country club.

As we drove, Tony brought me up to speed on what they'd done in the earlier interviews and what he was looking to get today.

"We've had three sessions with him, and I feel like we're just this close to something really good," Tony said, holding his finger and thumb a couple of millimeters apart. "Then he goes back into his shell. He's a sharp old dude, and I mean that in the most respectful way. He's seen a lot in nearly a century on planet earth. Be a shame not to capture his take on some of it for posterity."

"When does he freeze up?" I asked, wondering what subject matter I'd need to tiptoe around.

"Questions about when he was young lock him up sometimes, but the stuff about the war always shuts him down if you're not really careful about how you get into it," Tony said. "Though it's kinda hard to know if that's him or Beth. She gets all edgy when they're on that subject. She's never wanted him to know about her grandfather and the big family scandal about him running away to avoid having to go. Like it would matter. It's weird. She never even knew him."

"Sins of the fathers, or grandfathers," I said. "You'd be surprised how deep family guilt can go. How 'bout you, Tony? Tell me about your family."

"Not a whole lot to tell," he said. "Never had a dad in the picture. My mom did her best, but she struggled. She didn't have much education and she was young when she had me. I know she loved me and that counted for a whole lot, but I also grew up knowing everything could fall down around our ears at any given second. We moved around a lot and then she got sick. She didn't go to the doctor right away, 'cause we didn't have health insurance. She was working nights as a checker at a mini-mart. The old woman who lived upstairs looked after me. Her name was Mrs. Collier. She tried, too, but she was an old, tired woman trying to look after a young, spunky kid. It got harder and harder for me to be in that apartment; it smelled like old lady lotion and disappointment. I slept on the couch in her living room and she slept like the dead, so I started sneaking out at night and just wandering around."

"And then?" I prodded.

"Mom died and I went into the system," Tony said, his voice matter-of-fact.

"I'm sorry, Tony," I said. "I lost my mother when I was

in high school, but I was lucky. I still had my dad, for a few more years anyway. How old were you?"

"Just going into my freshman year," he said.

"So you were in foster homes after that?"

"Yep. I went through a few before I got lucky, too, and ended up in a good one."

"Here in Morningside?"

"Yep. The Robertsons."

"I know the Robertsons," I said. "How is it I never knew you?"

Tony shrugged. "I heard people talk about you, but you were away at college. Grad school, maybe?"

"Knowing Michelle and Eric Robertson, I don't think I have to ask if they were kind to you."

"They were," Tony said. "They *are*. I still see them a lot. They care about me and I care about them, but it's not the same as blood family."

"Blood family's not always a lovefest," I said. "But I know what you mean."

"I gave Michelle and Eric a lot of trouble," Tony said. "That's my biggest regret. I wish I could go back and do it over. But I was lost when I went to live with them. And if it hadn't been for them and for Beth I'd have gone under. She saved me. Wish I could do the same for her."

"Does Beth need saving?" I asked.

Tony hesitated and I took my eyes off the road just long enough to glimpse his pained expression.

"She might."

*　　*　　*

Charlie Martin didn't even try to hide his disappointment that I'd come in Beth's stead. But as we talked I came to understand why people found him interesting. He had the air of someone who'd seen about everything there was to see and none of it surprised him, upset him, disappointed him—or pleased him.

When he learned what I do for a living he pursed his lips and hunched a shoulder. "Needn't waste time on me," he said. "I never had much family to begin with and such as it was, they're all gone now."

"Where were you born, Mr. Martin?" I asked. "Are you a North Carolina native?"

Charlie gave me an appraising glance. "What's that got to do with the price of eggs?"

"Nothing," I said, taken aback by his response. "I was just wondering. You don't have much of a southern accent."

"I was born in North Carolina, near a little settlement town called Murdock, in 1918. Born there, half raised up there. But after my folks died I hit the road. That was a long time ago and I've been here and there and everywhere since, so I probably talk a little bit like everybody I've ever been around. Even picked up a little German and French back during the war, but I've forgot most of that."

"Murdock is pretty near Crawford. Did you know any of Olivia's people? The Hargetts?"

"Never knew anybody by that name," Charlie said. "Beth asked me that already. Like I say, I was gone from there when I was just a kid."

Nineteen eighteen made Charlie Martin ninety-four years old. He was remarkably spry and his mental faculties seemed sharp.

In my job I strive to put the events of an individual's life in the context of the times, and it's become an automatic response for me over the years. The mention of a date triggers a list, and sometimes a sort of dreamy period ambience in my head.

"Nineteen eighteen," I said, musing. "Lots of brutal battles. World War One ended, only to have Russians start up a civil war. A flu pandemic killed millions. Gandhi advocated for poor farmers, the Great Train Wreck in Tennessee killed a bunch of people, the Red Sox won the World Series, Houdini performed his vanishing elephant act, and Charlie Chaplin was onscreen as the Tramp in *A Dog's Life*, costarring a little dog named Scraps."

"Sounds about right," Charlie said, "but I was born so far out in the backwoods, not much of that would have been known about by my people."

"Did you have siblings?" I asked, and Tony gave me a look that let me know I needed to move things along.

"It was just me," Charlie said. "Guess that makes me the stump of my family tree. When I go the line goes."

"Any cousins?" I asked, and earned another exasperated look from Tony.

"Don't rightly know," Charlie said. "Like I say, my folks weren't much on family."

"I'm told you rode the rails for a while after you left North Carolina," I said, hoping to nudge him forward a few years.

That got him going. "Oh yeah, boy. It was an adventure back in those times. Not like during the worst of the Depression when the trains and camps were crowded over with desperate men. By the time I started hopping trains even the railroad bulls had let up a little. You still had to worry about getting kicked off the train, but not so much about getting clubbed or shot dead."

I risked another scolding look from Tony, my curiosity about Charlie's hobo days tingling like an itch. I'd read about hobo culture, but never had an opportunity to talk to anyone who'd actually lived it.

"Did people go solo, or travel together in groups?"

"Both," Charlie said. "Some kept to themselves 'cause they were just that type, but others had somebody watching their back. Me and a buddy left out at the same time and we pretty much stayed together the whole time we were travelin'."

"What was your friend's name?" I asked.

"Hershel," Charlie said. "Hershel Tillett. We worked when we could find it and pilfered when we couldn't. Saw twenty-seven states. Then Hershel caught the patriotic bug and we joined up together to go fight the Nazis."

"Did you stay together during the war?" I asked, and got an approving nod from Tony.

"Through training," Charlie said. "And we went to the same unit, but Hershel got wounded bad straight off and shipped back home."

"Did you keep in touch?"

"For a while, but you know how it is. You drift. I imagine he's long dead now. Not many of us left."

I could tell Tony was pleased when this segued into a discussion of other war buddies. Charlie hesitated now and again when the memories seemed too painful, and so I'd back off to ask questions about his leave time or what he'd been able to see of France or some more adventurous aspects of his time overseas. After about an hour Tony called it a wrap.

"You're pretty slick, young lady," Charlie said. "I didn't mean to get off on all that rigmarole."

"Think of it as your gift to posterity, Mr. Martin," Tony said. "Like you said, there's not many of you around who've lived through the things you've seen."

Charlie nodded, but his thoughts seemed to be on other things. "How is Beth getting on?" he asked.

"She's terribly sad," I said, "and I think maybe she's still in shock. But she'll be okay in the end."

Charlie puckered his lips and looked down at his hands. "I surely hope so. I hate that she has to go through this." His voice went raspy and low. "She's a fine young woman."

Tony was stoked. "That was fantastic," he said as I backed out of the parking space in front of Charlie's apartment. "You won him over. I woulda never thunk it! I didn't believe anybody but Beth could get him to open up."

"Maybe because I was genuinely interested," I said. "You and Beth were right, he's got some amazing stories. He'd be a good subject for a whole film."

"I've been thinking the same thing—a short, anyway. Want to get a cup of coffee and talk about it?"

I figured it was part of Tony's creative process to bounce ideas off someone, and I had no big plans for the evening. "Sure, I'll just call Esme to let her know I'll be late for supper," I said, stopping in the parking lot to dig my cell out of my bag.

"No problem here," Esme said after I'd told her the situation. "I'm going out for a bite to eat with Denny so you're on your own anyway. There's lentil soup in the fridge and plenty of salad makings."

"Great," I said, trying to feign enthusiasm.

"Sophreena," Esme said. "I know you're right now thinking you'll have an apple fritter with your coffee at Top o' the Morning and call it supper."

I sighed. "Stay outta my head, Esme. I'll see you later tonight."

"How did you and Esme meet?" Tony asked. "You two seem like kinda unlikely business partners—or friends, either, for that matter."

"You're not the first to say so," I said, pulling out of the parking lot and onto River Road. I gave him the oft-repeated story of how we'd met. "It was down in Louisiana and I was interviewing Esme's mother, who had been a domestic for the family I was tracing. We got off to sort of a rocky start, but over time we came to appreciate one another and the rest is history."

Of course, it was the *rest* that was the juicy part, the part that was Esme's very special contribution to the business. I wasn't about to let on about that to a filmmaker.

Top o' the Morning was busy. After-work coffee-daters took up most of the tables inside. Thankful for the unusually warm October day, I snagged one of the small tables that had been jammed into a space outside, partially obstructing the sidewalk and the alley, which I was sure violated some kind of town ordinance. No one had ever complained, though. Morningsiders were serious about their caffeine and there'd be marches on town hall if a bureaucrat messed with Top o' the Morning. Tony went in to place our order while I guarded the table. I couldn't wait to tell Esme she'd been wrong and that I'd gotten a tuna sandwich with my coffee. She didn't need to know it was in *addition* to the apple fritter.

I stowed my bag under the table and glanced around, prepared to give a friendly nod to those I knew. Bonnie Foster sat at the table directly behind me with a man I didn't know. She glanced up and gave me a smile that seemed to take effort, then turned back to the man, her eyes locked on his face like a laser. I wondered if this guy had anything to do with the business. Somehow he looked the expensive-suit lawyer type, even though he was dressed in khakis and a polo shirt.

I tried not to eavesdrop, really I did, but Bonnie was getting agitated as they spoke and finally she thumped both fists on the table and said, "Alan, give it up. She's got to face it. It's all bound to come out."

"Not if we keep our mouths shut," he snapped. "You don't know it all. And anyway, you're as guilty as I am about all this, so don't go all high-and-mighty on me."

It was all I could do to resist spinning around to gape at them. This had to be Blaine's buddy, Alan. A cadre of Blaine's fraternity brothers had attended the funeral but I hadn't sorted out names and faces.

Alan made shushing noises, though he'd been the one who'd raised his voice. I couldn't hear what he said after that but his tone was conciliatory. I heard the scrape of a chair and glanced out of the corner of my eyes to see Alan standing. "Let's move over there," he said to Bonnie, pointing to a

more secluded table along the alleyway that led to the parking lot. "The sun's in my eyes."

In fact, though the late afternoon sun was slanting in
through the alleyway, it was bathing everything in a soft
golden aura, so unless the guy had Dracula-level light sen-
sitivity, he was really looking to get away from prying ears—
mine. A pity. Just when it was getting interesting. What were
they guilty of? Not murder, surely. That wouldn't be the kind
of thing they'd be talking about sitting out in the open at a
coffee shop. Plus, they both seemed genuinely saddened by
Blaine's death.

Tony returned with our order and we spent the next half
hour brainstorming the concept of a film on Charlie Martin's
checkered life. Tony kept saying we could take this or that
approach and finally I asked. "Do you mean that as the royal
we?"

He looked startled by the question. "Guess I was taking a
lot for granted," he said. "Things just went so well today and
you seemed really into it. I just thought . . ." His voice trailed
off and he put his hands out, palms up.

"Well, I'm not saying I'm *not* interested," I said, popping
the last bite of apple fritter into my mouth. "The only thing
is, Esme and I have jobs lined up over the next six months. I
don't know how much time I could give it."

"Okay, let's be honest here," Tony said. "The guy's ninety-
plus. If we don't get what we need soon it won't get got."

"Is there a market for a film like this?"

"Absolutely," Tony said. "Plenty of places would be interested. Historical museums, war memorials, places like that.
Lots of outlets, just not much money. I was sort of thinking

whatever we could get after expenses would go to Charlie. The way he lives, it looks like he could use it."

I sighed. "Well, if we can work out the timing I'm on board, but this is going to have to be my last pro bono project for a while. I've got to make a living."

"I hear ya," Tony said. "I love filmmaking, but I can't spend my life freeloading off friends." He glanced down the street and suddenly grew intent. "Look at that sunset," he said, half rising from his chair. "That angle coming in on the dome of the town hall is perfect. I'll be right back; I need to get this shot."

I looked over the notes I'd taken while we were talking and suddenly I became aware of someone standing by my table.

"Hey, Sophreena, how's it going?"

Peyton Branch looked like he hadn't slept in days. His hair was mussed, he had bags under his eyes, and his skin looked sallow. He stood there with his hands jammed into his pockets and looked as if just existing was a chore.

"Peyton, how are you?" I asked. "I haven't had a chance to talk with you since, you know, what happened to Blaine. I'm so sorry."

"Yeah, me, too," he said. "It's not real yet."

"Sit down," I said, pointing to the chair Tony had vacated.

"Just for a minute." He perched on the edge of the seat, his leg bouncing as if he had to power himself to keep functioning. "How's Beth? You seen her?"

"Earlier today. She's struggling, but Olivia's taking good care of her. She just needs time."

"Yeah, time," Peyton said, huffing out each word. "That's what Beth always needed. Time."

"I don't know what you're trying to say, Peyton." I studied his face, but found no answers there.

He puffed his lips out like a tuba player then let out a long breath. "Neither do I," he said, finally. "I need a cup of coffee." He gave me a wry smile and rose, patting my shoulder. "Good to see you, Sophreena. If you see Beth, tell her I know—" He stopped as he glanced over and spotted Alan and Bonnie. "Never mind. Just say I hope she gets what she deserves. That's the message. Just say I want her to get what she deserves."

He turned and walked away, leaving me with a tuna sandwich/apple fritter lump in my stomach.

Tony returned, excited that he'd captured the shot he'd been hoping for. "I've been chasing a good sunset for days, but the weather hasn't been cooperating." He settled back at the table, took a sip of his cold coffee, and made a face.

We talked a few more minutes and set up some tentative dates for filming more interviews with Charlie, but I was distracted.

I noticed Peyton come out of the shop and approach the table where Bonnie and Alan had just stood, readying to leave. They had a quick conversation that looked intense from where I was sitting. Bonnie swiped her hands in front of her as if cutting them both off, then she headed for the street, where she'd parked her car. Alan and Peyton were still talking, arguing, it would seem. They exchanged a few more words then headed for the back parking lot.

"This may all be for nothin'," Tony said, snapping me back. He stowed his notebook in his backpack. "I don't even know if I'll be able to talk Charlie into it. He wasn't really keen on talking to me in the first place. He only did it for Beth."

I hugged my sweater around me and rubbed my arms. "Okay, well, you work on that. And speaking of the weather not cooperating, without the sun it's getting cold. Let's go."

We gathered our cups and napkins and deposited them in the trash, then headed for my car. As we rounded the corner of the building I heard a thump and a grunt and saw Alan slam Peyton against the brick wall, holding him by the front of his shirt.

"Don't you get it? Keep your mouth shut," Alan said, through clenched teeth. "You want her to have this on her—"

He turned and saw Tony and me and released Peyton, then stalked off to his car without a word.

"You okay?" I asked Peyton. "What was that about?"

"Friendly disagreement," Peyton said, smoothing his shirt. "It was nothing."

As Peyton turned and walked away, Tony stepped up beside me. "Sure didn't look like nothin'," he said.

Peyton's overturned coffee cup was on the ground, the hot liquid forming rivulets in the pine straw. A waft of vapor rose into the cool twilight air.

"Definitely *not* nothing," I said.

eleven

Esme and Denny were having peach cobbler when I got home. I didn't think I could eat another bite, but the aroma was intoxicating—and I wanted to be polite.

I waited until Denny had finished the last bite, so as not to ruin the pleasure for him, then asked, "What do you know about Alan Corrigan? And do you know where he was when Blaine was killed?"

As often happens, Denny answered a question with a question. "Why do you ask?"

I told him what I'd overheard at Top o' the Morning and about the altercation between Alan and Peyton. "I don't know what all their relationships are about. And maybe it had nothing to do with the case, but it seems worth mentioning."

Denny nodded, turning to stretch his legs out and assuming his thinking pose, arms crossed, a half-clenched fist pressing against his mouth.

"Definitely worth mentioning. As far as I know, Alan Corrigan was on his way back to Chicago when Blaine was murdered. I haven't done due diligence and verified he was actually on the flight, but he was for sure in Chicago the next morning because I spoke to him on a landline at his home there."

"Well, like I said, it probably had nothing to do with the case. I know you've got to be inundated with tips."

Denny barked a sour laugh. "We need a big-city police force to run them all down. Phones are lit up like a Christmas tree. Unfortunately we've only got two officers to sift through it all. So far it's been wild rumors and crackpots mostly. We're still hoping Beth will get at least some memory back. That's our best hope. Though it might behoove her to hang on to her amnesia. There's something really troubling there, but I can't get at it."

"You're not telling me you suspect Beth, are you?" I said with a half laugh.

Denny looked up at me for a long moment, his face serious. "I'm not saying that, but I'm saying something was wrong with the scene at her house. I haven't figured out exactly what yet. I admit it's been a while since I've done yard work. I've lived in an apartment for a few years now. But I think I remember how it's done. There was something in that yard that was out of place, but I can't put my finger on it. It frustrates me no end. You ever have that happen where you know there's something you're supposed to be understanding, but it's just too slippery or too convoluted for your mind to get hold of?"

"Happens to Esme all the time," I said, earning myself an over-the-glasses glare from Esme.

The front door opened and Jack called "Soph? You home?"

I called back and Jack headed to the kitchen by echo-location. "Well, here's your lawn care expert," I told Denny. "Maybe he can help you out."

"You got a big job for me?" Jack asked.

"Not unless you'd consider a windowsill with a half-dead aloe plant a job," Denny said. "But maybe you could help. If you've got time, that is." He nodded toward the stack of folders Jack was carrying.

"Oh yeah, sure," Jack said, hefting the folders. "Nothing urgent. It's my family history stuff and they're all still dead and not going anywhere. I just need Sophreena to double-check some things for me. How can I help you?"

"Okay," Denny said, "I know I don't need to remind any of you that I wouldn't want what we talk about here to get out."

"Have we not earned your trust by now?" Esme asked, her voice brittle.

"Yes, you have, Esme," Denny said, reaching over to cover her hand with his—a thing not many men could do. "But the heat on this one is intense so I needed to say that out loud, okay?"

"All right then. You said it. Go on," Esme said, not entirely mollified.

Jack pulled up a chair and I poured him a coffee, doctored it the way he liked it, and slid it in front of him.

"You all know firsthand how Beth was behaving that night. She can't remember much about that entire day, but she does remember she was doing yard work that afternoon. And there's something about the scene as we found it that doesn't make sense to me."

"Such as?" Jack asked.

"I'm not sure. That's the thing. Do you have any clients up on Crescent Hill?"

"Yeah," Jack said. "There are a few, like Beth, who enjoy doing it themselves, but most folks up there hire it out."

"So could you walk me through your procedures, tell me what you'd do this time of year?" Denny asked, taking a small notebook and pen from his pocket.

"Sure," Jack said. "We do quite a bit of trimming in the fall, cutting back shrubs and hedges, but a lot of it is leaf management. Blowing, raking, and bagging or composting the leaves so they don't smother the turf."

"Anything special about how you'd handle a job up on Crescent Hill as opposed to other houses in town?" Denny asked.

Jack frowned. "Yeah, that terrain is a little different. There's usually what I call the upper and the lower property. Most of the houses, Beth and Blaine's included, have a fenced-in backyard that's mostly grass, with maybe a few trees for shade or ornamentation. There's always a gate somewhere along the back of the property with a walkway or trail that leads down to the lake. Those areas are generally not manicured at all. The leaves are left to compost naturally."

"And what do you do with the leaves from the fenced part of the backyard?"

"We blow them or rake them onto a tarp and, depending on the client's preference, we either drag them out to the natural area beyond the gate, or around to the front if it's about time for the leaf sweepers to come around, or else bag them for pickup."

Denny nodded. "Beth says she remembers she was raking

leaves in the backyard, and we saw that she'd trimmed some of the shrubs near the foundation because she hadn't picked up the trimmings, and her loppers were lying there on the ground."

"What else?" Jack prompted.

"There were two rakes, both of them lying on the ground as well, and a leaf blower, still plugged into the wall outlet."

"First off, I don't approve of treating tools like that," Jack said, touching his lips to the rim of the coffee cup to check the temperature before taking a sip.

"That doesn't sound like Beth to me," I said. "She's usually very meticulous."

"That's what I'd expect, too," Denny said. "Though I imagine we can blame that breach on her falling and knocking herself senseless."

Jack nodded, now quaffing coffee. "So under normal circumstances," he said, "the tools should have been attended to, the lopper and trimmer blades wiped, any debris cleared from the blower and the cord wrapped, the rakes hosed off and hung to dry, and the tarp folded and stowed."

"There was no tarp," Denny said. "There was no tarp," he repeated slowly, digging his phone from his pocket. "Where'd the tarp go?" he asked, the question obviously not meant for us. He swiped through a series of photos, then turned the phone's screen toward Jack. "What'd you see here?" he asked.

Jack squinted at the display. "I see where a tarp *was*," he said. "That perfect voided corner in the grass there with the leaves all around it, that's not organic. Maybe she'd already put the tarp back in her shed."

"Nope," Denny said, swiping to another photo. "Here's the shed interior. No tarp."

"Maybe she'd dragged it out to the natural area and hadn't brought it back in?" Jack suggested.

Denny shook his head and swiped through more photos. "No tarp."

"What exactly does that mean?" Esme asked.

"No idea," Denny said. "But I gotta think it means something. A tarp would've made a very handy conveyance for a body. I told you there were several samples of blood collected from Beth's backyard. Could be all the samples will turn out to be from her injuries, but somehow I don't think that's the case. At any rate I'm gonna be waiting at the lab door for those results."

"What does that mean for Beth?" I asked, feeling a tightening in my chest.

"I don't know," Denny said. "That's the problem. Maybe she witnessed something, maybe she was attacked, too, and her brain has just shut it all out. In which case she may be in danger. Or maybe it means something else entirely. Maybe she *did* something she's suppressing. I don't like it, but I'm afraid I'm going to have to take off the kid gloves with her."

"Well, I don't like it, either," Esme said. "Not one bit. You know that young woman didn't kill her husband. She's not capable of something like that."

"Esme," Denny said softly, "you never know what people are capable of given a particular set of circumstances. At this point even Beth herself doesn't know what happened. Sometimes people do things in the moment they regret for the rest of their lives."

Esme rubbed at her temples. "Sometimes longer than that," she murmured.

"I thought I'd be happy when I finally found this," Jack said. He nodded to the folders stacked between us on the sofa. "I mean this is the whole reason I started my family history search to begin with, to find out if I really was descended from Robert Ford. And now I've got the proof right there." He tapped the folders and his face puckered as if he'd tasted something vile. "It seems I'm in the direct line of descent from the man who shot his friend and fellow outlaw, Jesse James. I don't know how to feel about that."

"Conflicted is a good choice," I said. "We've talked about this before: Our ancestors were flesh-and-blood human beings with all the glorious and ignominious traits humans are capable of, sometimes within the same person. Have you got everything nailed down?" I opened a folder but Jack reached over to close it.

"Let's not do this right now," he said. "It doesn't seem so important after that conversation with Denny. I hate to even say this out loud, but I wonder if he's right about Beth. Something *was* wrong with her that night."

"Yes, she had a concussion!" I said, hardening into defensive mode. "Listen, I've idolized Beth for practically my whole life. Once when I was with her at the grocery store she told the clerk to add a nickel to her bill because she'd sampled a grape to make sure they were ripe. If she wouldn't filch a grape, she's sure not going to murder her husband."

"Maybe it's *because* you've had her up on a pedestal you can't look at this with a clear head. I like Beth and I'm not questioning her moral compass. But from what Bonnie's told me I'm not sure everything was as rosy at the Branch house as they wanted people to think."

"Maybe not," I allowed. "I, of all people, know family relationships can get awfully tangled up." I pointed a finger at him. "Which does *not* mean I think Beth's guilty of anything. And friendships can be complicated, too." I told him about the altercation I'd witnessed between Alan and Peyton and about what I'd overheard between Alan and Bonnie.

"I don't know how Peyton fits into the group," Jack said, "but the others were all college chums. They were all in the same little posse; you know how that goes in college."

I did. I was still tight with a number of friends from my undergrad days. There's a natural clumping mentality at that life stage. Most kids are away from home for the first time and while they enjoy their first taste of real freedom, they also need the security of a structure akin to family.

Jack went on. "It was Blaine, Alan, Bonnie, a guy they called Neutron, don't know his real name, but he lives in Silicon Valley now. Then there was Sarah somebody, who married a doctor and moved off to Minnesota or Wisconsin or some cold state, and another guy, whose name I forget, who moved to Australia."

"Wow, you and Bonnie must talk a lot," I said, not particularly pleased.

"More lately," he said. "She was sitting out on her deck a couple of nights ago when I was putting up a motion sensor light on mine. There's a rude little neighborhood raccoon who seems to think my planter pots are there for his entertainment. Anyway, Bonnie looked lonely and when I called a hello she invited me over for a glass of wine. She seemed to need to talk, so I mostly just listened. She was all nostalgic about their college days. Simpler times, I guess."

"Beth wasn't part of their crowd? You didn't mention her."

"I take it Beth was sort of on the fringes. She was a more serious student than the rest of them. From the sound of it they were all playing musical chairs with the relationships. Bonnie went out with Blaine for a while herself, but it never went anywhere. Ditto Alan. And Alan had a thing for Beth before Blaine started going out with her, though he never actually made a play for her, and Blaine moved in."

"Wow, regular little Peyton Place, wasn't it?" I said.

"Yeah, there was more him and her and she and him—they and them, for all I know. I think I sort of tuned out at some point." He stretched and stifled a yawn. "I'm beat and I've gotta get up early tomorrow. I'll leave this stuff here with you. Look it over when you get a chance to make sure I haven't screwed up somewhere along the way and my documentation is square. Would you?"

"Sure," I said. "And as far as your ancestor goes, maybe you should give Robert Ford the same understanding you so freely give others. When people get hemmed in they have to make a call right on the spot. Sometimes they own it and sometimes they regret it."

Jack nodded. "I'll keep that in mind. How about you? You got any further on the search for your mother's people?"

"A few bread crumbs to follow," I said. "I've found an elderly couple who were friends of my grandparents around the time of my mother's adoption. They're in an assisted living facility in Kansas City and their memories aren't the sharpest, but their daughter's agreed to help me do a virtual interview with them soon. Maybe I'll learn something useful. I'm sure my mother's adoption was illegal, maybe *highly* illegal, which is why there's no paper trail and no one wants to talk about it. But my grandparents are gone now and so is my mother, so what difference does it make?"

"Legally, probably none, but to you it seems to make a lot of difference, else you wouldn't still be pursuing this like a terrier after a rat."

"Lovely image," I said. "You really know how to make a girl feel special."

"I'm a sweet talker," Jack said, rising with a half grunt. "Lunch tomorrow at the diner? Maybe I can think of a more flattering comparison after a night's sleep."

"Okay," I said, trying to suppress an answering yawn. "Noon at the diner."

"Good night, Soph," he murmured, then leaned down and planted a kiss on the top of my head. I felt his lips on my scalp, even through my mass of hair.

Well. This was new.

twelve

ESME WAS ALREADY IN THE WORKROOM WHEN I GOT UP THE next morning. She was holding her head, a sure sign she was being hectored from another dimension.

"I didn't hear the blender," I said. "No smoothie this morning?"

"I was waiting for you to get up," she said, heaving a long sigh. "Celestine is applying the whip now, urging me on to read her diaries." She gestured to a plain, lined tablet of the sort used in schoolrooms back in the day.

"I'm sorry, Esme," I said, rubbing her shoulders. "I know it's hard on you when this happens. Maybe we should just pack these up and let Olivia be the one to read them. I'm not sure we're going to get any useful information about what happened to Olivia's father anyway."

"No," Esme said, holding up a hand. "No, I won't turn my back on Celestine. She's a sweet lady and I want to do my best to help her, but I just can't get a grip on what it is she wants me to know. We can pack up some of it, but not the diaries. I'm going to read every word the woman wrote."

"Why don't these spirit people just come out and tell you stuff?"

"I've told you, Sophreena, I don't lay claim to being any kind of expert on the afterlife, but I've learned some things since this first started happening with me when I was a child. Some questions I can get clear answers to most times. Like where something is. Where's the will? The heirlooms? The gravestone? So apparently lots of people get awarded with a cosmic GPS when they cross over. But anything having to do with relationships, or events, or any kind of story or feeling, and it all becomes a miasma. Things get lost in translation. Either they can't get it out or I can't understand it. It causes a muddle of miscommunication."

"Sort of like with living people," I said idly, running my fingers along the cover of one of Celestine's diaries.

Esme laughed. "Hadn't thought of it like that, but I guess that's right. I've wondered over the years if it's something about language. We depend on it so much and yet I know we've all had times when we find it inadequate. Maybe language mostly dies with us or else it becomes irrelevant. Sometimes I get actual words, but most times I get symbols, images, metaphors, and signs, or just a feeling or an emotion. Problem is, it's up to me to decide what it means and I can be awfully dense about it sometimes."

"And you can be brilliantly perceptive about it, too, Esme. What exactly are you getting from Celestine?"

"Just a feeling she wants me to hurry up and read these diaries and that something is not right."

"Hm," I said, "it'd be nice if she could be a little more specific, eh?"

"She's trying. I feel like I'm getting to know her by reading all these and I can see why Olivia was so fond of her. She was a caring person. Listen to what she wrote in October of 1942":

They had a sale on school shoes this week down at Rolene's General. Seventy-nine cents a pair for little oxfords. They're not Red Goose or Buster Brown, but they look good and sturdy. It came to me the Calvert young-uns are down to wearing shoes with newspapers stuffed inside them where the soles wore out. I know their sizes cause I'm in charge of getting up all the children's measurements for the Christmas swap at the church. But the Calvert kids will be barefoot by then. So I bought a pair for Georgie and one for Polly, too. But then when I got home I had to study on how to get them to the children. The Calverts are proud and I wouldn't do a thing in this world to shame them as I know they try hard as they can to make do for their children. But it is hard times and George has been sick and not able to work much this past year. So it came to me I could put it to Minnie that I'd like to trade her the shoes for some of her flour sacks in the pattern I need to finish up a dress, which is nearly the truth. I've got right smart of chicken feed sacks saved up that I was going to make me some dresses out of, but now I'm thinking we'll do up some curtains and pillowcases for Renny with them. And I really do love best of all the flour sack patterns with the little yellow *flowers the Occo-Nee-Chee flour comes in. I use Silk Floss flour, even though it's priced a little more dear as it makes a lighter biscuit and Riley is particular about his biscuits. I don't get a chance to get any of that print unless I swap out with somebody and with Minnie squeezing every penny that comes her way the Occo-Nee-Chee sacks is all what she's got in her larder. She was pleased to trade me and we laughed about how glad we are the government is claiming all the burlap for the war effort. We're behind that because we want to do our part, but also we surely do love all the pretty cotton flour sacks and feed sacks they're giving us now and they're welcome to the tow sacks.*

"That's sweet," I said. "I've run across several passages like that where she's done nice things for people. She was always careful not to make anybody feel beholden or embarrassed. I love that about her. In my mind backhanded charity is about as bad as benign neglect."

"Um-hm," Esme said. "I know plenty about backhanded charity. The family my mother worked for had a daughter several years older than me and sometimes they'd give me her castoffs if they were in a giving mood. Then my mother would have to listen as the lady of the house chirped on to all her friends about how generous she'd been to her maid. Mama never turned down the clothes, because I needed them and she made sure I said my thank-you-ma'ams but I know it was hard on her to take their brand of charity." She turned back to the diary. "Seventy-nine cents for a pair of shoes! Can you imagine that?"

"That was 1942 dollars," I said, my brain automatically generating a list. "Nineteen forty-two, a war year: *lots* of battles, horrors yet unknown in Europe, FDR is president, gas, rubber, sugar among other things, are rationed, victory gardens, daylight savings time begins, the Manhattan Project, Japanese-American internment camps, the Cocoanut Grove nightclub fire, actress Carole Lombard crisscrosses the country promoting war bonds and is killed in a plane crash. And at the movies both *Casablanca* and *Bambi* premiered." I stopped for a breath.

Esme was not impressed. She's seen my parlor trick too many times. "Yeah, that," she said. "And as if the war abroad and all the wartime deprivations at home weren't enough, Celestine was worrying over the situation just across her own yard. Listen to this part":

I'm fretting for Renny. She's trying so hard to be a good wife and doing her best to learn to please Johnny but it's never enough. Not that Johnny treats her rough but he's never satisfied with what she does nor how she does it. He gets real short with her and I can see it hurts her feelings to the quick. But it's clear he loves her dearly. He can be sweet with her, too, especially after he's had one of his little fits and been hateful and said hurtful things. Then he feels bad and is nice as pie for a while, but he doesn't learn the lesson. It's the same thing over and over again. Riley has tried to talk sense to him about it but all he gets for his trouble is Johnny sulking or giving sass back. It's a worriment. Poor little Renny looks wore-out most of the time and her weight has fell off, which is a troubling thing with her being so tiny to begin with. I even tried talking to Johnny myself, not that I had any expectation he'd listen to me anyways. He told me, "Sister, you need to look after your own house and let me take care of my own." Made me want to snatch him baldheaded since he is seldom even in his own house these days but out roaming the countryside carousing with his wild friends until all hours of the night. But I swallowed my words and told him all I wanted was him and Renny to be happy. Which is not at all a fib since that is my biggest wish.

"Sounds like Olivia's parents' marriage hit the skids right away," I said, glancing up at the clock. "And speaking of Olivia, we're due at her house in an hour. Shall I go in and make our smoothies?"

Esme gave me a look. "Sophreena, there are some things best left to the professionals. I'll go make the smoothies and you pack up the stuff we've already examined here on this end of the table." She swept her hand to include two or three boxes' worth of letters, photos, and memorabilia.

"Fine," I said, as Esme headed for the kitchen. "Always happy to be the workhorse," I muttered under my breath.

"I heard that," Esme said, without a backward glance.

Being careful to keep the materials in the proper order, I packed them up and sealed them into archival water-resistant bins. This is a part of the job that gives me great satisfaction. I like knowing the family materials have been rescued from the oblivion of crumbling cardboard boxes.

My smoothie, in an alarming tint of green, was waiting for me when I went to the kitchen. "What's in this?" I asked.

"Some things are best left a mystery," Esme said. "Just drink it down. It's tasty and it's good for you."

"Long as I don't start glowing in the dark," I said, taking a tentative sip. It was tasty. I was noisily vacuuming the last few drops from the bottom of my glass with a straw when the phone rang. The caller ID announced Coco.

"Could you come down to my studio for a few minutes?" she asked, skipping the small talk. "I've got a situation and I think you'll know how to handle it."

"You got some kind of family history emergency?" I asked with a laugh. "That's my only real area of expertise, you know."

"Not exactly," Coco said, lowering her voice. From the muffled sound of it I imagined her cupping her hand over the receiver. "But there's a family that may *be* history if things don't get hashed out."

Esme raised an eyebrow and I shrugged. "Is this urgent, Coco? We're supposed to be at Olivia's soon."

"I'll be back in just a minute, Sweetie," Coco said to someone on her end, then I heard jostling and the welcome bell at the Morningside Craft Co-op and realized she'd stepped outside. "I need you to come now, Sophreena. I've got Tina Gibson here with me. She knows some information about the day Blaine Branch died but she's—" She hesitated and I thought for a moment we'd lost our connection but then she went on. "It's complicated, Sophreena. Just come, okay?"

I hung up and gave Esme a recap. "Go," she said. "Come on along to Olivia's when you can. Coco's not one for drama."

"Seriously?"

"Well, okay, she'll chew the sets when it's about her, but not about something like this. You'd better go find out what's what."

Tina Gibson was not quite herself. In fact, she was somebody else entirely. Tina was an upstanding member of the community and head of the Arts Council. She always took great care with her appearance and carried herself with a cool reserve. Today? Not so much.

Although I didn't know her that well, she and Coco had been friends for a long time and that counted for a lot in my book. Coco was trying to comfort her as Tina sobbed and swiped at her mascara-streaked face.

"What's wrong?" I asked, still standing in the doorway of Coco's studio.

Coco brushed past me and put the BACK IN FIVE MINUTES sign on the shop door. She twisted the lock and headed back into the studio, beckoning me inside.

"Sophreena, I called you because I know you can keep a confidence," Coco said. "I told Tina she could trust you."

"She didn't need to convince me," Tina said with a hiccup. "We've known one another a long time, haven't we, Sophreena?"

I allowed that we had, though I didn't see fit to point out that was a mixed bag. Tina was older than me by a few years and had been one of the popular girls. Unlike Beth, she'd not been universally loved. She wasn't a bad person, but she was unsure of herself, which made her occasionally do unkind things if that's what it took to stay with the in-crowd. She'd never done anything mean to me, so I had nothing personal against her, but we hadn't been pals by any means.

"Listen," I said hesitantly, "I don't know exactly what's going on here, but if you know something that's important to the investigation into Blaine's murder you need to come forward."

Tina looked to Coco, her eyes widening, then she wailed. "I told you this was a mistake," she said. She ran her hands into her hair, normally styled into a purposefully messy cut. Today there was nothing purposeful about it. She grabbed a hank of hair on either side of her head and let out another wail. "I'm ruined," she said, choking out a couple of pitiful sobs.

"Tina," Coco said softly, "just tell Sophreena what you told me. She's your best hope right now."

Tina sucked in a big breath, holding it longer than I would have thought possible. The woman had diver's lungs. Finally she let it out in a big puff. "I am *so* screwed," she muttered. "What does it matter now?"

She looked completely dejected and I felt compelled to say something reassuring. "Tina, I'll do anything I can to help. Now, what's going on?"

"What's going on is that I've made the worst mistake of my life," Tina said, now more morose than hysterical. "And that's saying something."

Coco pulled over a chair and motioned me into it, then moved her stool close to Tina so she could rub her shoulder for encouragement.

"I was with Blaine the day he died," Tina said, her face a study in misery.

"Go on," I said, trying hard to keep my face expressionless.

"I picked him up at The Sporting Life, in the back parking lot. I dropped him off a couple of hours later near his house," Tina said. "I was trying to talk him into making a contribution to fund an art scholarship for the high school."

"For two hours?" I said. "That's a lot of lobbying."

An angry look came over Tina's face, but it soon deflated into misery again.

"Were you having an affair with Blaine?" I asked, figuring we might as well cut to the chase.

"No!" Tina said. She held her chin high for a moment, then she slumped. "But I would have. It was only a matter of time. We were working up to it. How in the world could I have been so stupid? I wasn't in love with Blaine. Sometimes I didn't even like him much. I love Mike. I love my husband. I know that's hard to believe, given what I'm telling you, but I would just die if Mike found out about this. It would hurt him so much. I can't explain how I let this happen. I think maybe I just wanted some excitement and I was flattered when Blaine flirted with me. How pathetic is that?" She looked at me as if she actually expected an answer.

I'm normally a compassionate person, or at least I like to think so, and this woman was clearly in pain, but I was angry on Beth's behalf—and on Mike Gibson's. Mike was the ultimate nice guy. So, since she'd asked the question, I answered. "Truly pathetic," I said.

I instantly regretted it. Tina dissolved again into a heap of blubbering and Coco gave me a scolding look, which I had to admit I richly deserved.

"Look, Tina," I said, reaching over to touch her knee.

"I'm sorry you're in this situation and I hope it doesn't blow up your marriage but you've got to come forward with this information on Blaine's whereabouts that day. It could help the police solve the case. You need to talk to either Jennifer Jeffers or Denton Carlson."

"Denny, please, I'll talk to Denny," Tina said, sniffling. "Jennifer doesn't like me. That's my own stupid fault, too. I wasn't very nice to her in high school."

I thought of telling her Jennifer didn't like Esme and me much, either, but I didn't want to give aid and comfort at that point.

"Could you ask Denny to keep this to himself?" Tina asked now. "Will Mike have to find out?"

"This is a murder investigation, Tina. Denny will have to tell the other detectives anything that has a bearing on the case, but he might be able to spin it to make it look less—" I searched for a word, but could only come up with *sleazy*, which didn't seem a wise choice, so I just let it hang.

Tina nodded. "Okay," she said, drawing in a shuddering breath.

"Would you mind me asking you a couple of questions? Maybe you could think of it as practice for talking with Denny."

"Okay, I guess," she said, digging around in her purse for a tissue. I glanced over at her tote and my eyes bugged.

"Are you carrying a gun?" I asked.

"Oh that, yes," Tina said. "Mike got it for me for protection last year when I was having so many night meetings. I've got a license and I'm qualified with it. I go to the range and everything."

"I didn't realize Mike was such a gun guy," I said.

"He is," Tina said, nodding vigorously. "I mean he doesn't hunt, but he shoots for sport. He and Blaine are even on the same team at the gun club. *Were* on the same team. I don't really like having it. I'm always afraid if it came down to it a bad guy could take the gun away and use it on me. But I don't have the heart to tell Mike I don't want to carry it."

It seemed there were a great many things she didn't want to tell Mike. I bit my tongue and held in my opinions about toting lethal weapons around in pink designer handbags and moved on to my questions. "You say you picked up Blaine in the store parking lot, right?"

"Yes, he texted me the night before and told me what time to be there."

"Do you know how he got to the store? His car was in the shop."

"Yes, he said his brother and a friend were picking him up," Tina said, calming now that we were getting down to cold facts.

"That was nice of Peyton," I said absently as I was mulling the timeline.

"Not according to Blaine," Tina said with a sniffle. "He was hacked off three ways from Sunday when he got into my car. Apparently he and Peyton and whoever this other guy was had a bad fight about something. Blaine was madder than I've ever seen him." Her face twisted, threatening waterworks again. "Which may have saved me from myself. I think he would have made his play that day but he was too mad to even bother with me. He was in a terrible foul mood, which really put me off." She looked up, hope shining in her bloodshot eyes. "I mean that, it *really* put me off. Maybe I wouldn't have gone through with it. If Blaine hadn't gotten killed I mean. Maybe I would have stopped it right there. I was *that* put out."

"I'm sure you would have come to your senses," Coco said.

I wasn't so ready to let Tina off the hook, but I thought of Esme's many admonitions about how sarcasm doesn't become me and moved on with my questions. "Did he say what the fight was about or who the other person was?"

"No, but he asked me if I'd ever had a friend betray me, so it must have been somebody he knew well."

I suppressed a scornful laugh. That was a fine question coming from a married man who was sneaking around to meet up with a married woman, but I didn't think Tina was in a place to see the irony. "Where were you for the hours you were with him?" I asked.

"We drove over to Chapel Hill to eat lunch. Or I ate mine; he mostly drank his. And I did ask him about the scholarship fund," Tina said, turning to Coco, who was clearly more sympathetic than me. "He said I should talk to Bonnie Foster about it since she seemed to think she was the brains of the operation. He said it real bitter. He was so surly. He was usually smooth and charming. But not that day."

"And where did you drop him off?" I asked.

"Two blocks from his house," Tina said, "so Beth wouldn't see him getting out of my car."

"And that's the last time you saw him?" I asked.

"Yes, that was the last time. He said he'd call me and I hoped he would and hoped he wouldn't. You know what I mean?"

I nodded. "How many times did you have these little meet-ups with Blaine?" I asked, trying, and failing, to be delicate.

Tina winced and I made a silent vow to put a cap on the snarky while she searched her memory. "Four times within the last two months," she said finally.

"And you're sure Mike didn't know about this? Or at least suspect?" I asked. Though I couldn't imagine mild-mannered Mike as a murderer, Denny was right: Who knew what people were capable of given the right motivation.

"I'm sure," Tina said flatly. "Mike trusts me completely."

And the wailing began in earnest.

Once in my car I called Denny and gave him the quick-and-dirty on my talk with Tina—so to speak. I'd left her with the warning that she should contact Denny immediately and that I'd be giving him a heads-up. I also advised her to talk to Mike before the rumors got to him, but I wasn't sure she'd do that.

She'd looked up beseechingly as I got ready to leave, her lip quivering, green eyes round and vulnerable. "Haven't you ever made a mistake, Sophreena?"

I had. Many. Though I hoped none that had the potential to cause so much hurt. But Tina's obvious pain and genuine remorse got to me and I really hoped she and Mike could survive the fallout if this came out.

I started the car, then remembered Marydale had more papers we'd ordered for Olivia's scrapbooks and decided I might as well pick them up since I was here.

As I opened the shop door I reached up to touch the bell

to keep it from announcing me. Marydale wasn't up front so I figured she was in the workroom, and I didn't want her to stop what she was doing to rush out for a nonexistent customer. As I walked toward the back I could hear muffled voices. I couldn't hear the words but the tone was contentious. The doorway to the workroom has only a curtain and I pulled it aside to see Marydale and Winston sitting at the worktable. Marydale had her little Westie, Sprocket, cuddled up on her chest and Winston had the other dog, Gadget, asleep on his lap. Both people and canines looked up, startled.

"Winston came by to help me rearrange these shelves," Marydale said, her words coming quick. She gestured to the hodgepodge shelving units that had grown up willy-nilly over every inch of wall space.

"They're not efficient," Winston said. "We're trying to figure out what configuration works best."

I looked from one to the other. Were they acting weird or was it just me? I pulled a chair over and out of the corner of my eye caught them exchanging a meaningful glance— meaningful to them, anyway.

Normally we share everything in our little club and I considered telling them about what I'd learned from Tina, but I knew Coco would probably tell Marydale at some point today and it was so sad and tawdry, I didn't have the heart to rehash it at that moment.

"The order for Olivia is over here," Marydale said, setting Sprocket down on the floor. He sniffed and went to curl up in his bed in the corner as Marydale pulled the package from a bin. "That's one downside of rearranging. I know where things are now. I'll have to learn a new system."

"Change is good," Winston said. "It's just hard some-times."

I wasn't sure the conversation was about shelves any-more. I took the package and stood to go.

"Hang on a minute, Sophreena," Marydale said. "Some-thing happened this morning and I've been debating what to do about it. Let me run it by you." She motioned for me to sit back down. "You know Arlene Overton, right?"

I nodded, feeling a shiver of dread at the name. Arlene Overton was the poster woman for cranky, prudish, mean-spirited town gossips.

"I know, I know," Marydale said, reading my face. "She came in this morning with her sister, Susan. Honestly those two should be in some kind of genetic study. Susan takes after their mother, who was the sweetest woman you'd ever want to know. Never had a bad word to say about anyone. But Susan must have sucked all that water right out of the gene pool, because Arlene didn't get a drop of it. Anyhow, you know Arlene lives right next door to Beth and she was going on about why have the police not arrested that juve-nile delinquent because she knows good and well that's who killed Blaine Branch. How she has a mind to tell Sterling Branch or make a call to the State Bureau of Investigation to tell them the local police are botching things, or maybe con-tact a reporter or whatever."

"And this juvenile delinquent is?" I asked, already know-ing the answer.

"Tony," Marydale confirmed. "Poor Susan kept trying to tell her she shouldn't be accusing people without knowing all the facts, but Arlene went blathering right on. She swears she heard Tony's motorcycle backfire that afternoon. She was grumbling that she's been hearing it for weeks every time he rode up Blaine and Beth's driveway and that it unnerved her because it sounded like a gunshot. So she knows Tony was at Blaine's house the day he died. She said there was some kind of ruckus going on over there in broad open daylight and that it must have been Tony causing it, never mind that she can't see a thing through the hedgerow between their houses. Anyhow, she claims she's told the police and still they haven't brought Tony in for questioning. Then she said—right out loud in front of a store full of customers—that she wouldn't be surprised if Beth and the *hoodlum* were in on it together."

"She's nuts," I said.

Marydale nodded. "Poor Susan was so mortified she hustled her out of the shop before I had a chance to throw her out, which I would gladly have done. The problem is, we know she's a hateful old fishwife but not everybody does. So should I say anything about this to Denny? Would that make it better or worse for Tony?"

"I'll talk to Denny about it if you want," I said. "Arlene Overton may be a whack-a-doodle but if she's got any useful info I'm sure Denny would want to know."

"What about Tony?" Winston asked.

"Oh, I'll *definitely* be talking to Tony," I said.

thirteen

TONY WAS FILMING WITH ESME AND OLIVIA WHEN I ARRIVED. Esme hadn't warmed to the idea of the video scrapbook and had fussed about our having to arrange our schedule to match Tony's. I was expecting her to be relieved I was there to take over. But it seemed somewhere along the way she'd discovered her inner ham.

"If we're going to do these video scrapbooks with our clients I need to learn about it, too, Sophreena," she said, patting her hair, which she'd done up in a complicated braid. She leaned in close to me as if she wanted to tell me something secret, but then I realized she was checking her makeup in the reflection of my glasses. "Do you know about this Ken Burns effect thingy?" she asked, slicking her pinky over her lips to freshen her gloss. She pointed to the scrapbook pages open on the table. "Tony sets it up so the camera pans over the pages while we're talking about them and it gives the finished product movement and vitality," she said, her hands indicating an undulating motion.

I turned to Tony. "What have you created?" I asked.

"A prima donna. But the camera loves her."

"Okay, then," I said. "I'll just sit in the corner over here out of the way."

"No, you'll make me nervous, Sophreena," Esme said, flashing me a silent message with her eyes. "Beth's out on the porch. Why don't you go visit with her while we finish up here."

As I passed through the family room I saw a bouquet of beautiful roses on the side table. I tiptoed over to take in a whiff of their fragrance. Then I noticed the card and the snoop in me couldn't resist. They were to Beth from Alan Corrigan. The card read *Everything will be okay if we stick together.* It seemed an odd condolence message, but who was I to judge? I never know what to say on those occasions.

Beth was sitting in a wicker chair with a quilt wrapped tightly around her, though the day was balmy for October. She was mesmerized by something in the yard but I didn't see anything of interest. I spoke her name softly so as not to startle her and she turned, the movement in slow motion.

"Oh, hi, Sophreena," she said. "I'm trying to remember. Why can't I remember that day? I get little bursts," she flayed out her fingers, "but then it's gone and I can't call it back. It's so frustrating."

"Would you like some company for a few minutes or am I disturbing you?"

"No, please," Beth said, pointing to a twin wicker chair. "Will you be warm enough?"

"Yes, fine," I said, looking down at my sweater and jeans, which were actually a little too toasty with the afternoon sun warming the space. I brushed at my black jeans. "I was holding Sprocket," I said. "Normally he doesn't shed so much; he must be overdue for a grooming."

"They're cute dogs," Beth said, returning her gaze to the yard. "I always wanted a dog but Blaine says they make a mess and are too much trouble. He doesn't want us to get one." She frowned and pulled the quilt tighter around her. "He *didn't* want *me* to get one," she corrected.

"You know, Beth, sometimes the harder you strain to remember something the more elusive it becomes. What *have* you remembered about that day? Do you mind me asking?"

"No, I don't mind," Beth said, looking up at me as if surprised to find me there. "I just feel weird. It's like I'm not processing things, or there's some kind of delay. I don't even know how Blaine got to the store that day. Or was he even at the store? Bonnie said she didn't see him, so maybe he didn't even go there. He had no car and he didn't use mine, and his bike was still in the garage."

I decided it wasn't my place to divulge anything Tina had told me. And even if I had been free to tell her, I wouldn't have relished the idea. Would Beth feel the loss less if she knew or would it double it? I went for a more innocuous question. "What was your regular Saturday morning routine? Maybe thinking of that will trigger something."

"We usually sleep a little later than normal, then have an easy breakfast before Blaine goes off to play the sport of his choice: tennis, golf, sometimes fishing or kayaking, or maybe shooting at the range. I usually catch up on housework, then craft or read or spend time with Mom."

I noticed that she'd slipped into the present tense again and this time she didn't correct herself.

"This might not work considering your memory problems are caused by your injury," I said, "but there's a technique I use with clients to help them remember names, dates, and events for their family histories. Would you like to give it a go?"

Beth hesitated, then nodded enthusiastically. "Yes, yes, I'll try it. I'll try just about anything at this point."

"Okay, well, let's start by having you get into a comfortable position, then we'll do a relaxation exercise." I took her through the drill, asking her to relax each part of her body and clear her mind, then slowly slid into questions. "Okay, so you're waking up on Saturday morning. What do you see? What do you hear?"

"I see my bedroom, our bedroom. I look over but Blaine's not there." She frowned, then opened her eyes. "Oh, but I don't *know* if that was Saturday morning. Maybe that was another morning."

"It's okay," I said soothingly, hoping I could get her back on track. "Just close your eyes again and let it come to you. Now what do you hear? Is the radio on?"

"Mmmm," Beth said, "yes, my clock radio, classic rock. Blaine likes heavy metal, which is horrible to wake up to, but his is off. There are voices, but not from the radio. They're in our kitchen maybe. It's a man and he's saying something like 'your time is up' but real calm like maybe there's a chess game going on. Blaine doesn't like chess much but he plays with Alan sometimes. I think the voice *was* Alan." She opened her eyes again. "Well, no, it couldn't have been Alan. That would have been the day before. Alan had already gone back to Chicago by then." She let out a huge sigh. "Thanks anyway, Sophreena, but this isn't working."

"Keep using the relaxation exercise on your own, Beth. Even if it doesn't aid your memory it can help with stress."

"I will," she said, then surprised me by reaching over to give me a hug so fierce it squeezed the breath out of me and I wheezed like an accordion.

Esme was still upstairs getting dolled up when Denny arrived that night to take her to dinner. His eyes were bloodshot, he had a two-day growth of stubble, and he moved as if his shoes were made of lead.

"I take it the investigation is still stalled," I said as he followed me to the kitchen and plopped down in a chair.

"You take it correctly," Denny said. "Though *stalled* isn't exactly the right word; let's just say it's proceeding at a glacial pace. I talked with Tina Gibson this afternoon. I wish she'd come forward sooner. It would have helped establish Blaine's movements through the earlier part of the day. And I'm going to have a chat with Peyton Branch tomorrow. He never told me he was with his brother that morning."

"Was he ever asked? I mean, with the shock of his brother's death and the funeral and all, did anyone actually interview him?"

"Jennifer did," Denny said. "She interviewed everyone in the Branch family. You don't think she'd pass up a chance like that, do you? High-profile case, high-profile family? If she gets credit for a collar on this one it'll be very good for her."

"And very bad if she doesn't, right? Bet she's not getting much sleep, either."

"Let me put it this way, I'm the pretty one right now," Denny said, using his hands to frame his haggard face.

"Are you going to be able to keep Tina's information confidential?" I asked.

"Confidential, no. I'll do what I can but I couldn't promise that. I felt sorry for her; she's obviously ashamed and scared about what Mike will do if he finds out. But she made her bed—though if she's to be believed, she didn't lie in it."

"Listen, Denny, I know I asked you this before, but are you sure Alan wasn't in town that day?"

"Second time you asked me about him. What's up?"

I told him about my talk with Beth. "The exercise wasn't very effective, but for a moment or two it did seem like she was remembering. Probably nothing."

"Probably," he said, "but I'll follow up on Corrigan all the same."

Esme came down at that moment looking every inch the beauty, and with Esme that's a lot of inches. Denny's face brightened. He stood and kissed her on her proffered cheek and confirmed what she already knew, that she looked gorgeous.

"You said you'd pick the place," he said. "Where are we headed?"

"We're going to a little Thai place over in Chapel Hill for dinner. I want to get you out of town for a couple of hours so you can clear your head. Then after dinner we're going for a massage, both of us."

"A massage?" Denny asked. "I've never had a massage in my life."

"Well, you're getting one tonight," Esme said. "I booked it, I paid for it, you're going, and you're welcome."

"Esme," Denny protested, "will I even fit on a massage table? In case you haven't noticed, I'm a big guy."

She gave him an up-and-down sweep of her eyes, then cocked her head. "In case *you* haven't noticed, I'm not exactly Tinker Bell and I fit fine. But we will need to tip the masseuse generously."

As Esme threw the end of her scarf over her shoulder and headed for the door, Denny turned back to me and whispered, "They may have to charge us by the acre."

"I heard that!" Esme called.

I settled in to read more of Celestine Hargett's diaries to pass the time before Jack arrived. He was bringing pizza and a movie. It wasn't a date, and it certainly wasn't on par with a massage, but it was something to look forward to nevertheless.

My heart raced a bit as I considered a massage and Jack in the same mix. I'd been struggling for a while now about how to get over crushing on him. It was silly. I gave myself the usual lecture about the value of true friendship over fickle romance, and part of me listened but the other part was still hung up on the massage thing.

I opened one of Celestine's diaries and tried to put my attention back on life in the 1940s. I'd unrolled the timeline I was making for Olivia on the coffee table, letting it fall off each end and curl onto the floor. I located the section the diary covered in case I discovered anything that needed to be ticked in.

I hadn't given up on finding out what happened to Olivia's father, but I was getting discouraged. I was hoping I'd find something that might give me a lead. But, like Esme, I was also enjoying getting to know Celestine Hargett as she confided things about herself, like in the 1942 entry I was reading now:

> *I have not much time to write tonight for I am about to give out and will have to be up at early-thirty to get Riley off to his new job at the post office. I cannot begin to tell how relieved I am that he did not make it into the army. I am ashamed of that as I know he wants to do his duty and is really downhearted about them turning him down. And I know there's others that are going willingly and plenty that don't have any choice but to go. Maybe I feel a little like we are shirking by not making that sacrifice, but I can't help how I feel. I just don't believe I could go on through life without my Riley.*
>
> *Johnny has told everybody for miles around that he will refuse to go even though he got his draft notice last week. And he makes no bones about it. He feels no sense of duty at all and says we've got no business over there to begin with and he's not going to get himself killed for nothing. That makes Riley double-shamed as folks can now say one Hargett can't go and the other one won't go.*
>
> *Paul Tillett, one of that big family of Tilletts from over around Murdock, rents our farmland and he has two sons, Robert and Raymond, who work it with him. Since they're farmers both his boys could get exemptions but Robert is eighteen and has already signed up and Raymond wants to go so bad he can't hardly stand it. He is not but fifteen and his mama says he's just a boy and*

she will never sign for him to go. But there's lots of boys around who are slipping off and lying about their ages to get in. I hope she can keep him out as one son in peril is quite enough for a mother to bear.

Renny found a little feist dog down by the river yesterday. He was about half dead and had a string tied around his leg so it's probably one somebody was trying to drown to get shed of it. Renny washed it and fed it warm milk and it's looking a whole lot better, but Johnny says she can't keep it. She begged him and was pitiful until finally he allowed as how she could keep it in the corncrib, but she wasn't to let it in the house and she's to keep it out from underfoot.

He's a pretty little thing and we're calling him Shoes. She called it something a little different at first and said it was Chinese for water, since she found him by the river. But Riley and me couldn't pronounce it right. The little fellow has four black feet so we've all decided Shoes is a good name.

The dog has made Renny happier than I've seen her in a long while now and I do wish Johnny would let her keep the puppy with her but he is stubborn as a mule and purely strange about things when it comes to Renny. I don't understand him. It is as clear as the nose on your face that he is plum crazy for her, but he turns down nearly about every chance to do little things that make her happy.

I remembered seeing a dog in the background of one of the family photos and made a note to scan, crop, and enlarge it and to ask Olivia if she'd known the dog named Shoes. I also made a note about Johnny Hargett having received his draft notice sometime before the date of the diary entry.

I had my laptop beside me on the couch and it made a whirring noise. I realized I still had the Crawford movie in the drive and reached over to pull the computer onto my lap.

Something was niggling at the back of my mind, but I couldn't get hold of it. I clicked the video to play and watched as schoolkids paraded by in lockstep, girls skipped rope, and boys wrestled. Then the action cut away to the pool hall, where several swaggering young men gave James Dean squints at the camera, preempting the actual James Dean by a decade. Then there were two old men playing checkers. The board was set up on a barrel and the scene was fogged over with a haze of cigarette and pipe smoke. There was much Coke-drinking and watermelon-eating and tricks on bicycles and roller skates. Almost all the men wore hats: fedoras, panamas, baseball caps, porkpies, or farmers' wide-brimmed straw toppers. They all seemed to need something to do with their hands when the camera turned on them. Some made a show of pulling a cigarette from the pack, or rolling their own; others checked their pocket watches or messed with their hair. One standout was a man who looked so old he could have been the captain of the *Mayflower*. He stepped toward the camera, definitely ready for his close-up, Mr. DeMille. A grin spread across his rubbery face, revealing not a single tooth, though he had a glorious handlebar mustache that commenced some impressive tilting and bouncing as he hammed for the camera.

I clicked the slo-mo button; I remembered the segment

with Olivia's kinfolk was coming up and I wanted to watch it carefully.

Once the old man had exhausted his mustache acrobatics, the camera found Olivia's parents. Johnny was even more handsome on closer viewing. Olivia had gotten his height, his fair complexion, and what I assumed were his blue eyes, though all I could tell from the sepia-hued film was that they were light.

Renny was camera-shy but Johnny seemed intent on having them both looking into the camera. The film was silent, but if my lipreading was any good he said "get over here" and reached around her, grasping her upper arm and pulling her up against him, all the while smiling lazily into the camera.

Renny did look at the camera, though her head was tipped down. Johnny reached into his pocket for his pocket watch. He dangled it from the fob, then twirled it up into his hand, clicking the button to open it just as it landed in his palm.

Renny reached up to rub her upper arms as if she were cold. My mind went into a click-stall-grind session until finally the gears meshed. It was the exact same gesture Beth had made after she and Blaine had said their good-byes at Olivia's front door the day we'd given Olivia her present. Blaine had pulled her toward him in almost the same way, more a sign of possession than affection, it seemed to me.

I heard the front door and recognized Jack's footfalls. I waited for his usual "Soph? Whereyaat?" but instead he appeared in the doorway, pale and agitated.

"What's wrong?" I asked, setting the laptop back on the sofa.

"Something weird happened at work," Jack said. "But I'm not sure if I'm making something out of nothing or if it's something the cops oughta know about."

"Well, out with it."

He sat stiffly on the edge of the sofa cushion, his arms propped on his knees, hands clasped tightly together. "One of my workers called me out to the greenhouse just as we were closing up. You know Solomon, right? He's my crew foreman and he does a quick inventory of the equipment and supplies every couple of days to make sure we haven't left anything behind at a site or had anything stolen. He's very fastidious about it. He called me out to look at a tarp he found."

"What was special about it?" I asked.

"First off, it wasn't ours," Jack said. "I buy blue ones so they're harder to overlook. This one was dun-colored. It was folded like we fold ours, only not as neat or tight as my guys do it."

"Okay, so you have an extra tarp from somewhere?" I asked. "I mean, aren't they pretty cheap?"

"Yeah, but just listen. We unfolded it, thinking maybe it would have the name of the company stenciled on it or something. If we'd picked it up by mistake I figured I'd return it. When we got it all opened there was something all over it, and Soph, it looks like blood. I remembered all those questions Denny asked about how we do yard care at the Crescent Hill houses and I sort of put two and two together and got some ugly math."

"Yeah, I see. I'm getting a pretty wretched four, too."

"But here's the thing: It might not be blood, it could be anything," Jack said. "Paint maybe or some sort of fertilizer or motor oil. I don't want to look like a complete wing nut if it's nothing."

"Where do you store your tarps?" I asked.

"Behind the greenhouse," Jack said. "Back near the mulch pile and the chipper. Solomon built a wooden rack to stack them in."

"I remember now," I said as I visualized the area behind Jack's greenhouse. "So if Solomon checks these things every day or two, this outlier tarp couldn't have been there long, right?"

"No, not right," Jack said. "Solomon's been on vacation. He just got back yesterday. It could have been there for up to two weeks."

"Where is it now?" I asked.

"Locked up in the greenhouse. You think I ought to call the police?"

"Denny and Esme will be back soon," I said. "If it's all the same to you I'd rather you tell him than have Jennifer Jeffers at my front door. We'll see what he has to say. Like you said, it could be nothing. In the meantime, I'm starved; let's eat and watch the movie."

"Uh," Jack said, opening his hands as if searching. "I forgot the pizza—and the movie. I'm sorry, Soph. Everything just went out of my head."

"It's okay," I said, picking up the phone from the side table. "We'll get pizza delivered, then I have a little movie here on my laptop I want you to watch. Maybe you can help me figure out the plot."

fourteen

A HALF-CENTURY-OLD FILM ABOUT EVERYDAY LIFE IN A ONE-stoplight North Carolina town wasn't exactly the thriller we'd planned on for the evening's entertainment. But after we'd polished off the pizza, Jack settled in next to me to view the section of the Crawford film I'd watched earlier. I didn't want to prejudice him toward the theory I was developing, so I didn't say anything by way of introduction.

Jack occasionally made comments about the clothes, hairstyles, or cars. When we came to the part featuring Olivia's kin I simply said their names. I stopped it when their part was over.

"Tell me what you noticed," I said.

Jack frowned. "Is this one of those tests to see how observant I am? Was there something freaky going on in the background that I missed 'cause I was looking at the people on camera?"

"No, nothing like that. I just want your impressions."

"Okay," Jack said, drawing the word out. "Well, for one thing I'm glad I'm living now instead of back then. I don't care what people say about the good ol' days. That looked pretty hardscrabble if you ask me."

"What else? What about Olivia's people?"

"Well, her uncle and aunt looked like salt-of-the-earth types. Her mother seemed self-conscious, a little out of place maybe. And I'd say her dad was one of those showboat guys who likes to be the center of attention and in charge. Is that what you mean?"

"Yeah, that's exactly what I mean. And tell me if I'm reading too much into this." I told him what I'd observed of the exchange between Beth and Blaine by the front door at Olivia's house. "Could it be that these women, grandmother and granddaughter, were each being abused? Psychologically, at least."

Jack considered then shrugged. "Sure, it's possible."

His ready reply took me aback. I'd been expecting, hoping, that he'd tell me my theory was a stretch. "But surely Beth wouldn't put up with that kind of thing, right?" I protested. "She's an accomplished person. She earns her own living. It's not like she's trapped in a marriage out of financial want. And they have no children. Why would she stay and take that?"

"You know my sister, Kelly, right?" Jack said. "You wouldn't think she'd stay, either, would you? But she did. And in her case it wasn't just psychological. Kelly married young. Fell for a guy with a few rough edges she thought she'd be able to file down. She stayed with him for nearly four years, hiding bruises under makeup and wearing long sleeves. She didn't tell anybody, not even me. She couldn't bring herself to leave him until the night he pushed her out into oncoming traffic in front of a coffee shop because she put too much cream in his coffee. Hadn't been for an alert driver, she'd have been killed. She packed her bags that night and finally developed a stone ear for all his promises about how it would never happen again."

"That's so awful. I can hardly believe it. Kelly's such a strong person," I said.

"Yeah, she is—now," Jack agreed. "She met Mark a year later. It took him a long time to earn her trust but to his credit he hung in there and proved his mettle, and six years and two kids later he's still proving it. Looking back on it Kelly herself can't even understand why she stayed as long as she did. I think this is one of those things that looks a lot different from the outside than the inside."

"Well, I may be wrong about Beth and Blaine, but I'm convinced Olivia's mother, Renny, was controlled by her husband, maybe even physically abused. And in those days even when women got up the courage to speak out there was little in the way of help. Lots of times even cops would dismiss a complaint as a family matter and wouldn't intervene. Maybe that's why Renny wouldn't leave Johnny. She'd defied her parents to marry him, given up everything of her old life, and she was probably too ashamed to admit she'd been so wrong about him."

"Yeah, well, Beth and Blaine seemed like the perfect couple from all appearances, but like I say this thing looks different from the inside. I guess it wouldn't do to just come out and ask her, would it? And anyhow, what difference does it make now?"

"None, I suppose. Except it could be motive. If Beth was being mistreated anyone who cared about her would want that to stop—one way or the other."

"You got candidates?" Jack asked.

"No, not really," I said, though my mind was already constructing a list of those who might be most outraged: Daniel, Tony, even Olivia, however unlikely a suspect she might be. I thought of all those petite women who—if legends were to be credited—could call upon mama-adrenaline to lift a car off a pinned child.

Thankfully, these unpleasant musings were interrupted by the sound of Esme and Denny laughing in the front hall. Denny came in, looking far better than he had when he'd left.

"How was the massage?" I asked.

Denny crooked his neck from side to side and shook his arms. "I can't remember when I've felt this loose," he said. "I was nearly able to forget the case for a while there."

I looked over at Jack, then we both gave Denny a rueful smile.

"Sorry," Jack said, "but I think maybe I'm about to put some of that tension back in." He told him what he'd found and the two of them immediately set off for the greenhouse.

Esme stood at the window, a wistful look on her face as she watched Denny's car back out of the driveway. "Ah, well, duty calls." She glanced at her watch. "It's early yet; let's you and me read some more of Celestine's diaries so we can get all the books back to Olivia before we leave for Wilmington. How far did you get?"

"Is Celestine still urging you onward?" I asked, avoiding the question.

"Oh, honey," Esme said, flapping a hand. "She was even there while I was having my massage, and not happy I was trying to relax when there was work to do. Even that Tibetan new-age music they play couldn't drown her out. Same message—*It's not right*—over and over again."

I told her the tidbits about the dog and the timing of Johnny Hargett's draft notice. Then I told her my theory about Johnny and Renny's relationship.

Esme considered. "I don't doubt it," she said. "Looking at the way he was with her in that movie set my teeth on edge. My husband was just like that, a peacock, full of charm and strut and pretty to look at. I was young and silly and beguiled by all that. Until we got married and I tried to turn him into a husband. He couldn't catch on to the nuts and bolts of that job and the swagger lost its allure real quick. Nobody to blame but myself, though. Mama warned me not to marry a musician."

Esme had married young and was still young when she became a widow. Her husband had been killed in a car crash on his way to a gig. After he died Esme took back her birth name and swore never to put her trust in a man again, until Denny came along and convinced her, with our help, to go to coffee with him.

"Yeah, well, here's the other part," I said. "I see some similarities between that relationship, Renny and Johnny I mean, and how Beth and Blaine acted that day at Olivia's." I told her about what I'd seen in the front hallway and how it paralleled what I'd seen in the Crawford movie.

"That's a big leap based on one little interaction," Esme said.

"I agree, but it might explain why Beth got so upset when we watched the Crawford movie that day. Remember? Olivia thought it was seeing a happy couple that undid her, but now I'm wondering if she saw her own pain reflected back. I sincerely hope I'm wrong. I know it's complicated, but it's hard for me to accept that Beth would stay in that kind of relationship."

Esme stared off into space for a moment. "*Complicated* is one word for it," she said. "I might have ended up in that same boat if Roland had lived longer. I don't think he'd ever have hit me, considering I was a head taller than him and fifty pounds heavier. Plus he'd have been too worried about damaging his hands and not being able to play his sax again. But he tried his best to keep me in what he thought was my place and little by little I was letting him box me in."

That shocked me, but I tried to keep it off my face. Esme was the last person in the world that I could ever imagine being subservient to anyone.

She shook her head as if to clear it, pulled a diary off the stack, and flipped it open to look at the date. "This one takes up the time frame when Johnny decamped," she said. "I'll start in on it and you finish the one you were reading."

"Deal," I said. "I'll fix us a cup of tea."

"Chai for me, please," Esme said, settling on the end of the couch and kicking off the high heels she insists on wearing, as if six foot two weren't altitude enough.

By the time I came back she'd stretched out with a blanket over her legs, taking up the entire sofa, and was deep into her reading.

I set her chai on the table and she murmured an absentminded thank-you. I went back to skimming the diary I'd been reading, sucking in the words like a baleen whale straining to find the bits of info that might be useful in constructing Olivia's family tree.

We read in companionable silence, stopping occasionally to read aloud to one another. The more we read, the fonder we both were of Celestine. So I had to share her excitement when she first suspected Renny was pregnant with Olivia:

> *Renny is putting back on a little weight here lately. That's a good thing because she had fell off to where I was worried she was going to waste away. I am awful glad but nervous, too, as I figure it means something more than her having an extra biscuit once in a while. I believe she is in a family way, which is thrilling and worrying at the same time. It tickles me to death to think we might have a little one around here, but I worry for Renny's health and I worry even more for what kind of daddy Johnny will make if he does not grow up right quick like. I was hoping he'd surprise me and make a good husband to Renny, but that has not been the way things have gone. Oh, but putting all that on the side, a baby! That would be joy heaped on top of joy.*

"I imagine that must have been hard for Celestine in some ways," Esme said, her voice wistful. "She'd wanted children herself and it hadn't happened for her."

I heard the tremor in Esme's voice. "Did you want children, Esme?" I asked.

"I did," Esme said quietly. "Very much. But I was waiting for some sign that Roland was ready to be a father."

"And then he died."

Esme tilted her head. "I think I'd given up on babies long before Roland died. Then life just went on like it will and then it was too late."

"Looks like the sign never came for Johnny Hargett, either. This is from a couple of months later, listen":

I've never seen my Riley like this. He's got a fire stoked up inside and it is good Johnny is off on one of his rambles as I fear what Riley might do to him if he could get his hands on him right now. Renny is already struggling to carry her swollen belly and has been sick to her stomach right much. She usually comes over and lets me rub her shoulders and make her a tonic, but she'd kept to her house for two days and I got worried and went over to look in on her this afternoon. Riley was just getting home from the post office and he stepped over there with me in case she had some little chore he might do for her. She had a black eye. She claimed a switch from the maple tree snapped back on her when she went to fetch firewood, but she was telling a story and she's no good at fibbing.

Riley got real quiet then he made her tell him and she said it was her fault, that she'd said something she ought not have said and that Johnny had lashed out before he could stop himself. She cried and cried and said he didn't mean to do it and he'd promised her solemn nothing like that would ever happen again.

I never had any high hopes for Johnny, but even I wouldn't have thought such as this was in his nature. We are heartsick. Johnny was not raised to think he could do his wife like that. His daddy was a kind man, tender and respectful of their mother. Johnny Hargett knows this is not right.

"Well," I said, "there we have it. And there's your answer to what Celestine has been trying to tell you when she says *it's not right*. I suppose there's no way to gussy this up for Olivia."

"No, I guess not," Esme said. "On the other hand, maybe she'll realize it was a *good* thing he ran off. These things generally go from bad to worse if they're left to run their course. Renny was in danger, whether she knew it or not. Her parents were halfway around the world by then, so Riley and Celestine were all she had. Thank God for them."

"Yeah," I said, flipping through the diary and skimming. "I don't see anything here about what happened between Riley and Johnny over this. There's a long gap here, the longest I've seen. She didn't write for a couple of weeks and then this":

> *Johnny is gone. He has told everyone in the county he wouldn't go and fight so no one was surprised he would run off. It is a terrible shame to bear, but folks don't know the half of it and it's best they never know it all. Renny is pitiful. I don't know how to comfort the girl except to let her know she always has a home here with Riley and me. She's still hoping Johnny will come back, but Riley and me know better. My heart is heavy but we will all have to pull together in the traces and make a good life for this baby.*

"I must have the book that comes just after yours," Esme said. "Celestine writes here that an elderly lady named Mrs.

Yarborough saw Johnny boarding a train with a knapsack. Mrs. Yarborough was fond of Renny and let it be known that if she'd suspected the scoundrel was running out on Renny and his baby, she would've flogged him with her cane. She was also highly offended he'd gotten on the same train as young men in uniform. Celestine says Mrs. Yarborough's eyesight was poor and she was easily confused, but that it was good Renny believed her, so she'd accept Johnny was gone for good and she could get on with making a new life for herself."

My cell phone rang and almost simultaneously Esme's started singing from her purse. Jack and Denny were both calling in with a report. Once Denny had seen the tarp he'd called out the crime techs. The preliminary test showed the substance on the tarp to be blood, but there were no details beyond that.

"They're packing it up to take it to the lab," Jack said. "This may still turn out to be nothing. Denny says it could just as easily be animal blood, but I don't think he believes that. Plus, he called Beth and she confirmed they had a dun-colored tarp. I've gotta wait here to lock up so I guess I'll see you tomorrow."

Esme and I clicked off our phones at almost precisely the same instant and compared notes. Jack had read Denny right. He fully expected the results would show the blood on the tarp belonged to Blaine. That didn't *prove* that Blaine was killed at their home, but it certainly gave weight to the theory. And it raised a lot of questions, most centering around Beth.

"She'll be okay," Esme said, reading my mind.

"How do you always know what I'm thinking?"

"Just because I never birthed children doesn't mean I don't have a mother's heart. I'd never try to replace your mom, but there's no law says you can't have two."

"I think Mom would be happy about that," I said.

"She is," Esme said, with certainty.

"You've heard from my mother?"

"Calm down," Esme said. "No messages, no unfinished business. But she's a soul at peace and I'm certain she's very proud and happy with the choices you've made in your life—so far anyway," Esme said, tipping her head to give me the look over the top of her reading glasses.

I smiled, thinking of how much my mother would have loved Esme. Mom was always drawn to the unusual. "Okay, thanks for that, Mama Deux," I said. "And the choice I'm making right now is to toddle up and get some sleep. You?"

"I'll read on a little longer," Esme said. "Now that I know what Celestine was trying to tell me, maybe I can find a way to give the poor woman some comfort."

I put on my PJs and crawled into bed—and was instantly wide awake. My mind ping-ponged between conviction that Beth had been abused and thinking I'd gone off the deep end. By the time I drifted off I was certain I'd hyped this up in my own mind, influenced by what we'd learned about Beth's grandmother. Beth and Blaine surely had their problems, and given Blaine's wandering eye, he was no candidate for Husband of the Year. But a cad was one thing, an abuser quite another.

I finally drifted off into a hard sleep and dreamt of little feist dogs wearing children's school shoes and soldiers throwing civilians from trains. And then Celestine was there in a flour sack dress, shaking me and telling me *it wasn't right* again and again. I tried to slip from her grasp but she held firm. I woke to find Esme's hands on my shoulders, her face inches from mine.

"That's not what she meant," she said, her voice raspy. "It was something else, something horrible. Wake up, Sophreena."

I squinted against the light as Esme switched on my bedside lamp. She sat down on the edge of my bed as I pushed myself into a sitting position and tried to get my mind in gear.

"Oh, Sophreena, we have *done* it now," Esme said, clucking her tongue. "I don't know how we're ever going to tell Olivia about this."

"What?" I asked, wide awake now.

"I know what happened to Johnny Hargett," Esme said. "Oh Lord, Sophreena, what a mess. I wish we'd never gone looking. Celestine wrote it all down in her last diary, on the very last pages. It's like her dying declaration." Esme opened the notebook she'd been clutching. "Listen to this":

> *By the grace of God I have lived a long and mostly happy life. I was blessed with a good man to share my joys and trials. He was a good man, the best man I ever knew of and I want you to remember that, Olivia, if ever you read this. Riley and me made a promise long years ago we would never speak of this to another living soul, and we never did. But I am getting myself ready to cross over the river Jordan and this is weighing on me something terrible. I do not want to take it with me when I*

*go. I know this might make you despise our names and
remember us badly, Olivia, but I pray not as we did the
best we knew how and always loved your mother and you
with all we had in us.*

*If you have read my books I kept you will already
know that Riley and me found out that your daddy was
ill-treating your mama when she was carrying you. Riley
spoke to him about it and he made a solemn vow it
would never happen again and that he would straighten
up and do right by the both of you. And things went
along pretty good there for a little while, but then Johnny
got a notice that he'd be under charges if he didn't report
for the draft and he went on a bender and everything fell
apart. We heard terrible noises and hollering and Riley
went running out to the little house to stop whatever was
going on. He told me later if he hadn't come he believed
Johnny would have killed your mother. He was crazy out
of his head.*

*I took care of your mother and Riley hauled Johnny off
down to the river and out onto the train trestle where they
used to go when they were boys. Riley wanted someplace
where he could hold him and not have him run off, and
where he could cool down some himself because he was
so mad he didn't trust himself. He started in talking to
Johnny, trying to make him understand what he was doing
was wrong, but Johnny was too full of whiskey and fear
and hatefulness to listen. He told Riley that Renny was his
wife and he could do with her whatever he pleased and
it wasn't nobody else's business and that he'd teach Riley
to butt in and then he hit Riley so hard in the stomach it*

doubled him over. They got into an awful fight and then Johnny tried to get past him, yelling about going back to the house to teach Renny to keep family matters to herself. Riley tackled him and they fought hard and that's when it happened. Riley hit Johnny and he went right through the uprights and over the side of the trestle and fell to the river below. Riley heard a scream and a noise like something soft hitting something hard, sounds that stayed with him all his life. It was sounds he heard in nightmares and in his waking hours, too. Riley went as fast as he could down to the riverbank, but he couldn't find any sign of Johnny. The water was high and the river flowed fast that time of year and it is filled with big rocks and all kinds of entanglements from the roots of trees and such. Riley walked the banks all that night and we did it together all day the next day, but we never found a sign of him. Riley knew Johnny was dead, as nobody could have survived that fall. But he needed to find him for all kinds of reasons that probably don't make good sense all these years later. Riley couldn't stand it that he didn't have a Christian burial beside where their mama and daddy found their final resting place. Riley was destroyed. He blamed himself. He grieved for his brother and yet hated the thing his brother had become.

We had an awful dread the body would be found, and then were sick it wasn't and Johnny was out there by himself to meet his maker without even a send-off with some love in it. He most likely got tangled up in roots or in some of the junk people used to dump into the river before there was landfills. We couldn't bear to think *about that, about Johnny being left in that cold dark river all alone.*

Riley struggled about whether to report what happened to the sheriff. Not out of fear for his own self, but because of your mother. He asked me did I think Renny would take this all on herself and believe she caused it by telling. I said she surely would. Your mama was like that, especially in those days when she was so young and with her feelings so tender because of her condition. We decided we couldn't let your mama know what had happened. We agreed we'd let her think Johnny had just gone off again, at least until after you were born and your mama was stronger.

Then the talk around town picked up about Johnny running off to avoid the army and it seemed like that would be a better thing than the truth of it so we didn't dispute it. Renny had shame to bear, we all did. But she was saved from a terrible guilt that would have followed her all her life long that she was the cause of what happened. That helped me and Riley hold up under the burden of it. You can't ever know what this did to your Uncle Riley. He was never the same after that and he paid for his part in it a thousand times over. I pray you won't harden your heart against him, but if you do you have to give me my share, too. Him and me talked it over and decided the best way we could make it up was to watch over your mama and you and do all we could for you. And I want to think we did.

We loved your daddy, Olivia. We did. But it was like he had some kind of sickness and we couldn't help him.

We didn't know about any syndrome-this and disorder-thats back in those days.

I expect you'd like to know if your mama ever knew any of this. The answer is I just don't know. She surely never heard one word from Riley or me, but she was a smart woman and there was times when I was pretty sure she suspected something like this. Maybe not that Johnny died, but that Riley had run him off or something like that. But after you came along she turned her face to you and never did dwell on bad things. She loved you with everything in her, and me and Riley loved the both of you. That's one reason I'm leaving this behind. I think you've got the right to know it all and it can't hurt any of us now. I am old and I am weary and I've carried this long enough so I will lay it down here on this page. I'm not brave enough to tell you while I live. I'll leave it up to a wisdom greater than mine to lead you to read this or to keep it locked away in some dark corner or put it in a burning fire unread.

With my dearest love until we meet up yonder,
Aunt Celestine

"Holy crap," I breathed.

"Uh-huh," Esme said, closing the book with a snap.

fifteen

I WAS RAISED CATHOLIC BUT MY ATTENDANCE AT MASS IS
spotty and usually prompted by a rough patch in my life.
Though my own life was humming along pretty well right
now, I was feeling a lot of anxiety about people I care about
and I find comfort in ritual.

Esme didn't say anything when I came down fully
dressed, but she gave me a nod of approval. Esme, as usual,
was dressed to the nines for church in a shirtwaist purple
knit dress with a sage-colored belt so wide I could have
worn it as a tube top. She had matching green spike heels
and a multi-strand necklace of lamp-work beads in every
conceivable color. For the life of me I could never figure
how she pulls these odd combinations off, but she looked
stunning.

"I'll probably see Olivia at church," she said. "I'll ask if
we can stop by this afternoon. We may as well get this over
with."

"I haven't exactly figured out how to tell her yet."

"Not the kind of thing you blurt out at Sunday dinner between 'this fried chicken is really crispy' and 'pass the mashed potatoes,' is it?"

"No, it's not, and there are still a couple of things bugging me."

"Only a couple?" Esme said. "For you that's pretty good."

I ignored the jib. "What about the old woman, Mrs. Yarborough, the one who saw Johnny getting on the train?"

"You read what Celestine said about her, poor eyesight and prone to confusion. She was probably just mistaken. And anyhow, Celestine knew it wasn't true."

"And the arrest record?" I said.

"You know very well most forms of identification back then had no photograph. I can think of all sorts of scenarios where vagrants might have found Johnny's body and filched his ID," she said with a shiver. "But I don't like thinking too hard on that 'cause it's too grisly."

"Yeah, it is," I agreed. "I just want to make sure we give Olivia the most solid information we can get."

"What is it you're always preaching about firsthand reports?" Esme asked.

"That weight must be given to a description of events provided by a source with firsthand knowledge as long as they have no motive to misrepresent the event," I recited. "But it doesn't take the place of getting hard evidence."

"Which we can't do in this case, since only three people in the world knew what happened and they've all passed on. And since you academic types are so dead set—you'll pardon that expression—against accepting my word for anything those folks might have to say *after* they pass, we're stuck with what we've got."

Esme left for church and I still had a half hour—and an idea. I went into the workroom and powered up my laptop. I called up a series of maps and traced the path of the river that ran through Crawford, noting the counties downstream. Starting with the county closest to Crawford I checked death records for the time period in question. This was a long shot, as most records from that era haven't been digitized yet, but sometimes you get lucky—and this time I did. Sort of. Two counties south from Crawford I found a death certificate for a John Lamont HARNETT. The date of birth matched Johnny HARGETT and the one-letter discrepancy was likely a typo or a misreading. The box checked for notification of next of kin said UNKNOWN; cause of death listed was drowning. The date of death was also listed as UNKNOWN, but was estimated. The date fell two weeks after Johnny and Riley had their altercation on the railroad trestle.

I thought of what Esme had said about the paper identification from those days. There surely would have been water damage. And how many people could there be in that small area with the first and middle-name combination John Lamont and the same date of birth. It was far from definitive proof but I was reasonably sure I'd found Olivia's father's death certificate. But there were still two conflicting pieces of information I needed to sort out: the arrest report and the sighting of Johnny by Mrs. Yarborough.

I dashed off an email request for a copy of the original documents, hoping they would contain a physical description, and made a note to check the newspaper archives for more info. I sat back in my chair, feeling both relieved and terribly sad. If this held up we'd answered Olivia's most pressing question, but it was a disturbing story.

*   *   *

Olivia met us at the door and I noted the pink was back in her cheeks and she moved more spryly, almost like her old self. She was smiling but I could tell she was holding back, a part of her partitioned off with worry about Beth. It made me think of a saying Marydale spouts now and again about her two grown-up kids and their life challenges: *A mother can only be as happy as her unhappiest child.*

We went into the dining room and Olivia showed us the scrapbook pages she and Beth had done. They were beautiful. The items on the each page had good balance and weight and they'd used embellishments judiciously to help tell the story rather than obscure it. There was copious script on each page documenting everything known about each photo and weaving the family narrative through.

"Wow, you get a gold star," I said.

"It's mostly Beth," Olivia said.

"Where is Beth?" I asked.

"She's upstairs, resting," Olivia said. "She went to church with me this morning and it was hard. People either wanted to say their condolences all over again, or they pretended not to see her at all."

I feared this was the least of what Beth was going to get as the investigation into Blaine's death wore on, especially after word got out that their home was the likely scene of the crime. And with Arlene Overton running her mouth about her crackpot theory.

"What was it you wanted to tell me?" Olivia asked. "Esme said you'd found something. I'm dying to hear."

Esme looked at me, but I found myself tongue-tied. The genealogist in me was ready and eager to give a report. The friend in me was not. If this had been a couple of generations removed from Olivia, it would have been different. Clients can be more detached as they move back in time to more distant antecedents. But this was Olivia's father and though she'd never known him, this information about both his life and his death would be upsetting. And worse still would come the revelations about her sainted uncle Riley and aunt Celestine and what they'd kept from her throughout her entire lifetime.

Esme saw me struggling and said to Olivia. "Let's sit down to talk. We've found out what happened to your daddy and it's going to be a hard story to hear."

"Should I get Beth?" Olivia asked uncertainly.

"Let us tell you first and you can decide," Esme said.

Olivia's smile faded. She sat down at the table and folded her hands in front of her as Esme opened up the diary and spoke softly. "I'm going to read you something your aunt Celestine wrote a few months before she died. You need to hear this in her words."

Olivia listened, her face occasionally contorting. There were silent tears and shuddering breaths, but that was all. No histrionics. When Esme was done reading we sat in silence to let Olivia collect herself.

"Poor Uncle Riley," she said, fishing a tissue from the pocket of her jogging suit. "How he must have suffered. He was such an upright man. This must have eaten at him over all those years. And my mother! Why couldn't she have told me about the abuse? *She* didn't do anything wrong."

"I don't know why she chose not to tell you," I said. "Maybe she thought she was protecting you somehow. Things were a lot different back then. These things weren't talked about."

"Not so different," Olivia said, swiping at her nose with the tissue. "Even now people don't talk about it. And the abusers still get away with it. I don't understand it. My mother was a strong, smart woman. She went back to school after my father left her—well," she said, gesturing toward the diary, "I guess now I have to say after he died. She took correspondence courses, and then Aunt Celestine and Uncle Riley looked after me for a semester while she went to Greensboro to finish up her degree. She was a grade school teacher for thirty-seven years."

"I imagine she was a proud woman, too," Esme said. "And it seems like it's harder for proud women to admit they've let themselves get into situations like that. I'm sure she was doing what she thought best, Olivia, for both of you."

Olivia nodded. "You're right," she said at last. "Sometimes people blame the victim. No wonder they're afraid to come forward. And here I am doing it myself. I suppose I should feel sad that my father died, but I didn't know the man, and now that I know how he treated my mother I'm glad I never knew him." She frowned. "Is there something I should *do* about this? I mean, should I report it to somebody?"

"The principals are all deceased," I said, "and any evidence would be long gone, so I can't think what would be accomplished, but I'll check into what our legal obligations are if you'd like."

"Okay, you do that. But I'm not going to allow this to be a secret any longer. Otherwise I'd be doing to my family and friends what my mother and aunt and uncle did to me. This is our family's history, the good and the bad."

I didn't want to leave Olivia in this frame of mind, so we talked a little while about more pleasant aspects of her family history. Then I reached into my bag for the photo of Shoes, the dog. "On a happier note, did you know this little guy?"

Olivia smiled as she picked up the photo. "Ah, that's Shoes. My best buddy."

"You knew the dog then?" I said.

"Oh, I'll say," she said, sniffling into her tissue again. "That dog went everywhere I did, until he died of old age when I was about twelve. He slept in a little basket by our fireplace. He was a great little companion for a kid living out in the country."

"Do you know how he came to join the family?" Esme asked.

"You know, he was always just there," Olivia said. "Mama had him even before I was born. I don't know where or when she got him."

I pulled the page I'd scanned from Celestine's diary out of a folder and read it to her, selectively editing out her father's edicts about keeping the dog.

"Well, how 'bout that!" Olivia said. "All those years I should have been calling him Shui, instead of Shoes," she said, pronouncing the word *schway* the way her mother had doubtless taught her. "But Shoes suited him, too, in more ways than one. He was forever taking my shoes off and hiding them somewhere. I think maybe he believed it would keep me home with him instead of me going off to school. You know, somehow that dog could tell time. I swear he could. Every day he'd trot down to the end of the road to meet the school bus and he'd arrive just as I stepped off. Perfect timing, every single school day, rain or shine."

I got the eye signal from Esme that it was time to go. Olivia walked us out and as we were saying our good-byes Marydale's car pulled up with Winston at the wheel. Marydale got out of the passenger side and opened the back door. Beth got out, holding Gadget. She didn't have on a jacket and it was obvious she'd been crying.

Olivia rushed toward her, holding out her arms. "Beth, what in the world? I thought you were upstairs taking a nap."

"I was," Beth said, her voice almost robotic. "But I heard voices downstairs and I came down to see who it was. I wasn't eavesdropping," she said, turning to Olivia, "but I heard the whole story. It's so strange. Just strange."

"She walked over to my house," Marydale said. "I think she needs to get inside and maybe you could make her some hot soup, Olivia."

"Yes, yes," Olivia said, putting her arm around Beth's shoulders.

Winston reached over to retrieve Gadget. He practically had to pry the dog out of Beth's arms.

Esme and I both turned to Marydale after Olivia took Beth inside, but she put up a hand. "I don't know what she overheard, and I'm not going to ask," she said. "She wants to talk to you, Sophreena, but she says to give her a little time first. She was awfully upset. I think maybe she's starting to remember some things about the day Blaine died, too."

"Like what," Esme asked.

"We don't know, exactly," Winston said, casting a sidelong glance at Marydale. "She wasn't making sense. Something about history repeating and being a brother's keeper but none of it was tied together right. It was like she couldn't even hear Marydale or me talking to her." He looked over at Marydale again and I had the distinct impression they were hiding something from Esme and me. This was the first time I'd ever felt anything but total honesty in our tight little club.

I didn't like this feeling one bit.

sixteen

Esme has a thing for outdoor decorating, and ever since she's come to live with me our house gets decked out for all the seasons. We'd come home from Olivia's and set in working on the autumnal display. I was checking every few minutes to make sure I didn't miss a call from Beth, but no word yet. As we arranged a cornstalk teepee on our front porch Denny called to ask if he could stop by.

"Why does he bother to call?" I asked. "Surely he knows by now he's welcome."

"He calls ahead because he is courteous—and because I have explained to him those are the rules," Esme said. "I don't like being taken for granted."

"You mean you don't want to be caught when you're not all spiffed up," I said with a grin.

"There is that," Esme allowed. "But that's not all of it, Sophreena," she said firmly. "I never expected to be in a relationship again in my life and I don't like the idea of giving over my independence to any man, even Denny Carlson."

"He's a good man, Esme," I said.

"I know," she said with a sigh. "And he's handsome, and he's taller than me."

"How many men have all that going for them?" I asked. "And he's willing to put up with your quirks?"

"He doesn't know about *all* my quirks, Sophreena, as you well know."

"Why don't you just tell him?"

"Oh no," Esme said, holding up a hand. "Absolutely not! I'm not going to have him thinking I'm some kind of circus freak."

"You're certainly not a freak, Esme," I said. "You're a sensible, caring person. A person who just happens to have a gift."

"You say gift, other folks say peculiarity. And some days even I say it's a blue ruin."

"Well, you know I don't agree," I said, as I hung a pinecone wreath Esme had made onto our front door. "You do a lot of good with your gift. And you've trusted our friends with your secret and they've been totally accepting."

"Our friends are accepting people," Esme said, "otherwise I wouldn't have told them in the first place. But not everybody's like that."

I thought Denny Carlson was exactly like that, but I could see Esme wasn't going to be moved by any argument from me right now.

A few moments later the man himself pulled up and parked on the street. He ambled toward the house, his long legs covering the walkway in a few strides.

"Good job," he said, admiring our harvest display. "Makes me hanker for a cup of hot cocoa or something."

"Well, come on in," Esme said. "I can make you one."

"Strong black coffee might do better," Denny said. "I go on duty in an hour and I need every synapse firing."

Esme put on the coffee and then got out a saucepan. "I think I want a cup of cocoa now that you've put the idea in my head. I like to make it the old-fashioned way, none of these foil packets with those gravels of marshmallow. That's sacrilege."

"I called Jack this morning to let him know we're done with his place," Denny said, settling at the table.

"I'm sure he's relieved," I said. "He was creeped out big-time."

Denny nodded. "Don't blame him. And there's still plenty to be disturbed about. The blood on the tarp was human blood and the type was the same as Blaine Branch's. We're still waiting for the DNA, but I have a hunch it's his—a strong hunch. I know that doesn't sound like cool, analytical thinking," he shrugged, "but I believe sometimes you've got to go with your gut."

"Yes, I believe that, too!" I said, giving Esme the wide eyes.

She returned a snort that muffled a French swearword.

"Anyway," Denny went on, "I followed up on Alan Corrigan. Thanks for that lead. Turns out he was actually still in town the day Blaine died. He took the red-eye out of RDU that night. Jenny questioned him by phone and he says the last time he saw Blaine was that morning. Him and Peyton gave Blaine a ride to the store. I talked to Peyton and I'm convinced there's more to the story, but they've both clammed up. 'Nother thing," he said, stopping to take a deep draft of the coffee Esme set in front of him. "Jenny's got a burr under her saddle about that kid, Tony Barrett. Beth's neighbor has called the station probably ten times or more, insisting he was at the house the afternoon Blaine died. She claims she heard his motorcycle backfiring. Jenny remembers Tony from back when she was the liaison officer at the high school. He was trouble back then and I believe she's letting that color her judgment, but I expect she'll be dragging him in for questioning."

"Are you telling us we should give him a heads-up?" Esme asked, stirring the pot as the aroma of hot cocoa permeated the kitchen.

"Not at all," Denny said, giving me a wink. "I'm simply saying if you were to talk with him anytime soon you might mention that it would be a good thing if he could account for his movements for that entire day."

After Denny left, Esme went up for her traditional Sunday afternoon nap. I put away our outdoor tools and checked my phone for the dozenth time to make sure I hadn't missed a message from Beth. I was just closing up the shed door when Tony pulled his motorcycle into our driveway.

"Hey," I called out, wincing as he turned the key, expecting the motorcycle's backfire.

"You got a minute?" he asked, peeling off the helmet and shaking out his mop of hair.

"Just about that," I said, making a show of looking at an imaginary watch. "I've got to be somewhere in a little bit. What's up?"

"I wanted to show you some of the footage from the interview with Charlie."

I motioned him inside and he set up his laptop on the kitchen table. "You're a great interviewer," he said, as he powered up the computer. "Even better than Beth, but don't tell her I said that. After seeing this I really want to go forward with this project on Charlie."

"I'm glad, Tony," I said, "but remember what I told you about my schedule. We leave for Wilmington on Thursday and I'll be gone for at least two weeks."

"Yeah, yeah, I know," he said, punching at the keys. "And we still have to convince Charlie, but watch this, then tell me you don't think it's worth the hassle."

He played a series of rough clips and I watched, at first distractedly and then mesmerized by the emotions playing out on Charlie Martin's face. It was powerful.

"He's a charismatic old dude, isn't he?" Tony asked, clicking a key to put his computer to sleep.

I sighed. "Yes, okay, it's worth going after. We'll work out the logistics. I'm sure Olivia won't mind putting you up a while longer."

"Hey, I'm a paying tenant now. I finally got paid for a wedding video job I did a while back. I got my motorcycle fixed and, after some fast talking, I got Olivia to let me chip in for the electric and water I'm using at least."

"I'm really glad to hear your bike won't be backfiring anymore," I said. "And speaking of which, are you sure you didn't go by Beth's house at some point earlier on the day Blaine died?"

"No, not till you all sent me over there to check on Beth just before dinner that night. You already asked me that. Twice. Why are you bringing it up again?"

I told him someone thought they'd heard his motorcycle backfire. I tried to keep it offhanded and didn't mention names.

"Let me guess," Tony said, his chin jutting out. "That lady next door. Man, what did I ever do to her? She hates me for some reason."

"She hates pretty much everybody; try not to take it personally," I said. "Thing is, she's pushing her claim pretty hard, so it might be a good idea to work up a timeline and whatever documentation you can gather that shows where you were at any given time on that day."

"Okay, here we go again," Tony said, throwing his hand up in exasperation. "Anything bad happens, pin it on the juvenile delinquent." He clicked some keys on his laptop again. "Like I told you before, I was out shooting b-roll stuff. I may have gone somewhere *near* Beth's house, maybe even near enough for that old hag to hear my bike, but I didn't go to the house and I didn't see either one of them that day until Beth came to Olivia's for supper that night. Here," he said, turning the laptop so I could see the screen. "Here's my b-roll from that day." He hit the fast-forward button and I watched as he zipped through a series of shots in and around Morningside. I was relieved. The video was time-stamped and it covered most of the afternoon of the day of the murder. Still, there were several gaps where he'd presumably been moving from place to place, and since the time of death had been difficult to pin down, the gaps were problematic.

"Wait," I said, as an image on his laptop caught my eye. "Slow it down." I squinted at the screen view of a couple of guys in a kayak out on Potter's Creek. They paddled in unison, veering toward the shoreline of the river. I recognized the spot. It was about a quarter mile down from The Sporting Life.

"That's Peyton Branch and who's that with him?" I asked.

"It's that college friend of Beth and Blaine's, the one who came to visit from Chicago. Alan somebody," Tony said.

I watched as the two men continued to paddle toward the shoreline. They made a sharp turn and I saw Peyton's hand reach down to the water. A moment later he lifted a paddle from the water and pulled it into the boat and they reversed direction, moving toward the pier in back of Blaine's sporting goods store.

"Somebody must've lost an oar," Tony said.

"Yeah, an oar," I said, my mind spinning.

After Tony left I decided Beth must have changed her mind about talking to me. I was seriously considering laying a fire in the family room fireplace and snuggling up for a nap, but then Olivia called, sounding frantic. I told her I'd be right over.

As I was searching for my keys, Jack called to ask if I wanted to hang out. I told him I couldn't and got perverse pleasure in how disappointed he seemed. I told him I'd call him later if he was willing to play it by ear.

He was.

This was the wonderful thing about being friends instead of a couple. We didn't get hung up on expectations or pout about being neglected or any of that stuff.

That's what I told myself.

Olivia met me at the door and practically marched me to the backyard. She grabbed an afghan off the back of the sofa when we went through the family room. Beth was sitting in one of the Adirondack chairs next to a cast-iron fire pit. It was filled with red embers so it must have been going for quite a while.

Beth smiled at me, but her eyes looked vacant. "Thanks for coming, Sophreena." She motioned toward a matching chair and I sat down. Olivia handed me the afghan.

"Mom," Beth said, frowning as if she needed to concentrate to get her words into the proper sequence. "I'd like to talk with Sophreena for a few minutes. And then I want to tell you and Daniel some things. Would you call him and ask if he could come over? Tell him it's important."

"Beth, you're scaring me," Olivia said.

Beth made a tutting sound. "There's no reason to be afraid, Mom. Not anymore. Just tell Daniel to come and we'll all have a talk later, okay?"

"Okay, honey," Olivia said, wringing her hands. "I'll leave you two alone." She started back into the house, but stopped a couple of times to look back as if she thought Beth might change her mind and ask her to stay.

When she'd closed the door I waited. Beth stared into the fire for a long time. Finally she brought her chin up slowly and looked me square in the eyes, a deep frown furrowing her forehead.

"I always liked you, Sophreena," she said. "Did you know that?"

"Well, not really, but I'm glad to hear it," I said.

"I mean it," Beth said. "When we were kids I used to like

it when our families got together. I always found you had interesting things to talk about and you were smart and funny. There was the age difference then, but now we're both adults and we're on equal footing. And I know I can trust you to keep a confidence. I can, can't I?"

"Yes," I said. "If what you have to tell me doesn't hurt anyone else, I'm good at keeping things to myself."

Beth nodded. "I'm sorry we've never gotten to be closer friends. You may have noticed I don't have any close friends."

"Well, that's certainly not true, Beth," I said. "You've always been one of the most popular people I know."

Beth smiled ruefully. "I have a lot of very lovely acquaintances," she said. "And back in high school and college I did have friends. Wonderful friends." She stared into the fire again. "But later I wasn't allowed friends," she said at last. "Do you understand what I'm saying?"

I did. And I thought I could make things easier for Beth by just coming out with it. "Blaine wanted you under his control. He isolated you. It's the pattern of controlling men."

Beth's eyebrows went up. "You knew?"

"No, I had absolutely no idea. Not until recently. I always thought you were the happiest couple around."

"We were," Beth said with a wry laugh. "For an occasional fifteen minutes at a stretch."

I decided that since Beth had asked me here to talk, she might welcome a chance to simply get it all out. "How bad did it get?" I asked.

"Bad," Beth said, her eyes flooding with tears.

"Physical?" I asked.

Beth nodded. "Lately."

"Who else knows?"

"Alan Corrigan and Bonnie Foster suspect. They saw how it was from the beginning. Blaine was showing signs of this kind of thing even back when we were in college. But I just thought he was jealous and honestly I was a little flattered by that at first."

"Who else?"

"Peyton knows."

"Is that why you and he were arguing? Was he pressuring you to keep this quiet?"

"I can't talk about Peyton," Beth said with a sigh. "I just can't go there right now, Sophreena. I don't have the energy."

"That's fine, I'll drop it," I said, reaching over to pat her leg and give myself time to delicately frame my next question.

"Beth, does any of this play into how Blaine died?"

"No," Beth said, startled. "No, how could it? I just needed to tell someone. I've held this in for so long. And when I heard you and Esme this afternoon telling Mother what happened to her father, I couldn't believe it. History repeating itself like that. Isn't it strange? But, no, I don't see how this could have anything to do with Blaine's death. No one knew how bad it had become. No one but Peyton. And that only made things worse."

I wondered just how far the historical parallel went. After all, it had been her grandfather's own brother who'd ended up killing him over just this issue. Though in the present case it seemed Peyton's issues were with Beth, not with his brother.

"So the violence had escalated lately?" I asked.

Beth nodded. "And I let it."

"Beth," I said, "you know it wasn't your fault. You're a smart woman."

"Yes," she said, the tears spilling over and running down her cheeks. "I consider myself a reasonably intelligent person. Which makes it all the more perplexing. And makes me feel more a failure. Why couldn't I fix it?"

"It wasn't up to you to fix him, Beth," I said. "But I've got to confess it is hard to understand why you stayed."

Her chin began to tremble and she crumbled. "Do you know what this would do to Blaine's parents if it ever got out?" she asked, her voice ragged. "Sterling and Madeline have been wonderful to me. And they thought—*think*— Blaine was the perfect son, the perfect husband. It would kill them if this came out. Maybe literally in Sterling's case. And they'd hate me for making the claim. Plus, I can't face people knowing I was a victim. I won't have it. I'm asking you to honor your word and keep this to yourself. I'm going to tell Mother and Daniel; it's time I did that. And Esme will be able to comfort Mother, so you can tell Esme, but no one else is to know." She looked at me like a drowning woman begging for a life jacket. "You have to swear to me, Sophreena."

I swore.

seventeen

CARRYING A SECRET CAN WEIGH YOU DOWN. PLUS IT CREATES A gap between those who know and those who don't. I could already feel the effects as I drove home.

Beth had asked me to stay with her while she told her mother and Daniel, and it was an emotion-wrought hour. As frequently happens, I held two opinions at once: that both Daniel and Olivia had absolutely no inkling and were completely in shock *and* that they had suspected all along. Olivia took the news with physical pain, holding her middle and rocking back and forth. Daniel's anger had smoldered like the embers in the fire pit. I'd had the thought—inappropriate and ghoulish—that it was a good thing Blaine was already dead or else Daniel might have killed him.

I stayed long enough for the shock to wear off, then left them to their family time.

When I got home I recounted everything to Esme and she took it with her usual rant to mask the pain of it.

"I knew I didn't like that guy," she said. "He was too slick by half and he wouldn't ever look you in the eye. Shame! That's what that was all about: He was ashamed and he had plenty to be ashamed about. We find out now after he's dead and gone and can't be held accountable. I know it's wrong to speak ill of the dead and no matter what the man did he didn't deserve to have someone take his life, but I've got to say, the more I find out about him the less regret I feel about him being gone from this earth. And all those people at his funeral, talking about him like he was a saint? Well, that surely won't stand once this comes out."

"It can't come out," I said firmly. "We're not to tell anyone, not even the club. Beth doesn't want any hint to reach Blaine's parents and sully their memories of him."

Esme started to protest, then puckered her lips. "I understand," she said, resigned. "I don't like it, but I understand."

After supper I called Jack and asked if we could go for a walk on the lakefront and was gratified by his eager yes. I dug my heavy coat out of the back of the closet and rummaged on the shelf for a scarf and gloves.

After five minutes of walking the gloves were in my pocket and my coat was unzipped. There was a nip in the air, but not enough to warrant my togs, especially at the pace Jack was setting. He was in an ebullient mood.

"Does it make me a jerk to be happy Blaine wasn't killed at my place?" he asked. "I mean the poor guy's just as dead no matter where he was killed."

I thought of what Esme had said about her waning regrets about Blaine's demise. I knew she didn't mean it. Esme's go-to reaction to tragedy or injustice is to find someone to blame and let all the negative energy flow. When she's purged she comes back to her old, compassionate self.

"You're not a jerk," I said, wishing I could tell him I'd been right about Beth and Blaine's troubled marriage. Wishing I could learn more about his sister's experience and maybe understand it better. But I couldn't and I wondered if he felt the distance that created between us. I thought of Marydale and Winston and how weird they were acting. I wondered if they knew, or at least suspected, about Beth's marriage, or maybe something even worse. Had Beth remembered something about that day? Something she'd told them when she'd gone to Marydale's house so undone this morning?

"Still a big question, though," Jack said, snapping me back to the moment. "How'd that tarp get there? It had to be somebody familiar with the place, how we fold our tarps, where we store them. Denny and his cops have questioned all my employees and they're all in the clear. But it still puts a taint on the place."

"It'll be okay," I said. "The police are piecing things together. Sooner or later a loose thread will appear and someone will pull it and the whole thing will start to unravel and reveal what the killer worked to conceal."

"I know you believe that," Jack said, "but this isn't a genealogy search. There's somebody out there with a vested interest in keeping things tied up tight."

I gazed up, admiring the scattering of stars across the velvet sky. "Yes, but if you're patient, and you keep trying to understand how one thing relates to another, sooner or later you get a picture, though it's not always a pretty one." I told him about what we'd discovered about how Olivia's father had died.

"So that's why you were at Olivia's," he said. "I thought maybe it had something to do with your suspicions about what was going on with Beth and Blaine."

I cringed. I didn't want a lie between us, but I couldn't betray Beth's confidence, either, so I sidestepped.

"Olivia was very upset when we told her," I said.

"Can't blame her there," Jack said. "That's almost biblical—brother against brother. Speaking of which, I saw Peyton this afternoon and he looks like crap. I think he's taking this harder than anyone thought at first. The guy looked like he hadn't slept in days—or showered, either."

Jack frowned, his attention caught by something ahead, and I squinted to see what it was. "Is that Olivia?" he asked.

"Yeah," I said. "What is she doing down at the water? Didn't she learn her lesson last week? She exhausted herself getting down to the lake and back."

"She looks like she's moving pretty good now," Jack said.

We quickened our pace but were still too far away to call out to Olivia. She went out onto her pier, where our sight line was blocked by an overhanging limb. When she came back into view she was carrying something long and straight cradled in her arms. She headed back up the series of concrete steps to her backyard. She was moving slowly, but without hesitation.

We walked on and when we came even with Olivia's house I saw that the lights were on in her garage studio and there was smoke coming from the stack of the woodstove.

"Surely she can't be welding," I said. "Let's go up and make sure she's okay."

We climbed the steps and as we came to the door I called out so we wouldn't startle her. Once inside I saw she was carrying several short lengths of board from the chop saw to the woodstove.

"Olivia, what in the world are you doing out here at this time of night?" I asked.

"I can't rest, Sophreena," Olivia said. "I am so sick and tired of resting. And when I put my head on the pillow every rotten thing I've learned in the last twenty-four hours starts looping in my brain." She gave a sidelong glance toward Jack as she tossed the planks of wood into the stove.

"I know finding out about your father was a shock," I said deliberately, letting her know I'd kept Beth's confidence. "But it was a long time ago."

"I know," Olivia said, pulling off a glove to push a fuzz of hair back up under her bandanna. "But it was upsetting just the same and I needed something that brings me comfort, and for better or worse this is it." She made a sweeping motion, taking in the piles of scrap metal.

"Were those boat paddles you just put into the stove?" I asked, noticing the shape of one of the pieces still left by the saw.

"Yes, I had to get new ones. Those were so old they were starting to splinter. And I didn't have any firewood; that's one of those tasks that got overlooked while I wasn't well. So I figured burning the old paddles would warm things up enough for me to stay out here a while tonight."

"You aren't planning to start welding, are you?" Jack asked, then tried to soften his tone. "I mean, are you sure you're ready for that?"

"Don't worry, you two," Olivia said. "I know my limitations.

I'm going to work at my drafting table for a little while, that's all." She pointed to the corner where a large sheet of paper showed scribbles of angles and shapes that formed a structure that would have vexed Rube Goldberg. "I have in mind a piece I want to make when I *am* able. Sort of a celebration of new life thing."

"Sounds cool. I can't wait to see what you come up with," I said, meaning every word. "Now, does Beth know you're out here?"

"Yes," Olivia said slowly, glancing at the stove, where the paddle pieces were now fully aflame. "She and Daniel are having some brother-sister time," she said, giving me a meaningful look. "They know I'm out here. But do they know I walked down to the lake? No, they don't, and I hope you two won't tattle on me. The other day it was warm out and I just got overheated. I thought maybe I could do better on a cool evening. I made it fine and I'm really proud of myself, so don't ruin it for me."

"Your secret's safe with me," I said.

"I know it is, Sophreena," she said, reaching over to pat me on the cheek.

When I got home Esme was doing dishes—loudly. This was a clue. Whenever Esme is being hectored by a spirit or nettled by a message she can't understand, she cooks or she cleans, both with a lot of clanging around and fussing.

"What now?" I asked.

"Celestine. Still," Esme said. "You cannot talk sense to the woman. She keeps on at me, it's *not right, not right*. I've tried every which way I know to placate her, but it's not working. I've told her everybody understands how it all came about and nobody blames her or Riley. That Olivia is sad, but not mad. I've even tried to let her know about Beth's situation to give her extra assurance that Olivia understands, but it's no good. She won't let it go."

I picked up a dish towel and started to dry and put away dishes. "Maybe she means something else entirely. Maybe she's trying to say that keeping it a *secret* wasn't right."

Esme considered, then shook her head emphatically. "No, that's not it."

"Well, maybe not for her," I said, "but I don't enjoy having to keep Beth's secret. I felt guilty when I was with Jack."

"Yeah, well there's plenty of things you're keeping from Jack," Esme said, pursing her lips. "But I know what you're saying. Same with Denny. And what if the abuse did have something to do with Blaine's murder? It's a motive, a strong motive, and Denny ought to know."

"I agree," I said. "But we can't break a confidence."

"No, we can't," Esme said. "But just between us, let's explore this. Who could have known Beth was being abused and been willing to go vigilante to stop it?"

I leaned against the counter, making circles around a large serving platter with the cloth. "Well, there's Daniel. He's very protective of Beth and it was clear he didn't have much use for Blaine. He seemed shocked when Beth told him this afternoon, but maybe he's a good actor. He'd be a good candidate except we know he was at the farm all that afternoon."

"We know he *says* he was at the farm all afternoon," Esme corrected. "Then there's Tony. He didn't even try to hide his hostility toward Blaine."

"But he was out filming and has time-stamped footage to vouch for his whereabouts most of that afternoon."

"*Most* of the afternoon? And can't those things be monkeyed with?" Esme asked. "Anyway, you're forgetting he went over to Beth and Blaine's that night to check on Beth."

"I'm not forgetting, but Blaine was probably already dead by then."

"They don't know when he died. There's a big window. And you remember when Tony came back he was favoring his arm, like he'd been in a scuffle or something."

"Daniel had an injury, too," I said. "He had that long scratch. Olivia asked him about it and he said he got it on a gate at the farm."

Esme pointed to the platter. "You're gonna rub a hole through that, you keep on," she said.

I put the platter into the cupboard, my mind still winnowing through suspects. "Okay, there's Peyton. According to Beth, he's the only one who knew the actual extent of the troubles. But from what I can gather he was trying to protect Blaine's reputation, not Beth. I always thought Peyton was a good guy, but it seems he's on the wrong side of this one. Family loyalty's one thing, but talk about blame the victim. And Beth says Alan Corrigan and Bonnie Foster both probably suspected, though she doesn't think either of them knew how bad it really was. They were friends of Blaine, too, so who knows what they were thinking."

"If they had a brain in their heads their first concern should have been Beth's safety. But you never know about people. Seems strange that Alan fella didn't tell Denny right off he was still in Morningside that day. And there was that little set-to he got into with Peyton at the coffee shop. What do you suppose that was about? And Bonnie? Does she stand to get the store now?"

"I don't know," I said. "That's a whole other angle, isn't it?"

"Yep, yet we can't discuss any of this with Denny without breaking our word. I wish we could talk it over with the club at least. I don't like keeping things from them."

"Me, either," I said. "I've already felt like Marydale and Winston were acting peculiar."

"You know, now that you mention it, Winston hasn't brought us bread or anything in quite a while. What's up with that?"

I shrugged. "I don't know. But I think they may know something they aren't telling."

"Yeah, and so do we," Esme said. "In the words of my dear departed friend, Celestine, it's *not right*."

eighteen

MONDAY MORNING DAWNED SUNNY AND BRIGHT, WITH THE promise of Indian summer temps. Esme had gotten up at early-thirty and was on her way to Olivia's. They'd be working on the scrapbooks, but Olivia would also want to talk about the situation with Beth and she seemed more comfortable talking with Esme alone.

I had so many questions roiling in my mind, I couldn't concentrate. I pulled on sweatpants, layered a fleece jacket over a T-shirt, and headed out for a morning walk. Without Esme along I got to set my own pace instead of having to double-time it to keep up with her long-legged strides. I settled into a lazy stroll and by the time I got to the coffee shop I hadn't even broken a sweat. And my psyche was no more settled.

I crossed over to Keepsake Corner to say hello to Marydale. Coco was there, too, and they both gave me a customary hug. As we chatted I decided I must have been imagining the tension with Marydale and Winston. Everything seemed as it always had been.

"Sophreena," Coco said, "you were a lifesaver with Tina the other day. I didn't have a clue what to say to her."

"I'm just glad she talked with the police on her own," I said.

"Yes, well, she talked to Denny on the phone, but she ended up being interviewed by Jennifer, so that didn't go too well. As you know, Jenny can be sort of a snit sometimes. But, anyway, Tina told her she'd been with Blaine that day, though she made out like it was all business. And she did tell Mike, like you urged her to, but I think she gave him basically the same story. Still, if he's not a complete knucklehead he's got to know there was more to it than her trying to get money for the Arts Council."

"Mike is such a sweetheart. I sure hope they can get through this," Marydale said. "Though I've got to say I am sorely disappointed in Tina."

"Me, too," Coco agreed, "but I honestly don't think anything like this will ever happen again. Tina learned a huge lesson and she realizes now what she's got and how close she came to throwing it all away."

Marydale nodded, then frowned at me. "Where's Esme?" she asked, as if I might have left her somewhere by accident. As if.

"She's at Olivia's working on the scrapbooks," I said. "And just being there for her in general." I told them what we'd found out about Olivia's father. And maybe because I was so relieved to be able to share at least that much of the cause for Olivia's distress, I filled in every grim detail.

"Crikey!" Coco squeaked, a phrase she'd picked up from the year she'd spent in Australia during what she called her post-divorce global gallivant.

"Oh, dear Lord," Marydale said. "This was a horrible gift."

"No, it wasn't," I said. "It's not what she wanted to hear, of course, but I think she's relieved to know and it's helping her understand a lot of things about her mother and her aunt and uncle."

"What do you do about this sort of thing?" Marydale asked. "I mean, there must be a crime in there somewhere."

"I told Olivia I'd find out, but I don't think there's much urgency. Esme and I are going out to Crawford with Tony this afternoon to get some footage of the town and the house where Olivia grew up for her video scrapbook. Maybe I'll stop by the courthouse and talk to somebody while I'm out there, though I can't imagine there's much to be done about it all these years later."

"No, I suppose not," Marydale said, then cocked her head. "I don't know how I feel about this video scrapbooking deal you're getting into. That's liable to put me out of business if it catches on."

"Not to worry; it'll never replace physical scrapbooks, Marydale," I said. "There's nothing like that tactile feeling of paper and actual photos and artifacts. Think of this as complementary. You'll see how nicely they work together."

A group of customers came in and I said my good-byes and made for the coffee shop. I grabbed a cup of my favorite light roast and settled at one of the outdoor tables, happy the cold snap of the last few days had been sent packing by a stubborn sun determined to have its last days of Indian summer. I pulled out my phone and started punching in a list of the places I wanted to make sure Tony included in the afternoon's shoot. I was so absorbed I didn't notice someone was standing by my table until a shadow fell over the phone's screen. I looked up to see Michelle Robertson smiling down at me.

I hadn't seen her in a long time and she'd aged noticeably, the salt hairs now outnumbering the pepper ones. "Nice to see you, Sophreena," she said.

Michelle had been a librarian at Morningside's public library when I was growing up, and she'd patiently helped me with my many and varied research projects. I'd been dead serious about learning how to research, especially after I started helping my mother search for her origins.

"How have you been, Michelle?" I asked. "Can you sit and talk for a few minutes?"

"Just a few," she said, taking a seat. "I retired last year and instead of all the free time I've dreamt about all these years, I'm busier than ever. I'm tutoring kids at the elementary school and I have to be over there in fifteen minutes."

"I was just making a list for a project I'm working on with a new friend. I think you know him, pretty well in fact. Tony Barrett."

Michelle sighed heavily. "Ah, Tony. I love that boy and I'm so proud of him. He's come so far; but he gave us trials and troubles aplenty there for a while."

"So he tells me," I said. "But he seems to have left all that behind."

"Yes, I believe he has," Michelle said, serious now. "It makes it all worth it. He's got so much talent and so much empathy for people. I think maybe that's what made him act out so much when he was going through his rough spell. He just feels everything, too deeply sometimes. We've enjoyed

spending time with him since he's been back in town. I wish
we could have had him stay with us, but Eric and I moved to
a condo last year and it would have been tight quarters."

"I think Olivia likes having him at her house," I said, wondering if I dared probe any further about Tony's background.
"He's helping out."

"He would do that," Michelle said. "That was never an
issue with Tony; he always wanted to do his part at home."

"Do you mind me asking what happened that got him
sent to juvy? He's pretty free to talk about it, but I didn't ask
him any particulars."

"He'd tell you if you asked. He's never tried to hide it. It
was a fight, just a horrible fight. He broke a boy's jaw. So severely the kid had to have surgery to correct it."

"That's not good," I said.

"No, it wasn't," Michelle said. "And, not to excuse what
Tony did, because it was wrong, period. It was no way to
handle the situation, but I wish some people had been more
willing to consider extenuating circumstances. The boy in
question, Douglas Brower, had been terrorizing some of the
smaller kids for months. He was a bully, plain and simple,
but his parents thought he could do no wrong and complaint
after complaint just kept getting swept under the rug. You
know the Browers?"

I did. They were a prominent family, though not totally
accepted by what passed as high society in Morningside,
because they were latecomers. They'd lived here only about
fifteen years.

"Well," Michelle said, "one day Tony saw Doug picking
on a little kindergartner who was so scared he was crying and

had wet his pants. Tony lost it. He had a lot of anger built up in him and once he started the fight, it all came out. There was no excuse for it, but as I say, I wish people had been more willing to look at all of it. Instead Douglas got a private tutor until he was well enough to go back to school and pick up where he left off being mean to other kids, and Tony got sent away for six months. It hardly seemed fair."

She took a peek at her watch. "Oh good grief, I'm going to be late if I don't scoot. Call me, Sophreena, and let's get together so we can really catch up."

As I watched her hurry across the street I caught sight of Daniel coming out of the coffee shop with another guy and a woman. They stopped on the sidewalk and I saw that the woman was Madison Branch. She didn't seem to know what to do with her hands and alternated between jamming them into the pocket of her hoodie and wringing them. The other guy was Alan Corrigan. They talked for a few minutes, each so intent on the conversation they didn't notice anyone or anything else. A woman pushing a jogging stroller had to come to a full stop and give them a loud "excuse me" before they moved from the sidewalk and continued the conversation on the strip of grass by the street. They all nodded in unison, then walked off in opposite directions.

Why was Alan still in Morningside? And since when were he and Daniel so chummy? I thought I recalled Daniel saying he hardly knew Alan. And what in the world was Madison Branch doing with them?

None of it was my business—which made it all the more intriguing.

I had picked up my cup and keys and stood to go when

I noticed a familiar figure approaching from the parking lot. Jack's description had been an understatement. It was Peyton Branch and he looked like he needed a straitjacket more than he needed caffeine. His hair was sticking up like he'd just crawled out of bed after a restless night and his clothes looked like he'd slept in them. He walked by my table and didn't seem to register my presence, or anything else, for that matter.

I called after him and he turned, but I couldn't tell whether recognition had dawned. "Peyton, are you okay?" I asked, pulling out the chair Michelle had vacated and gesturing for him to sit.

"Are you okay?" I asked again.

"Yeah," he said. "I'm fine as I can be under the circumstances."

"It's gotta be hard," I said. "How are your parents doing? And Madison?"

"Well, I know I'm supposed to say they're bearing up well, or they're healing or whatever it is people say. But since you asked, the truth is my mother cries just about twenty-four/seven and my dad is out in the stables or out riding nearly every daylight hour. Madison is holding on by a thread. Like she didn't have enough problems before any of this happened."

"I'm so sorry," I said. "I know this has got to be hard for you. For all of you."

Peyton nodded, but seemed distracted. "How's Beth?" he asked, staring off into the distance at nothing.

"She's—" I hesitated a moment, then decided that if he was offering up the hard truth, I might as well reciprocate.

"She's not good, Peyton, for a lot of reasons. You may as well know she confided in me about how things were with her and Blaine. Are you pressuring her to keep quiet about that?"

"Is that what she said?" he asked, his mouth setting in a hard line.

"No, she didn't, but I know you two have been quarreling."

"No offense, Sophreena, but that's between me and her. And I hope you're not going around blabbing this stuff all over town."

"First off, Peyton," I said, annoyed with him, even if he was grieving, "I don't blab. I would think you'd know that about me by now. Beth told me in confidence and I'll keep it in confidence. The only reason I said anything now is because I know you already know about how it was with your brother and Beth. I'm worried about her. She's close to the edge as it is, so pressure from you could push her over. But, you're right, this is between the two of you."

Peyton put his head all the way back and stared up at the sky. "Sorry," he said, so softly I almost didn't hear him. "I'm not myself these days."

He looked so very tired. I suddenly didn't have the heart to press him. So I tried for something safer, but also perhaps enlightening. "I saw you were out kayaking with Alan Corrigan last week."

"How did you know that?" Peyton said, his forehead pleating into a frown.

"Was it a secret?" I asked, trying to keep my voice light.

"No, 'course not," Peyton said. "I just didn't remember seeing anybody when we were out."

I told him about Tony's video, but the frown only carved in deeper. "Guess there's no such thing as privacy in this town," he said. He tapped the table lightly with his hand and started to rise, then saw something that made him stop, halfway sitting, halfway standing. His eyes went wide and I turned to look.

Beth was heading our way, coming in from the sidewalk. She wore only a thin cotton tunic and below-the-knee leggings. She had on simple flats that, on closer inspection, turned out to be bedroom slippers. It was nice out, but not *that* warm. She'd clearly been crying and looked like she was about to start up again.

I stood and she ran into my arms with a strangled sob. I looked around, hoping her arrival hadn't caused a spectacle, and was relieved to see only empty tables this far back from the sidewalk. I guided her over to the very back table and sat her down where I could sit opposite and block anyone else's line of sight. Peyton followed, without invitation, and sat down beside me.

"I've been looking for you, Sophreena. I remembered," she said with a hiccup. "I remembered. There was someone there. It was bad. It wasn't right what I did."

I reached over to rub her knee and made shushing sounds. "Beth, it's okay, take a breath. You want me to get you some water or something?"

"No, no, don't leave," she said, grabbing my arm. Her hands were like ice and I could see she was starting to shiver. "Sophreena, I think maybe I did it. I think maybe I killed Blaine."

I saw Peyton's face turn to stone. He punched in a number on his phone and I was horrified when he said, "Yes, this is Peyton Branch. Pass me through to Detective Jeffers. Tell her I've got information about the Blaine Branch case."

Beth sucked in a breath and I grabbed for Peyton's phone, but he pushed my hand away and turned, keeping the phone from my reach. Then my indignation turned to something else as he spoke the next words. "Yes, Detective Jeffers, this is Peyton Branch. I'm coming in to make a statement. I'm the one responsible. I killed my brother."

nineteen

BETH AND I SAT IN STUNNED SILENCE AS PEYTON STALKED OFF without another word. Ideas and images were spinning and colliding like a freeway pileup in my brain.

"That is *not* right," Beth said in a whisper. "Peyton didn't kill Blaine. He couldn't have. He *wouldn't* have. Never."

More people were now being lured outside by the sunshine. I had to get Beth out of there. I thought of calling Esme to come pick us up, but then I saw Jack's truck pull into the parking lot. I took Beth by the hand and half dragged her away.

"Jack, could you give us a ride to my house?" I called, trotting toward him with Beth in tow.

He'd just climbed out of his truck and was clicking the lock on his key fob. "Can I get a cup of coffee first?" he asked, then took a closer look at my face and at Beth's unusual appearance.

"Yeah, sure," he said, punching the key fob again.

"Don't ask any questions," I whispered to him after I'd put Beth in the passenger side and closed the door. "I'll call you later."

Jack raised his eyebrows, but nodded in agreement. I crawled into the jump seat and we rode in silence except for Beth's occasional keening noises. Jack dropped us off and as I got out of the truck he touched my shoulder lightly. "Good luck," he said. "Call me later."

This willingness to trust is one of the things I like about him. Okay, one of things I really *love* about him.

Once inside, I made Beth a cup of hot tea and got her a pair of my socks and one of Esme's sweaters. The sweater swamped her and we both burst out laughing like hyenas on uppers, though it wasn't that funny.

"This is crazy," she said once she'd regained her composure. "The whole world's just gone crazy. Peyton has lost his mind. This is all my fault. Everything."

I was dying to interrupt her to ask what it was she'd remembered, but I thought it was best to let her tell me when she was ready. I was afraid if I pressed her it would slip away from her again.

"I can't go home like this," she said now, looking down at her ragtag outfit. "Mom is worried enough without seeing me like this, and this is the second day in a row I've run out on her. She'll be calling the guys in the white coats. I need to let her know where I am. And then could you take me up to my house, Sophreena? I want to get some clothes and things and I haven't been back there since, well, you know."

I glanced at the clock. Plenty of time before we were due to meet Tony. "Sure, but are you sure you're ready to go back? Could I go get the things for you?"

"No," Beth said. "I need to go there. I've remembered some things, but it's still coming in bits and pieces. Maybe if I go there I can get it all. I'm afraid, but I've *got* to do this before Peyton does something idiotic that can't be undone."

I feared it might be too late for that and I was beginning to entertain the idea that maybe Peyton had indeed done it. Not intentionally, but maybe a fight that got out of hand, like with Johnny and Riley. Peyton surely had something eating at him these days. Was it grief or guilt? Or maybe both?

Beth called Olivia, then we headed to Crescent Hill. I'd been to Beth's house lots of times, but I realized only now that it had always been for events with other people present, never as a lone visitor. Beth didn't have a key with her and had to retrieve the one she kept in a fake rock in the flower bed by her front door. The bed was planted with pansies that were still profuse with blossoms despite the cool temps lately. I commented on them while I waited.

"That's all Charlie's doing," Beth said. "He's got the green thumb. I kill everything I touch."

Her words seemed to echo back to her and she winced. Her hands were shaking and she had to make several tries to get the key into the lock. When she finally pushed the door open she backed away as if afraid to go in. I brushed past her and stepped inside. Everything was tidy, obsessively so.

Beth followed me in, then looked around as if she stumbled into an alien land. Maybe it was. "We built a life here," she said, her voice dreamy. "I thought it was going to be a good life. For a long time I thought that." She faced me, her eyes narrowing. "Sophreena, will I ever get myself back?"

"I don't know, Beth." I figured I owed her honesty.

We headed down the hall to the bedroom she and Blaine had shared. Beth took a small suitcase out of the closet and spread it open on the bed. She started going through drawers filled with meticulously folded clothes, then gathered a few more things from a closet where color-coordinated clothing hung on wooden hangers placed at precise intervals.

I am a huge fan of organized spaces and organized people, but this made me feel twitchy. It was a symptom of something very unhealthy.

Beth excused herself to the bathroom and changed into jeans, a shirt, and jacket. When she came out she sat in a chair by the window and pulled on a pair of boots. All the while her eyes were scanning the room as if some gremlin might jump out from behind a piece of furniture.

She stood abruptly. "Let's go out to the backyard. I want to remember. I need to remember."

As we stepped outside we both squinted against the light and Beth made a noise like a dry heave. She put her hands to her face and stood for a moment, then began, her tone flat. "I remember getting the tools from the shed to start the yard work," she said, nodding toward a small structure in the corner of the yard. "I like yard work. I find it soothing. Most everything between that time and when I woke up in the hospital the next day is either a vague notion or a flash that I can't hold on to. But this morning I remembered that we had an argument. Blaine was here and we had a fight."

"Let's try walking through it," I said, guiding her toward the garden shed. It had been recently painted and, as with the house, it was in apple-pie order inside. Every tool had its place and supplies were labeled and efficiently arranged on shelves.

"I've never seen a toolshed like this," I marveled.

"Blaine likes things tidy," she said. "Liked. Not just tidy, but organized with military precision. Life was easier if I kept things that way."

I scanned the walls and shelves. "Where did you store the tarp?" I asked.

"There," she said, pointing to an empty space on a bottom shelf. "I used it that day. I remember that. I raked leaves onto it and dragged them down past the gate. At least I *think* that's a clear memory, but it's possible I'm confusing it with some other time. I always did it that way."

"Is everything else accounted for?" I asked.

"The rake is missing, but it's probably still out in the yard." She placed her hand on an empty spot on the shed wall. "And the pruning loppers go here and the shears. And there's a short shovel that usually hangs on that peg over there, but I lent it to Charlie a while back and I think he still has it. Everything else is here." She turned from side to side, studying the shed's contents.

As we went back outside I looked up, shielding my eyes against the sun, and noticed a hunk of wood splintered out of the side of the shed. The raw wood stood out in stark contrast to the fresh red paint.

"What happened here?" I asked, reaching up to touch the spot. I pulled at the splinter and it gave way, revealing a hole that went straight through the board.

"I don't know," Beth said, studying the spot. "A rock from the lawn mower maybe? I never noticed it before." She walked around reenacting the steps she usually went through to ready for yard work. When she spotted the long-handled loppers on the patio she gasped. "That's what I remembered this morning," she said, her hands starting to shake again. "That's the flash I got but couldn't hold on to. Oh, Sophreena, we had a terrible fight. It was my fault. I was standing right over there, pruning that azalea. Blaine came out of the house and he was furious. It was something bad I'd done. But what was it?"

She bent over and held both sides of her head as if in pain. I moved toward her but she waved me away. "No, I have to remember. Now. Sterling and Madeline can't lose another son."

I backed away and Beth gasped. "He was angry because he'd found my birth control pills. That was it. He thought we were trying for a baby. He insisted and I let him think I was going along with it. That was wrong of me. But I couldn't bring a child into this," she said, staring at the back of the house. "Not the way things were."

I didn't reply, afraid she'd lose the thread again.

"He came toward me and I saw it," Beth said. "I saw it in his eyes. He wasn't the man I knew anymore. He was going to hurt me. And not like before, not just control me; he meant to end me. He came so fast and before I could move he hit me on the side of my head, very hard. I somehow managed to stay on my feet and then I did the thing I never thought I could do. I hit back. I had those loppers in my hand and I swung them as hard as I could at him. He was so shocked he didn't react right away. He jumped back but the blade nicked him. He touched his cheek and when he saw the blood on his fingers he went into a rage. He came at me again and I remember pain and I remember falling to the ground but after that everything's mostly blank. But

Sophreena, I *was* trying to hit him again. Maybe I connected as I was going down. Maybe he was hurt and stumbled off down to the lake while I was unconscious. Maybe I killed him."

"Beth," I said. "First off, you can't make an intentional move like that when you're blacking out, and secondly—" I hesitated, fashioning my words carefully. "I think it took more force than a swipe with glorified pruning shears by someone stunned and passing out. What's the next thing you remember?"

Beth frowned. "Things get really fuzzy after that. I think I must have been in and out for a while. When all that happened it was still light, but when I came to it was dark. During that time I think I had some awareness. I'm pretty sure I heard voices, and caught a glimpse of somebody moving around, but I could have imagined it, or been hallucinating or dreaming."

"Well, for now let's say you did," I said. "What did the voices sound like?"

Beth frowned. "A man's," she said, "or else a woman with a deep voice. Some shouting I think. Anger, or maybe I'm confusing that with Blaine yelling at me. Was Tony here?" she asked. "I think I heard his motorcycle backfire."

"He came over looking for you that night when we were getting ready for dinner at your mother's house. Was it that late? Could you have been hearing the voices then?"

"I don't think so. It was quiet when I woke up and it was full dark. I wouldn't have been able to see anything if somebody had been there then." She bent over again as if in pain and this time I pulled her by the arm, guiding her to a chair on the patio. She sat down heavily and looked as if she might be sick.

I went inside and got her a glass of water, which she chugged down like a woman who'd been in the desert for weeks.

"I have no idea how long I was out," she said. "But I'm pretty sure Blaine wasn't here when I woke up. I only have a hazy impression, not a real memory, of going inside to take a shower and clean myself up. And I guess I went to Mom's house, but I don't remember driving there or what I did when I got there. You'd know more about that than me."

I didn't want to plant ideas in Beth's head or skew her memories, so I decided not to push her anymore. "This is good, Beth," I said. "This will be very helpful. You need to talk with Denny about this."

She nodded. "The sooner the better, before it all slips away again. Just because Peyton's lost his mind, that's no reason he should lose his life."

I wasn't sure if any of this would help Peyton or if it would seal his fate. Now I was the one feeling sick.

I took Beth home and she put up a good front, looking and sounding more like the old Beth in front of her mother and Esme. I feigned being in a rush, telling Esme we needed to get ready for our filming session with Tony. Esme puckered her lips and looked at her watch, and I could see she was about to say we had plenty of time. I put my arm across the back of her chair and gave her shoulder a little pinch and she allowed as how we certainly did need to get a move on.

We headed home so I could change out of my walking togs, and I spilled to Esme as fast as my lips could move. She listened silently, other than some surprised grunts, gasps, and an occasional minced oath, ending with "Well, dog my cats!"

"I have no idea what that means. Translate."

"Means I'm thunderstruck," Esme said. "Do you think Peyton actually did it?"

"I've got to admit I considered it might be true there for a little while. There are some things that make it look bad for him. You know, like him *confessing*. But no, I don't think he did it. Peyton and Blaine had their troubles, but despite all that they were still brothers."

"Johnny and Riley Hargett were brothers, too. But all the same one of them ended up causing the other's death."

"Yes, but Riley was trying to protect Renny," I said.

Esme didn't say anything and when I stopped at a light she was looking at me over her sunglasses. "Mm-hm," she said. "He was protecting his sister-in-law who was being mistreated. Does that ring a bell?"

"Yes, but that's not the case here. In fact Peyton and Beth are at odds about something. They don't even seem to like each other very much; they've argued every time I've seen them together. What I can't figure out is why Peyton would say he did it if he didn't."

"Got me there," Esme said. "I hardly know the man. Before all this came up the only time I'd set eyes on him was when he was coaching from the sidelines at the football games. He always seemed cool and collected. Not the type you'd think would flip out and do something like kill his own brother."

"Something else," I said, talking fast as we turned the corner to our street. "When she was telling me what she remembered, Beth asked if Tony was at her house that day. She thinks she has some recollection of hearing his motorcycle backfire while she was passed out and maybe his voice, too. Now she's pretty sure it was still daylight out then and it was well after dark when Tony went over to check on her for the dinner at Olivia's. And he swears he didn't actually see her. But if what Beth remembers is right, I think we have to consider it's possible he did go over there at some point during the day, despite his denials."

"Well, that's not good," Esme said.

"It gets worse," I said. "I ran into Michelle Robertson at the coffee shop this morning. You know what Tony's juvy bust was for?"

"I'm nearly 'bout afraid to ask," Esme said.

"He beat up a kid who was bullying smaller kids. Beat him pretty severely."

"So, has he got a hero complex, or just anger issues?"

"Eye of the beholder, I suppose. I got the impression from Michelle there was no question the kid he beat up was a menace, but apparently he was from a family with juice while Tony was a foster kid with a loser reputation. You do the math."

"Are you sure Beth will call Denny and tell him what she's remembered?" Esme asked. "I don't like that there's getting to be so many things I have to keep from him."

"She'll call," I said. "She'll edit liberally, but she'll call. This could break open the investigation. The murder must have taken place right in her backyard while she lay there unconscious. That'll tighten the time frame."

"Assuming she was unconscious and not having a blackout where she was still functioning but she's blocked it out now. And assuming she's remembering and not misremembering. And assuming she's telling all she remembers. And assuming everything she's telling is the truth of how she remembers it."

"That's a lot of assuming," I said.

"Ain't it just?"

The drive to Crawford was an exercise in frustration. I wanted go on talking things through with Esme, and I was worried about Peyton and how things would go when Beth talked with Denny. But we couldn't say anything in front of Tony since there was a possibility—remote, I sincerely hoped—that he might have some involvement.

With effort I put some of it on the mental back burner as we drove into town. I started to recognize some of the Crawford landmarks from the old movie. Tony intended to reproduce some of the same shots and angles as in the forties film and he didn't need us for this part. We'd do voice-over later. We parked, coordinated a meet-up time, then Esme and I went off in search of information while Tony captured his visuals.

At the courthouse Esme and I divvied up the tasks. I headed for the land appraiser's office while she went off to vital records to check some missing birth, marriage, and death dates.

The clerk, a young woman who looked fresh out of high school, helped me find what I was looking for and I traced the four hundred acres of Hargett land through several divisions as it was split between heirs or sold out of the family.

The original tract still in Hargett family ownership was Olivia's piece, almost fifty acres. Her great-great-grandfather, Isaac Hargett, had paid less per acre than we'd pay for a spot in a parking garage today. The clearing had been done by men, mules, and gritty determination. I wondered what old Isaac would think if he could see it now.

Next I went down the hall to the clerk of courts office to see if I could find the disposition of Johnny L. Hargett's drunk-and-disorderly arrest. When I rang the little bell on the counter the same young woman came out from the back.

"Me again," she said. "Lisa's out; I'm covering for her. I'm Katy, by the way."

"Well, I hope you can work your magic here for me, too." I told her what I was after.

Her expression didn't give me much hope. "Records that old would be in the long-term storage in the basement. I don't even have access to those," she said. Then she brightened. "But there are some summaries that we've got on microfiche, for some years anyway. Let me go see what I can track down." She moved a pad of paper over to me so I could write down the name and year.

As fifteen minutes dragged on to twenty I started to worry again about what might be happening to Peyton back in Morningside. I deflected those thoughts by matching Oscar-winning movies to the dates on the record books lining the shelves behind the counter. Nineteen seventy-six, *Rocky*; 1975, *One Flew Over the Cuckoo's Nest*; 1974, *The Godfather Part II*; 1973, *The Sting*. I got hung up on 1972, then remembered it was the original *Godfather*, which in my mind made the 1974 selection a case of double-dipping.

"Sorry it took so long," Katy said as she came back in. She was carrying some papers, which I took as a good sign. "I did find the case. It was dismissed with time served, like most of 'em were. They didn't have but a two-cot, one-cell jail back then; guess they had to keep 'em rotating. But there's an arrest report if you want to call it that. It's not much, not even a form, just these handwritten notes, and if you can read a half-dozen words of it you're doing better than me. But this is all we've got."

I thanked her again and tried to decipher the chicken scratch handwriting as I walked down the hall to meet up with Esme. There had been an altercation at a pool hall. Johnny Hargett, according to the report, had been "drunk and mouthy." I smiled. Today a similar report would read that the subject was intoxicated and belligerent. My smile disappeared as I read the brief physical description. He was described as five feet, nine inches tall, approximately two hundred pounds, and his race was listed as "Other." Our Johnny Hargett was a tall, slender white man.

When I went into the vital records office Esme was chatting with a woman who could have been Katy's grandmother. She motioned me over. "This is Miss Imogene. She and Olivia grew up together."

Imogene nodded. "We did. And her mama was my teacher when I was in the sixth grade. She was a sweet lady. I haven't seen Olivia in years, but please tell her hi for me and tell her I'd love to see her next time she's in town."

"Will do," I said, giving Esme the eye signal that we had something to discuss.

"We'll let you get back to your work, Miss Imogene," Esme said. "Thanks for your help."

"Wow," I said as we moved to the small table where Esme had been working. "And I thought Morningside was a small town. Listen, I think your theory about someone else using Johnny's ID may be right." I told her about the conflicting description.

"Well, from what we've learned about him I don't have any problem with describing Johnny Hargett as 'Other,' but not when it comes to his race. He was about as Caucasian as you can get."

"So if we take your scenario we're only left with Mrs. Yarborough's spotting of Johnny at the train station."

"Which is thin evidence to begin with. She was elderly and had bad eyesight," Esme said, then fanned her hand in the air in irritation. "Okay, okay, and Celestine says she had a fanciful streak, which I take to mean she made stuff up out of whole cloth." Esme made an *um-hm* noise. And Celestine may have encouraged Mrs. Yarborough in that story. You know she wasn't wanting the real story to come to light, which we certainly understand, don't we?" Esme rolled her eyes toward the ceiling.

"Absolutely," I agreed. "Perfectly understandable."

I leaned back in my chair and sighed. "Okay, so my two concerns have been pretty much placated. Rest in whatever peace you can find, Johnny Hargett."

We didn't need to meet Tony for another half hour, so I decided to see if I could unearth some info on Charlie Martin. If Tony and I went ahead with "The Charlie Project," as Tony was already referring to it, we'd need some background. And since we were already in the right county courthouse, why not use the time to some purpose?

I had little to go on, so I didn't expect the search to be easy, but it quickly started looking hopeless. There was a virtual infestation of Martins in the county and numerous Charles Martins, but none seemed to fit the right age range.

"You losing your touch?" Esme teased. "You need my help?"

Since I'd taught Esme nearly everything she knew about records searches, I ignored the taunt and accepted the help.

Minutes later she brought a record book over to my table. "I found a Charlie Martin here, and the time frame sort of works, but I can't be sure it's your Charlie."

"You're doing better than I am," I said. "Let me see."

"Some kind of declaration, looks like it was for guardianship maybe. You're better at deciphering these things than me."

"Hershel Tillett?" I said, scanning the page. "That was Charlie's best friend's name, the one he joined the army with, but this can't be the same guy, he's too old." I read on, struggling with the faded ink and the barely legible handwriting. The upshot was that one Hershel Tillett was seeking to take a boy named Charles Martin into his household and serve as his legal guardian. Tillett declared that his two natural children, Hershel Jr. and Lucille, also resided in his household. Then there was a paragraph that was completely illegible.

"Wow, so his friend must have been Hershel Jr. But Charlie didn't say he actually lived with the family, though he did say his folks died when he was pretty young." I pulled my phone from my pocket to check the time. "Interesting, but I'll have to follow up later; we've got to meet Tony."

I took a quick photo of the page in question with my

phone camera since I didn't have time to get copies made, and we gathered up our things.

As Esme and I waited for the ancient elevator I started to worry again about what might be happening back in Morningside.

"What's gonna happen is gonna happen," Esme said, staring at the smeared elevator doors. "Troubling yourself about it won't change a thing."

"How do you know I'm troubled?" I asked. "I think I've been pretty chill, all things considered."

"Honey, you're so agitated folks might mistake you for a washing machine. I'm gonna start calling you Miss Maytag."

We rejoined a happy Tony. "Wow, I've never been so psyched about a lack of progress," he said. "Some of these places haven't changed much at all."

"Maybe they'd prefer to call it preservation," I said.

"Whatever," Tony said with a shrug. "I call it good footage."

But despite Tony's assessment of Crawford as we drove out to the Hargett farm, I was taken aback by the modernity of the place. I had a picture in my mind from reading Celestine's diaries and had half expected it to appear in sepia tone.

We walked around the property with Tony filming from every conceivable angle, then used the keys Olivia had given us to get inside to film the rooms of both houses. As time wore on Esme started to get flustered, muttering and occasionally putting her hand across her forehead.

"Who's Miss Maytag now?" I asked, when Tony was out of earshot.

"Shush, it's Celestine," Esme said. "She's getting all riled up again. It's this place. I need to get out of here and take a walk."

"I'll come with you," I said, glancing over to where Tony was absorbed in panning across the living room's fireplace wall.

"No, you stay here and supervise Mr. Spielberg over there," Esme insisted. "I just need some air."

I was concerned about Esme, but I knew better than to argue. I waited for Tony to finish filming the rooms, then checked the list on my phone and followed Olivia's directions on where to find meaningful family artifacts for Tony to film. This is one facet of family history documentation people sometimes neglect. We live our lives among things. Even when we were cave dwellers we had our favorite rock for breaking open nuts or a long limb that made a good walking stick. It often takes me by surprise how a seemingly insignificant thing, like a cookie jar with a broken lid, or lamp with a tattered shade, can be imbued with so many memories.

Tony and I worked well together. I put a white tablecloth on the long farmhouse table where Tony could film each artifact in panorama. I carried each back to storage as Tony finished filming. There was the biscuit bowl, a big crockery bowl with blue stripes around it, and a glass vase in which Celestine had proudly displayed the wildflowers Olivia picked for her, always including the stinky bitterweed little Olivia found beautiful, despite the vile smell. Then more objects, more furniture, and finally some architectural features of the houses.

When we'd finished I went in search of Esme while Tony packed up his gear. I called out and could hear her answering voice coming from somewhere far away. I followed it to the back side of the property, which sloped gradually downhill, past what I assumed had once been a thriving garden plot and was now a patch of rutted, fallow ground. I hiked past dilapidated outbuildings that were once chicken coops and corncribs and through a copse of trees along a narrow, snaking trail. I brushed aside bushes, picking at my jeans, until I came to a clearing. As I stepped out, the wind freshened and I could hear rushing water. I spotted Esme standing by a wide river gazing up at the old railroad trestle that still spanned the water. The rusting hulk looked as if it had been abandoned for decades.

I walked down to where Esme stood. "You okay?" I asked.

"No," she said. "I'm not. Poor Celestine. She is weary and restless and I can't help her. Look at this place." She made a sweeping gesture of the picturesque scene. Water tumbled over the rocks, some smooth, some craggy, that formed a stepping-stone path out almost to the middle of the river. The trees along the far bank were all decked out in autumn oranges and golds; dying shafts of sunlight the color of the inside of a lemon muted it all and gave it a faded soft-focus look. The river was fast moving and the susurration of water sluicing around rock should have been a soothing sound, but instead it seemed an ominous sound track to the story we had burned into our brains of how Johnny Hargett had died here. The bleak skeleton of the trestle silhouetted against the dying light of the sky seemed to harbinger despair and ruin to anyone who came close.

"We should go, Esme," I said. "This isn't doing you any good and apparently it's not helping Celestine, either."

"A few more minutes," Esme said, gazing out across the rushing water. "Abiding with her a while is the least I can do for her. I understand, now that I see the place, how it could be they never found the body. Look at that tree limb over there in the water," she said. "That thing's big around as my leg." She stopped and looked at me over her sunglasses. "Okay, big as *your* leg. And see how fast the current's carrying it. And look how wild it is along these riverbanks, even now. I expect it would've been even more overgrown back then."

"Yeah," I said, imagining Celestine and Riley walking these riverbanks, searching in vain for something they desperately wanted to find yet had a dread of finding.

Esme started a rhythmic nod of her head. "I know, I know," she said aloud, though she wasn't talking to me. "I know you say it's not right, but there was no evil in what happened here. It was a terrible thing but not an evil thing."

I sat down on the grass and waited as Esme continued to stare out across the water. After a while I heard Tony calling to us, and a few minutes later he emerged from the tree line. He stopped in his tracks and looked up at the trestle. "Oh, man! Is this the one?"

He didn't wait for an answer, but pulled out a small camera. "I doubt Olivia will want this right now, but maybe generations from now somebody will." He panned across the river and up to the trestle, then put the camera back in his bag. "That's it, lost the light."

He turned and started back up the hill. When he had moved a ways ahead I turned to Esme. "You ready?"

Esme heaved a big sigh. "Ah well, I tried. She's still un-settled and completely dissatisfied with me, but I don't know what more I can do. Let's go home."

As we neared the tree line I looked back to the river. The limb that had been floating downstream had vanished.

twenty

WE WERE QUIET ON THE DRIVE BACK TO MORNINGSIDE, EACH of us lost in our own thoughts. As Esme drove her SUV along the two-laned road the headlights probed the inky darkness, only reaching a little way into what lay ahead. I could identify.

I hadn't realized how deep the silence was until about halfway home, when Tony burst out. "Are you two mad at me or something? Did I do something wrong?"

"No, Tony," I said. "It's not you. We've just got a lot on our minds." And since I couldn't list for him all the things *actually* consuming our thoughts, I said, "We need to get Olivia's project wrapped up and turned over to her—and you. Then we've got to prepare for the job down in Wilmington."

"Not to mention being neck-deep in Blaine's murder investigation," Tony said dryly. "I'm not an idiot, you know."

"No, you're not," I said. "And since we're on that subject, I need to tell you something, Tony: The police are probably going to want to talk to you again."

"But I've already told them everything I know," he said.

"I think they may have some questions about what you saw when you went over that night looking for Beth."

"But I only went because you all asked me to," he protested. "And I didn't see anything. We've been over this. I showed you the footage from that day."

"And that's what you tell them so you can clear this up once and for all," I said, encouragingly, though the thought of those gaps in his timeline worried me. "And if it's Jennifer Jeffers you talk to, and you start feeling the least bit uncomfortable, you ask to be represented by a lawyer. I can give you a name."

"I can't afford a lawyer," Tony said flatly.

"No worries. She's a friend of ours and she owes us a favor," Esme said, which was big news to me. Crystal Conners *was* a friend of ours, but as far as I knew she wasn't beholden to us in any way.

We were tired and hungry when we got home. "I'm gonna fix us grilled cheese and soup," Esme said as she climbed out of the car. "Tony, you want to stay?"

"Thanks, but I'll fix myself a sandwich back at Olivia's. I want to get this footage set to render so I can do some cutting tomorrow. I think we got some good stuff today. Thanks for going out with me."

As we watched him get on his bike and ride away, I turned to Esme. "What favor does Crystal Conners owe us exactly?"

Esme raised an eyebrow. "I'm not gonna have Jennifer Jeffers jamming that kid up. I'll pay the fee myself if need be."

"So, you're convinced he didn't do it?"

"Didn't say that. Let's just say I accept this is a complicated situation, and I know that kid has two strikes against him already in some people's minds."

"You old softy," I said, giving her a nudge.

"Yeah, I'm a regular marshmallow. But if Tony screws up I'll kick his behind."

We went into the kitchen and started our supper with the practiced ease of two people who've prepped many meals together in a small kitchen. I thought back to how it had been when I moved back here after graduate school. I love my house and it is filled with glorious memories, but it was a lonely place with my parents gone. Everywhere I looked there was a reminder of what I'd lost. But since Esme moved in it's become a home again and we're making new memories to add to the old ones.

Esme had just turned up the heat under her trusty cast-iron skillet when Denny called, wanting to know if he could stop by on his supper break.

She told him that would be fine and as she was putting the receiver back in the phone's base the front door opened and Denny called out a hello. "I was out front," he said. "I took a chance you'd be here, but I *did* call."

"Letter of the law if not the spirit," Esme said. "Have you actually had any supper on your supper break?"

"No, I decided I'd rather see your smiling face," he said. "And I brought you some presents." He pulled his hands from behind his back, a book in one and a to-go cup in the other. "Latest mystery from your favorite writer and a chai tea from Top o' the Morning. I know that's not as romantic as flowers and chocolates, but I thought you'd like these better."

"You know me," Esme said with a smile. "Now sit down and I'll have you a grilled cheese in a jiffy."

"Okay, this is all great and wonderful," I said, unable to contain myself a second longer, "but, Denny, what's up with Peyton?"

"Peyton," Denny said, shaking his head as he sat down. "That lunkhead. I took his statement and sent him home."

"Just like that? So he came to his senses and didn't confess to killing Blaine."

"Oh no, he did," Denny said. "And for such a savvy coach that was about the worst call ever made. The school board gets a whiff of this and he'll be out of a job."

"But you don't think he actually did it?" Esme asked.

"Let me put it this way," Denny said. "I was born in the morning, but it wasn't *yesterday* morning. I know how to work a timeline same as you two." He pulled a small notebook from his pocket and opened it so we could see his scribbled diagram. "I know where Peyton was practically every minute of that day. There's a small gap right here in our window and he would have had the time if he was quick about it, but the problem is he overconfessed. He got nearly 'bout every particular of the crime wrong. So either he was gaslighting us or he didn't do it."

"Why did he *claim* he did it?" I asked.

"Oh, you know, the usual Cain and Abel stuff. He trotted out a few things, like he was auditioning motives to see which one would fly. First it was just general jealousy between the two. Then it was the fight they were in about their folks letting Madison come back home. But my favorite was that he killed his brother because he reneged on a promise to fund new uniforms for the football team."

"That's ridiculous! Who would kill somebody over that?" I said.

"Sadly, people have killed for less," Denny said. "But I don't buy it in this case."

"Did you talk with Beth today?" I asked.

"I did," Denny said, smiling up at Esme as she set a gloriously gooey cheese sandwich in front of him. "She's remembering bits and pieces, but I suspect you already know that." He gave me a sly look, which I ignored.

"Anything helpful?" I asked, wondering how much she'd revealed.

"Some," Denny said, sawing the sandwich in half. "What she told me helped solidify our determination that their house was the scene of the crime, and late this afternoon we got the DNA back from the blood samples we took from the yard. Some was Beth's; some was Blaine's. That's compelling. But I know Beth's holding back. I'm not getting the whole story. She remembers Blaine being there and she remembers falling and being knocked out, but she can't remember how it happened. She says she thinks maybe she tripped over the rake and hit her head on the rock border."

I looked up to see Denny studying me, his brown eyes searching my face. I felt like I might be telegraphing everything running through my brain on a little screen on my forehead. And the more I tried to look impassive, the more involuntary tics and grimaces took over.

"Soup's ready," I said, jumping up to ladle the tomato-basil into mugs, thankful to get away from Denny's mind probe. "Well, I'm glad about Peyton," I said. "Though I still don't understand why he would do something as stupid as confess to a murder he didn't commit."

"I'd say the only thing that makes sense is he's protecting someone," Denny said.

"Who?" Esme said, dealing out sandwiches to my plate and hers.

"No idea," Denny said. "Must be somebody he cares a whole lot about to be willing to risk so much."

"Madison?" I asked. "He's very protective of his sister."

"It's a theory," Denny said. He took another big bite of his grilled cheese. The thick slabs of sourdough looked like a canapé in his big hands. He let out a couple of appreciative *hmmms* and gave Esme a thumbs-up. "All I can tell you is somebody around here is protecting somebody. From who or from what I don't know just yet."

And there was that probing stare again, directed first at me, then at Esme.

I blinked, but Esme stared right back.

I slept late on Tuesday morning, so grateful I'd finally *gotten* to sleep I'd willed myself to prolong it. I'd tossed and turned for hours mulling over the situation with Beth, Peyton, Tony, and all the others impacted by, and maybe involved in, Blaine's murder. Plus, the trip to Crawford had gotten under my skin. I kept having visions of Celestine and Riley walking that riverbank, of a human being hurtling off that train trestle and landing on the rocks below. I imagined I could hear the sickening thud, the rush of water, and the mournful whistle of a train off in the night.

When I finally fell asleep my worries skulked into my dreams. There was that foreboding trestle, except it was Blaine falling to his death as Olivia paddled a boat across the river below, the wind sculpture on the back of her boat making a clanging cacophony instead of a musical sound. Celestine Hargett stood on the shore, her hair frizzy from a recent home permanent. She clucked disapprovingly at the scene before her. "That's not right," she said, "not right at all." Tony stepped out of the shadows. "Okay, cut!" he yelled. "The light wasn't right; we're going to have to do another take." Celestine protested. "But he's dead. You can't make him dead again."

When I jolted awake from that one I turned on the white noise machine on the head of my bed. In the wee hours of the morning I finally fell into a deep and dreamless slumber.

The next morning I knew right off Esme must have had a bad night, too. I found her in the workroom, packing up the last vestiges of Olivia's artifacts as she muttered to herself. "Mums, gladiolas, tulips. Okay, but I don't get it."

"You okay?" I asked, already knowing the answer.

"No, I am *not* okay," Esme said. "I am bothered. I am annoyed. I am pestered." She looked to the ceiling. "And I cannot help."

"Still Celestine, I take it?"

"Sweet Lord, yes. She's showing me flowers, all kinds of flowers."

"Hmm, you think maybe you're riffing off what Denny said last night about flowers being more romantic than books?"

"No," Esme said. "That's not it. We're not talking a vase of flowers; we're talking flowers everywhere. Like at a funeral or something."

"Maybe that's what it means. Think about it: Johnny never had a proper funeral. She said in her diary that troubled her and Riley. Maybe that's what she thinks is not right."

Esme's expression was hopeful. "I never thought of that. Oh, good night, I hope she's not expecting me to throw him a wake after all these years."

"Maybe it's just a spirit world funeral?" I offered.

Esme smiled and held both hands out. "Well, come on then, Celestine, I'll preach Johnny a funeral, though it'll be a short eulogy. And I'll admire all the pretty flowers with you, too."

"While you're playing preacher and florist, I'm going out to the kitchen for coffee and toast. Then I'll help you pack the rest of this."

The chore list Esme had started was on the kitchen table. There were several errands on the docket, plus tonight was the regular meeting of the genealogy club, so we needed to prepare snacks.

I was looking forward to our meeting. We'd be out of town for the next two Tuesdays and I missed everyone already. Despite feeling reassured by my visit to Marydale yesterday, I still felt there was something she and Winston were keeping from us. I had the thought that maybe they were keeping the same thing from us that we were keeping from them. I decided I'd ask Beth at the next opportunity if she'd confided in Marydale or Winston. Or maybe it was something else entirely. Something to do with Madison, maybe? Marydale is a mama bear when it comes to people she loves.

I could hear Esme out in the workroom still rattling off the names of flowers: *roses, daisies, hyacinths, daffodils, asters.* As I put my coffee mug in the sink I heard. "Ranunculus? Come on now, I don't even know what that one looks like. Sounds more like a medical condition than a flower. Let's give it a rest."

"Done?" I asked from the workroom doorway.

"I am but I don't think she is. We're on a break."

I glanced at the archival boxes lined up on the table and sighed. "You know, despite everything, I think Olivia's still glad we did this. Apart from that one horrible family secret she did find out some good things. Like that her grandparents made peace with her mother before they died."

"I guess you could say that," Esme said. "After Renny wrote them that she was in a family way, they seemed to have softened up some. And her mother did write in one of her last letters that they missed her and that when they came back to the States they wanted to visit her."

"Yeah," I said, drawing the word out. "'Course, Renny never told them Johnny was already gone by then. Do you think she knew? About what happened to Johnny, I mean?"

"I think she *had* to have known *something* somewhere deep down. They all three lived side by side with their lives intertwined for all those years." Esme stopped; her gaze drifted to the window and her voice sounded far away. "But they never spoke of it aloud. Never one word."

"That sounds like more than speculation on your part," I said.

"Never a word," Esme repeated. "But with total trust in one another for the rest of their days on earth. I think they all intended to take this to their graves, but Celestine couldn't carry the burden when she was left alone with it. I wonder if it would've been better if she'd taken the secret with her. Maybe she regrets she didn't. Maybe that's why she can't find peace."

"Well, you know my take on that. It's always better to know your own history, bad stuff and good stuff. It's all gone into making you who you are. Knowledge is power, so they say."

"Um-hm," Esme said. "They also say ignorance is bliss. And, anyhow, sometimes *they* talk through their hats."

I got out my calligraphy supplies to fill in the few remaining missing dates on Olivia's pedigree chart, using Esme's notes from the courthouse records.

"While you do that I'll go get dressed, then I'll call Olivia to see when would be a good time for us to bring the rest of this stuff over."

After I finished the chart I looked over the report I'd compiled one more time. The others had all done a smash-up job and we'd be giving Olivia a good solid start into tracing her family lines. I felt good about the job, despite all that had happened, and I was eager to see Tony's finished video scrapbook. The tape gun made a *rrrripp*ing noise as I sealed up the last box. Done. *Fini*. It would've been nice if we could have given Olivia a prettier portrait of her parents, but I still had to believe the unvarnished truth was better than the shameful silence.

As I went to close the notebook we'd used at the courthouse I saw the scribbled notes I'd jotted while trying to find sources on Charlie Martin. I knew Esme would be a while, so I calculated I could slip in a few phone calls. If I could find out something about Charlie's best friend in the world, that might go a long way in convincing him to do the project with Tony. I did a census search and found Charles Martin living in the Tillett household when he was two years old, but by the time the next census rolled around, the household had either moved or been broken up. I didn't have enough info to go further so I opted for some scattershot sleuthing and made a list of the telephone numbers I could find for Tilletts in a four-county area. I pulled out my cell and started at the top. If I got an answer I recited my well-rehearsed spiel, giving my name and occupation and, in my friendliest voice, telling the person I was looking for family information on behalf of a client. This was not technically true. Nor somewhatish true. Or true in any sense, really. To keep it from being a flat-out lie I hired myself, placing a quarter I found in the desk drawer in front of me as a retainer.

Cold-calling is a Hail-Mary play, but when it connects there's usually a big payoff. I reached five live people in the first seven calls, that in itself a miracle. Four were gracious and polite and were as sorry as they could be that they couldn't help me. And I knew they meant it. Southerners are earnestly reverential about family ties. The fifth call was answered by a man not-from-around-here, judging by his clipped accent. He told me to bug off, though he wasn't as judicious in his choice of words. I left messages on two machines, but didn't expect to hear back on either. I would have stopped there, but Esme was still getting dolled up so I decided to try one more number. And on that call I hit pay dirt—sort of.

The woman who answered had married into the Tillett family and didn't know much about the distant relatives of her deceased husband, and something in the way she said it let me know she didn't care to know more, but she did vaguely remember Hershel Tillett, Jr. She wasn't sure what had become of him, but she knew he had a granddaughter, Lacey Simmons, who was still in the area.

I thanked her, rang off, and googled Lacey's name. It took a few more information hops before I turned up a phone number for her on a social media site. She answered with a perky "Lacey, here" and I laid down my line of patter. Lacey Simmons seemed genuinely happy to receive my call. This didn't happen often and I took a moment to enjoy it. "I'm a bit of an amateur genealogist myself," she said. "Or at least I've been appointed the custodian of the family picture box and I've got the family Bible. Does that count?"

"It's a good start," I said, liking this woman's easy laugh. We had a nice conversation and she told me that yes, indeed, Hershel Tillett had been her grandfather and that, sadly, he'd passed away a decade ago. I asked if she'd ever heard her grandfather mention a man named Charlie Martin.

"His brother, you mean?" she asked.

"Brother?" I repeated.

"Well, stepbrother. Granddaddy's mother died in child-birth and his daddy married a widow who had a couple of kids; they were Cora and Charlie Martin."

"Do you know what became of either of them?"

"Well, Cora scandalized the whole county and ran off with an Italian peddler who came through. I don't know whatever happened to her or if she had a family. And Granddaddy and his stepbrother weren't together long. Sad to say, he died not too long after his daddy married his stepmama. It was from something you don't hear much about anymore. Whooping cough? Something like that. Whatever it was it got Granddaddy's sister, Lucille, too."

"Wait, what? So Charlie is deceased? I guess I have the wrong Charlie Martin."

"Well, there are a bunch of 'em. You can't round a corner out here without running into a Martin," Lacey said with a laugh. "And they all seem to favor the same two first names, Charles and Paul. There's at least a half dozen of each. It all gets very confusing."

I knew that was true from my search at the records office. I told her about our Charlie Martin. "He says he and your grandfather were pals. They rode the rails together as hobos when they were young men and later joined the army together."

"Hm, I wouldn't know about that," Lacey said. "I remember Granddaddy talking about his days as a knockabout— that's what he called it. But I never heard him mention anybody he knew being with him. Not that I remember anyway. I didn't pay much attention to the old people talk when I was a kid. I wish now I had. And Granddaddy never would talk about his time in the war. I tried to interview him about it once for a school project and he got upset and told me he just didn't want to think about it. I do know he had some cousins who joined up at the same time as him. Could this man be one of them?"

"Could be," I said. "When did you say your grandfather died?" I asked. "And how old was he?"

She gave me the dates and I calculated. Hershel would have been roughly the same age as our Charlie Martin.

The question I wanted to ask was *are you sure he's really dead?* But since that sounded like a casting call for a zombie movie, I tried a more normal question. "Was his death sudden?"

"No, poor Granddaddy sort of faded away. He was in a nursing home for several years. Toward the end he didn't even know any of us. It was very sad."

"I'm sorry," I said, only meaning it partly for her. I'd had a crazy notion maybe Hershel and Charlie were one and the same person. That maybe Hershel had taken on his brother's identity to escape from some debacle or other. So much for that theory. I scuttled around in my brain for a new one. In the forties lots of young men had the patriotic fever and wanted to sign up for service even if they were too young. It wasn't unusual for them to sign up under false names with false papers. Maybe Hershel gave his brother's birth certificate to a friend. I asked Lacey what she knew about his friends from his early days.

"Well, now I know he did have a gang he used to raise hell with when he was a young man. He admitted to being a rounder. And I know some of them were kin to him. But I can't recall names. Listen, I'm at work right now, but when I get home I could look through the pictures. I'm pretty sure some of them from those days have names written on the back. And I think there's one with a buddy of his right after they went to boot camp. I never saw that picture until after Granddaddy died."

I thanked her and clicked off my phone, making a note on my pad to follow up if I didn't hear from her tomorrow. If

Charlie, or whatever his real name was, had been an under-age enlistee, his wartime stories would be even more poignant fodder for the documentary.

Esme came in and I told her about what I'd been doing, all in a rush. "I think this could make a really compelling story if Tony and I can talk Charlie into doing it."

"Assuming Tony's not in the hoosegow by then for Blaine Branch's murder."

"Don't joke about that," I said.

"Oh, I'm not messing around," Esme said. "I was just on the phone with Denny. He says Jennifer's got her hair on fire. She's bound and determined to make an arrest, and at this point he doesn't think she especially cares who it is or if the charge holds up. She's desperate to show she's doing *something*."

"Will Denny be there when she talks to Tony?"

"He says he'll make it a point, but I'm going to call Crystal, just in case. And you call Tony and give him her number. Make sure he calls her if he feels the slightest need. That boy did not do this."

"Wow, you've sure changed your tune. Last night you weren't so sure of that."

"That was before I heard from his mother," Esme said.

"Michelle? His foster mother, you mean?"

"No, his real mother, his birth mother."

"But she's—" I began, then I got it. "Oh, I see. More inter-realm memos? What is she telling you?"

Esme sighed. "She's not telling me, just showing me. He's a good kid. And tenderhearted. That's what got him into trouble before. Like that time Michelle told you about when he couldn't stand to see that little kid getting picked on or like—"

"Like Beth?" I said, when she didn't go on. "He says it himself, Esme. Beth saved him. Maybe even literally saved his life, and he knew she was in trouble. Back then he was teetering on the edge. What if seeing Beth hurt made him totter?"

"He didn't totter, Sophreena. I won't believe that. His mama failed him in a lot of ways, though it wasn't from lack of trying. She had a lot of guilt about that but she's at peace now and she believes in him one hundred percent. And so do I."

"Okay," I said, nodding. "I'm with you."

"Good then, that's settled. Wish I could say the same for Celestine's issues. What was that slogan on those old florist commercials—say it with flowers? Well, I can tell you, that is *not* working for me."

After gathering up our lists, packing the last boxes into the car, and plotting our route for errands, we set out for Olivia's house.

"Olivia's at Marydale's shop right now," Esme said, "getting more supplies for her scrapbooks. She said she'd probably be home by the time we get there. She's really taken to those heritage scrapbooks, and I think she's taking special care with them because Tony's filming them. By the way, you did call Tony and tell him what I said, didn't you?"

"Yes, I called him," I said, pulling my sun visor down.

"Did he say he'd call Crystal?"

"Yes, but I'm not sure he will. He sounded—I don't know—maybe *resigned* is the word."

"I don't care for that word," Esme said. "And neither does his mama."

I started to pull in the driveway at Olivia's, then noticed her car wasn't there so I parked on the street behind another car, Peyton's shiny sports car. "What do you suppose he's doing here?" I murmured.

We each grabbed a box from the backseat and headed up the walk. I started to knock, but Esme told me not to bother because Olivia had said we were to go on in and make ourselves at home. She stuffed the box under one arm and barged right on in. I could hear voices coming from the living room, but I couldn't make out much, except that among Peyton's words I heard "keep it to yourself." I wanted to strangle him. This was the last thing Beth needed right now.

As we drew level with the doorway Beth and Peyton both startled. They were standing by the window and Peyton had been right in Beth's face, gesturing with both hands, his face florid. Beth was crying, but she quickly wiped the tears from her cheeks and turned to face us with a rueful smile.

Peyton gave us a murderous look, then grabbed his jacket off the sofa and stomped past without a word of either greeting or farewell.

"Are you okay, Beth?" I asked. "Is he harassing you?"

"You should call Denny," Esme said. "You want me to call him?"

"No!" Beth said, moving toward us with outstretched hands. "No, he's just—he doesn't know the whole story. It's a misunderstanding, that's all."

The front door opened and Olivia came in carrying a bag from Keepsake Corner in each hand. "Was that Peyton I saw leaving?" she asked as she came into the room. "He didn't even say hello." She nodded to us, then noticed Beth's state of distress. "What has he said to you?"

"It's nothing, Mother," Beth said. "Really. It'll be fine. Did you get all the supplies?" She forced a smile and pointed to the bags.

"Yes, I got everything we need and then some," Olivia said, still eyeing Beth with concern.

"And here are the last two boxes of your family things," Esme said.

Olivia put her arms around me and squeezed. "I thank you for this, both of you. I really do. It's been a wonderful gift. I never did like that word *closure*. I always thought it was new-age babble, but I see now what it means. I'm glad to know what happened to my father even if it was a tragic story. It's hard to move ahead when you're constantly looking over your shoulder and trying to understand how things that happened in the past are hindering you." She turned to look at Beth, and Esme and I both turned with her. Beth burst into tears and Olivia stepped over to put her arms around her daughter. She stroked her hair and shushed her as if she were a child. "It will all come out what happened to Blaine, too, one day," she said. "And when it does we'll square our shoulders and deal with it head-on."

In contrast to the emotional scene at Olivia's, the rest of the afternoon was filled with the most mundane of activities: returning library books, getting prescriptions filled, a pickup from the dry cleaners. We fell behind schedule and had to settle for stopping at the grocery store deli for a veggie platter as our contribution for the evening, which Esme would normally have found a criminal offense.

As the other four arrived they added their food offerings to the coffee table and took their customary spots in our living room. All except Marydale and Winston. Marydale usually takes the chair closest to the doorway, since she's forever jumping up and down to fetch things from the kitchen. Today she settled by the side window. Winston always takes one end of the sofa, but today he sat next to Jack by the front window. It was a trifling thing, and certainly we didn't have assigned seats, but it seemed indicative of some more consequential shift.

We chatted about our completed report on Olivia's genealogy as we ate. Everyone had heard bits and pieces, but this was the first time we'd gotten together since we'd found Celestine's description of what happened to Johnny Hargett.

"And you and Esme saw this trestle when you went out to Crawford?" Winston asked.

"We saw it," Esme said flatly.

"It looks Gothic, or maybe like something you see after the apocalypse," I said. "Or maybe it just looked that way to me because I know what happened there."

Then the talk turned to the investigation of Blaine's murder and I had to carefully consider my words. I could see Esme was doing the same, so I was surprised when next she spoke.

"The police are bringing Tony Barrett in for questioning again tomorrow. And if that doesn't go well they'll probably be coming around to talk to all of us about that night again.

Now, I'm not trying to tell anybody what to say—we've all got to tell the truth as we see it—but I want you all to know I'm one hundred percent sure that boy did *not* kill Blaine Branch."

I was astounded, and so was everyone else, judging by the looks on their faces. They all knew about Esme's gift and, like me, they'd progressed through skepticism to various levels of true belief over the years. Esme trusted them completely with her secret, but she'd never before been this blatant about influencing them with what she'd learned through this channel.

"I know he's been in trouble before," she said, "and I know his whereabouts for that day can't be completely accounted for, but I'm asking y'all to trust me on this. He didn't do it and if we can find any way to help him I hope we will. Now that's all I have to say about it."

As we cleared the food Marydale's two Westies got frisky. I stopped to play tug-of-war with Sprocket with a squeaky toy and Gadget took that opportunity to launch a raid on Sprocket's bed and steal the biscuits he buries under his covers. Then we walked the few blocks to Keepsake Corner to work on our own heritage scrapbooks and exchange our latest findings. The ritual was routine and familiar, but I couldn't shake the feeling something was off somehow.

After we'd pulled our boxes from the shelf in the back room and settled at the table we went around the circle. Jack and I were the only ones with anything new. Jack told how he'd found proof of his being descended from Robert Ford. And when it was my turn I pulled a manila envelope out of my bag. "This came in today's mail," I said. "I haven't even had a chance to open it yet, so we'll all learn about it together. You all know how long I've been searching for my mom's natural family. Well, while this isn't about her specifically, I'm hoping it will tell me some things. I had an in-depth DNA profile run and these are the results." I put the envelope to my head like Carnac, that old soothsayer character Johnny Carson used to do on his show. "I predict my profile will come back fifty percent European and forty percent Asian, with about ten percent something *other* thrown in."

"Should we start a pool?" Coco asked.

"I can't wait long enough for you to put down bets," I said, ripping the flap of the envelope. I shuffled through the sheaf of papers and scanned through the scientific text until I came to the part written in plain English. "Drumroll, please," I said. "I'm forty-eight percent European, northern European to be more exact. I'm six percent other and I'm forty-six percent Polynesian, from a subgroup identified in the Marshall Islands. Wow!" I skimmed through the remaining pages. "Then there's all this stuff about three subgroups and the various theories about their migration from Asia. And a map! For the first time in my life I can point to a map and say this is where my mother's people are from!"

"Cool," Jack said.

"Way cool," I agreed. I was excited—and apprehensive. I wondered if this was how Olivia felt when we started exploring her family history, and look how that had turned out. Still, always better to know. And anyway, I was already calculating how I might fund a research excursion to the North Pacific.

twenty-one

"No more procrastination," Esme said sternly, setting a cup of coffee in front of me as I tried to clear the cobwebs from my head. "We leave tomorrow. We've got to pack."

"I know," I said, "but I hate leaving Morningside right now with all this stuff going on."

"I don't like leaving, either," Esme said. "But we're not going to the back side of the moon. We can be back here in less than three hours if need be. Hey, did you hear back from that woman, the granddaughter of Charlie Martin's friend, what was his name?"

"Hershel Tillett, and no, she hasn't called me back. You know how that goes. I'll have to pester her again but there's no urgency."

"You lost interest already? Yesterday you were all in a tizzy about it."

"Oh, I still want to do it, but we won't be able to get any more interviews in before we leave town. And anyhow,

Charlie hasn't agreed to do it and I have a hunch Tony's gonna have a hard row to hoe talking him into it."

"Assuming Tony's able himself. I'm nervous as a cat about what Jennifer Jeffers is going to do after they talk to him today. Honestly, I wouldn't be surprised if she's harassing him just to get at me 'cause she knows I'm fond of the boy."

"Wow, paranoid much? First off, I think your fondness for the boy is a *very* new development, which I didn't even realize until yesterday. And second, maybe we don't occupy Jennifer Jeffers' thoughts as much as you seem to think."

"You know she hates us," Esme said. "You know it. And I can't for the life of me figure out what I ever did to her. Other than become friends with her partner."

"I think you and Denny are a little more than friends," I teased, expecting her to sputter.

Instead she frowned. "He's a good man, Sophreena. I like him more than I probably ought to."

"Why would you say that?" I asked. "You two make a great couple."

"Um-hm. Until he finds out I'm a freak. And how long do you think it'll be before I slip and he figures it out? You can't have this thing I've got and a normal relationship, too. I'm going to have to give him up before he finds out."

"Are you out of your mind? Look, you have perfectly normal relationships with me, Marydale, Winston, Coco, and Jack, and we all know. What makes you think it would be any different with Denny?"

"He's a cop, with a cop's mind," Esme said wearily. "You're too young to remember Jack Webb on TV saying *just the facts, ma'am*, but that's a cop's way of looking at the world."

"Don't you have one of your mother's homespun expressions to cover this? Like not getting your cart before your horse or something?"

Esme considered. "Well, she used to say, 'Don't trouble trouble till trouble troubles you.'"

"Okay, that one makes my brain hurt a little, but it sounds like good advice."

We'd gotten our computers, scanners, recording equipment, and other gear packed up and ready to go by the time Jack called to ask me to lunch. I wasn't about to turn that down. I promised Esme I'd be back soon to pack my clothes and load the car so we could get on the road early the next morning.

To borrow from Esme's line of patter, I enjoyed passing time with Jack probably more than I ought to. Over the past months my determination to keep my true feelings from him had grown ever stronger. But so had my confusion. Sometimes things he said or did gave me a faint hope he might feel the same. Then I'd realize it was only wishful thinking on my part.

When I heard Jack's truck pull into the driveway, I went out to meet him. He had his boat in the back of the truck and he'd gotten out to adjust one of the bungee cords holding it in place. "You'll be happy to hear I'm gonna repaint her," he said.

"Oh, I don't know if you should," I said, running my hand along the upturned hull. "I kind of like her the way she is."

"Good," Jack said, sheepishly. "Because I really don't want to repaint, but I do have to make some repairs."

"What's this from?" I asked, looking at a hole, surrounded by some splintered wood that had been water soaked and weathered into a gray patina.

Jack smiled. "Bullet hole. When I was about nine or ten my dad shot at a muskrat that was burrowing under our dock. His shot ricocheted off a rock. Muskrat one, boat, zero. I repaired it from the inside but can't bring myself to cover it entirely. Every time I see that hole I remember my dad's face that day as he watched the boat slowly sink."

I rubbed my finger in the indentation. "I saw something that looked just like this at Beth's," I said, half lost in my own thoughts. "In the side of their shed. I forgot to tell Denny."

"Why would you need to tell him?" Jack asked. "Blaine wasn't shot. And I doubt it was a bullet hole anyway."

"I'm pretty sure it was," I said, fishing my phone from my bag. "And the wood around it was still light colored; it hadn't weathered. I don't know that it had anything to do with Blaine's death, but if there was a gun, if Blaine had a gun then maybe—" I caught myself before I said any more out loud.

Jack gave me a peculiar look, but he didn't ask questions. We got into the truck and he drove slowly toward the diner. I called Denny but he was unavailable so I texted a message. "I hope that means he's in the interrogation with Tony," I said.

"Yeah, about that," Jack said. "I got a call from Detective Jeffers this morning asking if Tony had ever been to my place, my business, I mean."

I groaned. "What did you tell her?"

Jack shrugged. "That yeah, he'd been over and filmed a little, though he was mostly interested in asking about the golf course and its operations since that's our biggest client and a huge player in Morningside's development."

"What else did she ask?"

"Nothing," Jack said. "I was holding my breath figuring she was going to ask if he'd ever been back where we keep the tarps, but she didn't."

"Had he?"

Jack shrugged again. "I suppose. He'd been all around the place, but I couldn't tell you if he took any particular notice. And anyway, after what Esme said last night I wasn't going to volunteer anything."

I wished Esme could hear him say that. No hesitation. As if whatever Esme said could be taken to the bank.

"I'm still freaked out about that tarp being found at my place," he said. "I've been turning this over in my head for days. I'm convinced somebody put it there to hide it in plain sight. A tarp's harder to get rid of than you might think. Up on Crescent Hill there are no commercial properties, so no Dumpsters. I suppose somebody could have put it into a trash bag and slipped it into someone's trash can, but they'd need a trash bag handy, right? And they couldn't dump it in the lake with the body. It would've floated to the surface and attracted all kinds of attention."

"I've been thinking about how it was folded. Is your method special?"

"Well, no. I mean we didn't invent it or anything. It's just the way we do it. Painters sometimes fold their drop cloths that way, too. It would be like your preference for how you knot your scarf," he said, reaching over to yank the one I had looped around my neck. "Our way lets you tuck in the final fold so it'll stay through handling. If you fold them in simple squares they soon get messy."

"Boy, would you appreciate Beth's toolshed," I said, describing its state of tidiness.

Jack nodded. "Good tools should be respected."

As we met a car on Front Street the driver's hand lifted off the steering wheel in the Southerner's ubiquitous two-fingered wave. I didn't think much of it at first, since the gesture is almost automatic whether the driver knows you or not, but then I realized it was Daniel. I turned just as he passed and then I saw Alan Corrigan in the passenger seat.

"Alan's still here?" I said, more musing than question. "That's the second time I've seen them together this week. What do you suppose that's all about?"

"Alan's going to invest in Daniel's restaurant when and if he can get enough other capital together to start it up."

"And how do you know this?" I asked.

"Bonnie told me," Jack said. "She said she'd invest herself if she had any extra cash. I understand Blaine hit the roof when he found out Alan was in."

"When did he find that out?" I asked. "It might be relevant to the investigation."

"Naw," Jack said. "That was weeks ago. They had a big dustup about it but in the end Blaine told him if he wanted to throw his money away to have at it."

"Sounds like they patched up their differences then," I said, feeling oddly disappointed.

"On that score, I guess," Jack said. "But Blaine had another bone to pick with Corrigan. Everybody knows Blaine and his parents were at loggerheads over what his parents were doing to help Madison."

"Yeah, and what's that got to do with Alan?"

"Sterling Branch didn't want the family lawyer to handle this for some reason. I think maybe he was on Blaine's side of the argument. So Sterling hired Alan to come down and set up an amended trust for Madison. That's one reason Alan was here the night before Blaine died, and even then Blaine was still thinking he'd be able to talk Alan out of doing the job for his parents."

"Wow, Miss Bonnie tells you everything, does she?" I said, a twinge of jealousy working its way along my shoulder muscles, kinking them tight.

"I think she's lonely," Jack said. "And she doesn't have any family around so she's had no one to lean on through this whole thing. She sits out on her back deck every night now, even when it's cold outside. She just sits out there and looks up at the stars. I think she's worried about losing her life savings, too, if things don't pan out with the settlement. Or maybe it's something altogether different bothering her; I don't know. She doesn't tell me anything about her private thoughts."

That pleased me more than it should have and the guilt moved in. "I hope she'll be okay," I said. "I'm glad she has you to talk to. She's seems like a nice person."

The diner was crowded and we threaded our way among the tables to grab the last available booth. When I slid in I spotted Marydale and Winston sitting at a far table with Madison Branch. They were deep in conversation and hadn't noticed Jack and me come in. Madison looked upset or confused, or maybe angry. It was hard to tell with her. She had an unnaturally flat affect and the way she carried her body was a little off-kilter. Madison had always been a little different. She was an artsy type but thus far she hadn't been able to channel her abilities in a focused direction. I'd seen some of her paintings and she was talented, but the subject matter she chose indicated she was also troubled.

I wanted to observe Madison but it was a private conversation, and I had no business intruding, even visually. I grabbed a menu and studied it, though I knew it by heart.

Jack and I each ordered the soup du jour, and since this jour was Wednesday it would be a luscious thick cream of mushroom. I order a salad to go with it, out of sheer guilt, but Jack had no such compunction and asked for a side of double cheeseburger.

Jack asked about the job in Wilmington, which I expected to be a straightforward gig. "We'll interview the family members," I told him, "then spend the rest of the time on research and sourcing. No heritage scrapbooks, no filming. No scanning or indexing. They just want a well-documented pedigree chart and a decorative family tree. I don't think we're going to have any skeletons pop out of closets on this one."

"Sounds a little boring," Jack said, hacking his newly arrived cheeseburger into half-moons.

"Yeah, well, I could use a little boring after Olivia's job."

As we ate our lunch I checked my phone every few minutes. This is behavior I abhor in other people and Jack—properly—called me on it.

"I know, I'm sorry. I was hoping to hear something from Tony. I'm worried."

Jack nodded. "With good reason, I'd say."

I saw Madison Branch get up to leave. She hugged Marydale, then Winston, and gathered up her things. She seemed less agitated than she'd been when we came in, but I wasn't sure I was reading her right. If the buzz around town was to be given credence, she'd brought home a pre- scription drug addiction along with her other issues. Mary- dale said she'd been working hard to get herself clean and healthy again.

Winston spotted Jack and after the waitress brought their bill they came over to our booth. We exchanged what little bits of news we'd collected since last night, which wasn't a lot. They didn't offer up anything about Madison and I didn't ask, though I wanted to.

When they were gone I got that odd vibe again. "Do they seem weird to you?" I asked Jack.

Jack frowned. "Weird?"

"Acting strange?"

Jack puckered his lips, thinking. "Nope, they seem like always."

"I hope so," I said, watching as they walked back across the street to Keepsake Corner.

"News," Esme pronounced as I came into the kitchen.

"Good news or bad news? Is it Tony?" I asked, holding my breath.

"Oh, no, I'm sorry, sugar. But Denny promised he'd call me the minute he could. No, my news is about the job in Wilmington and I don't know if it's good or bad. Mr. Mar- kum's daughter called. We're going to have to reschedule. Her father's in the hospital."

"Is it serious?" I asked.

"Appendicitis. And I gather there were complications. He'll be okay, but he'll be hospitalized for at least a week. I told her we'd have to check our calendars and get back to her."

"Poor man. But I can't say I'm disappointed to postpone, with all that's going on here right now."

My cell phone rang and a beat later the special ringtone Esme had recently assigned to Denny started singing into the room. Salt-n-Pepa's "Whatta Man." I made a mental note to tell Denny to call her on the phone sometime when they were together so he could hear it. I fumbled my phone to look at the screen and saw Tony's number displayed. I pushed the talk button and asked if he was okay.

"Yeah, I'm good," he said, though his tone implied that wasn't entirely true. "I was wondering if I could stop by this afternoon to show you some stuff, a rough-cut preview of Olivia's video and more of that last interview with Charlie. I know you're going out of town tomorrow but it wouldn't take long."

"Come over now, ASAP," I said, not bothering to tell him our plans had changed.

Esme had stepped out onto the patio to talk and she came back in, hugging her sweater tighter around her to erase the chill.

"Well, apparently they didn't arrest him," I said.

"Not *yet*," Esme said, gesturing with the phone. "Denny convinced Jennifer she didn't have enough to hold him and that the DA would not be pleased if she made the arrest on evidence this flimsy. But she's still got the bit between her teeth."

Tony's motorcycle pulled into the driveway a few minutes later and Esme and I both went out, peppering him with questions before he could even get his helmet off.

"It wasn't bad," he said. "Well, it was bad, but I've had worse. Your guy," he said to Esme, "he's okay, but that woman is a—" He stopped.

"A buster of some tender part of your anatomy?" Esme said, raising an eyebrow.

"Yeah, that," Tony said with a tired smile.

Esme, it seemed, had warmed not only to Tony, but to the video format as well. And from the snippets I'd seen so far it had warmed to her, too. She was great at voice-over, her voice warm and full of inflection and resonance. Mine, on the other hand, was small, like me, and came off sounding like a cartoon rodent. She was also good at scripting, where the cadence and rhythm were much different than the cut-and-dried parlance we use for our family history reports.

I wasn't yet absolutely sold on the idea of adding video scrapbooking to our list of services, but I was keeping an open mind. Tony set up his laptop on the coffee table in the living room and after some finagling of wires and remotes, managed to get the picture up on our TV screen. He started Olivia's video scrapbook with some clips from the old Crawford movie.

"The company is still in business," he said. "They got swallowed up by a bigger company years ago, but I was able to get permission to use the clips." He brushed his hair back off his face. "I was gonna use 'em anyway, but since this is a portfolio piece I wanted everything legal-eagled."

He'd cut in the footage he'd taken yesterday, positioning the camera at the same angles as the old shots. "We'll have to do some voice-over here," he said, turning to Esme, naturally, "and then here we slide into Olivia's part."

Olivia came onscreen, telling what she knew of her family history, then there were interviews with Daniel and with Beth. Then came Esme's narration of Olivia's family history and those Ken Burns–style pans of the scrapbooks.

Now I was sold.

When I didn't speak for a moment Tony interpreted my silence as disapproval.

"You hate it," he said.

"No, Tony, I'm just speechless. This is better than I ever expected; no offense."

"None taken," Tony said. "As long as you like it. We've got more work to do on it, but so far, so good."

"So far, *real* good," Esme said.

"I know you don't have much time, but let me show you some clips from the interview with Charlie, too." He ejected a disk from his computer and popped in another one.

"Relax," I said, telling him about our cancellation. "All we've got to do this afternoon is unpack the stuff we already packed."

"Okay, cool. Maybe after you see this you'll buy into this project, too. Keep in mind this is all raw footage."

Charlie's now-familiar face appeared on the screen. He was stiff, almost sullen, in the beginning, but slowly mellowed as I coaxed him along in the interview.

When the screen went blank Esme sat back on the sofa. "Okay, well, now it's my turn to say *I'm* convinced. You've got an interesting story there."

"Especially if my hunch is right," I said.

Tony gave me a quizzical look and I told him what I'd found while searching for information about Hershel Tillett. "And based on that, I'm thinking Charlie may have been one of Hershel's underaged friends, or maybe even one of the cousins. I'll keep digging. And if Charlie Martin, or whatever his real name is, was a boy soldier, don't you think that makes his story even more compelling?"

"Depends on how young he was, I suppose," Tony said. "Lots of boys fresh off the farms fought that war. Or when you think about it, pretty much every war."

Esme groaned, and when I looked over there was the hand across her forehead again.

"I know, it's not right," she murmured.

Tony shrugged. "I know it's not right, but that's just the way it is."

twenty-two

Tony called early the next morning. "Charlie's agreed to another interview. Can you go this afternoon? We need to catch him before he backs out."

"He's agreed to the project?"

"Not yet. I figured, better to ease him into it. Get him used to talking to you. And maybe when Beth's feeling better she could help wrangle him into it."

In the hours I had until time for the interview, I dogged Charlie Martin's trail, only to end up in a succession of frustrating dead ends. I was more convinced than ever that Charlie Martin was somebody else, somebody who'd gone to war young and grown up too fast. I suddenly recalled what Celestine had written about their tenants' sons wanting to join up even though one was underaged. Was the name Tillett or was I getting my wires and my jobs crossed? We'd already taken everything back to Olivia, so I'd have to check the next time I was over there. Olivia might get a kick out of it if she found out that there was a link, however

tangential, between her family and Charlie's all those decades ago.

I called Lacey Simmons and got her voice mail. I left a
message asking if she'd had any luck locating the photos of
her grandfather's pals and told her—sincerely—that I'd *really*
love to hear from her.

I got out my calculator and tried out different age discrep-
ancies. Charlie Martin was in remarkable vim and vigor for
his age. Shave a few years and he'd be fit, but not extraordinary. And if that range was right, the enlistment age of the
erstwhile Charlie would have been somewhere around fourteen or fifteen. That was sad to think about, but it made for a
much more dramatic story.

I looked through my notes from the last interview with
Charlie and jotted down questions for the afternoon session
today, some of them subtly contrived to help me prove my
theory about Charlie's actual age and identity.

When Tony arrived we went over the questions, adjusted some, and added a couple of new ones. On the drive
to Charlie's place Tony seemed fidgety. "Are you nervous
about this or something?" I asked. "Afraid I'll scare him
off?"

"No, we're ready," he said. "And you're fine. It's something
else. I feel like I ought to tell you about it, but I don't know
why I should feel that way. I mean it's not like I owe you
what's in my head."

"You don't owe me anything, Tony," I said. "But if there's
something you want to talk about, I'm a pretty good listener
and I know how to keep my lip zipped."

"I know, else Beth wouldn't have told you about getting

used as a punching bag by her creep of a husband," he said, spitting each word.

"She told you?" I asked.

"No, I overheard her talking to Olivia and Daniel. They don't realize how much sound travels through the heat ducts in that house. I wasn't eavesdropping; you just hear whether you want to or not," he said.

"Did you suspect what was going on?" I asked. "Is that why you didn't like Blaine?"

"I didn't know-know, if you get my drift, but something about him wasn't right. He had this look in his eyes sometimes. It was stone cold with an afterburner of psycho. Foster kids got good radar about that look."

"You know Beth doesn't want anyone to know about this, right? I think she'd be very distressed if it got out."

"I don't get why," Tony said. "She didn't do anything wrong. But it's her business and she should get to say what she wants. So I won't say anything to anybody but you. I just didn't like holding it in, you know? And I overheard Beth say she'd told you and Esme about it because she knew she could trust you. It made me feel bad she couldn't trust me, too, but I don't blame her."

"Don't look at it that way, Tony," I said. "Knowing is a burden, really. You just said so yourself. She probably wanted to spare you that."

"Yeah, maybe. Anyhow, I don't want any of them to start acting different around me, or be mad at me for overhearing. So don't say anything."

I pinched my thumb and finger together and drew them across my lips.

*   *   *

Charlie wasn't at his place when we arrived and we had no way to reach him since he didn't have a phone. The only way Tony had been able to contact him was to come over or search for him around town, which was how he'd found him this morning.

"He's probably still over at the Methodist church," Tony said. "The pastor's wife hired him to construct some new beds and put in bulbs—tulips and some other flowers I can't remember the names of—along the walkway that leads from the parking lot to the church. She's hoping they'll bloom at Easter time."

Esme could probably recite the names of all the flowers for him, I thought. She'd still been suffering under a barrage of blossoms this morning, though she had a feeling things were building toward something more comprehensible. She'd been in the midst of cooking a big dinner when I left with enough banging and clanging to rival Olivia's big wind contraptions. That's the way Esme works out her issues with her *guests.* Sometimes, when she's feeling kindly disposed, she refers to them as PALS, which is her acronym for Previously Alive and Longing for Solace. When she's feeling neutral they're guests and when she's ticked off they're parasites. As much as Esme had come to admire Celestine, after last night she'd slipped from PALS status to guest and was teetering there.

"Should we wait for Charlie or come back later?" I asked.

"I'd say wait unless you've got something better to do," Tony said. "I don't want to give him any excuse to put us off."

I realized only then that I was the one who was nervous. I had no idea why. Yes, Charlie Martin, aka whoever, was an irascible old cuss, but I'd surely seen a lot worse. And I was confident that with enough patience, he could be brought around.

Just then Charlie rounded the corner of the building on his bike. He was pulling his cart full of tools behind him. The sight made me reassess my theory. Today he looked every year the age he claimed.

He nodded a curt greeting as he unlocked his door and huffed as he started to take his tools from the cart and put them inside. "People will steal the fillings out of your teeth around here," he grumbled.

Tony and I each grabbed what we could carry. I noticed there were two short shovels. One matched the quality tools at Beth's house and one was a lower grade and still had a sticker on it. So I guessed Beth would be getting hers back soon. When the cart was empty Charlie came back out and cobwebbed what appeared to be a logging chain around his bike and cart and secured it with an old-fashioned padlock the size of a softball.

He left the door standing open and Tony and I looked at one another and shrugged, figuring that must be our invitation. We followed him into a narrow vestibule, where Charlie stopped to hang up his jacket.

He slumped into a chair and motioned vaguely toward a threadbare sofa. I noted again how tidy the place was. The furnishings were spare, cheap and old, but everything was clean and orderly.

"How's Beth?" Charlie asked as we sat down. It was the first spark of interest he'd shown and I debated what to tell him.

"Is she okay?" he pressed. "I mean, I know she's not okay just yet, but will she be once this part's over?"

"I'm sure she will be," I said, though I wasn't clear on what *this part* was. "I expect she'll come around to see you soon. She just needs some time."

Charlie nodded, then dealt with a coughing spasm. "That's good then," he said when he'd gotten his breath back. He glanced around toward the kitchen, then tapped his hands on the arms of his chair. "You know, I think this is enough of this foolishness. I'm tired and hungry and nobody cares what an old man has to say about anything anyhow. Let's call this off."

Tony slumped, but I wasn't ready to throw in the towel. "You know, I'm hungry, too," I said. "Maybe Tony can go pick us up some lunch. What do you like?"

I wasn't remotely hungry, having had a big fat calzone and two tall glasses of tea just before I came over, but I tried to sell it, giving Tony's arm a little slap. "This guy's so into his filming he forgets a woman's got to eat!"

Charlie considered for a long moment. "Well," he said finally, "I like the pizza from that place over on River Road. Y'all like that?"

"I love it," Tony said, and was instantly on his feet. I handed him my keys and after he took our topping orders he was out the door.

I didn't want to ask Charlie any questions that Tony would want to capture on camera, so I mustered all the charm I could and tried some light banter.

Charlie was immune.

Fine. I wasn't really in a mood for small talk, either. What I really wanted to ask him about was his buddy Hershel

Tillett and how he, much too coincidentally, happened to share the same name as Hershel's deceased stepbrother. But he was already cranky enough. I figured if I brought up any of that and he realized I'd been snooping around in his background he'd throw us out for sure—and for good. I struggled on for another ten minutes or so, asking him about the various jobs he was doing around town. He was mending a screen door at Miss Etheleen Morganton's, repairing a fence for Ingrid Garrison, and helping out with building a meditation labyrinth at St. Raphael's.

I latched on to the last job and asked a bunch of questions. I was genuinely interested since St. Raph's is my parish. And, lax Catholic though I am, I loved the idea of the labyrinth and had even made a modest contribution. We talked easily for a while but when we'd exhausted that subject the awkwardness returned.

He got up from his chair with some difficulty. "'Scuse me," he said. "I'm gonna go wash up. Make yourself to home."

The small space was getting to me. I headed for the front doorway to get a breath of air. I bumped Charlie's jacket as I went by and it nearly fell from the hook. I reached up to catch it. It was heavy and lopsided and I saw why. There was a gun that looked as old as Charlie in one of the pockets. So much for Denny's warnings. I'd definitely be informing on Charlie on that one. I opened the door and took in a few gulps of air, then returned to my place on the sofa. I pulled my phone from my bag and started to check messages and email. What did people ever do with snatches of downtime before smartphones came along?

I was excited to see a message from Lacey Simmons. I tapped it open and skimmed through her apologies about not getting back to me, then came to the meat of the message. She had a total of twenty-seven photographs of Hershel posing with gangs of friends, but she'd only attached scans of the five that had names written on the backs and the boot camp one that had no names. I clicked to bring up the first one and read the names, none of which sounded familiar. I dutifully pulled out my notebook and scratched them down. I spread my fingers on the screen to enlarge each of the four faces and studied each carefully, making a star by the names of the two who looked baby-faced. I went through the other photos in a similar fashion. When I got to the final one fireworks started going off in my brain and the planet seemed to tilt.

Charlie came out of the bathroom, his thin hair wet and slicked back over his balding pate. He pulled his watch from his pocket and swung it by its fob, twirling it in a loop into the palm of his hand. The whole business seemed to happen in super-slow motion. He hit the latch button just as it reached his hand, studied the face for a long moment, then latched it and put it back in his pocket. Only then did he look in my direction.

The turmoil in my head must have been visible and as our eyes met he went ghostly pale.

"Hello, Johnny Hargett," I said. "Where've you been all these years?"

His eyes widened and he glanced toward his coat. Only then did it occur to me that maybe I'd just made a very large mistake.

Just then Tony came through the door. "Hope everybody's hungry," he said cheerfully, lofting the pizza boxes. He looked from me to Charlie, then back to me again. "What's going on? Please don't tell me the interview's off."

"Depends on who it is you wanted to interview," I said.

twenty-three

"I RECKON YOU'RE GONNA RUN RIGHT OVER AND TELL OLIVIA and the kids about this," the erstwhile Charlie said, his voice at once relieved and resentful.

"I'm not sure what I'll do," I said. "But sooner or later they're going to know. Don't you think it would be better all around if it came from you?"

"Tell who what?" Tony said, still holding the pizza boxes. "Could somebody please tell *me* what's going on?"

I held up a hand to quiet him. "Just give us a minute, Tony," I said, still focused on Charlie/Johnny.

He continued to stare at the scarred linoleum floor, then shook his head emphatically. "I can't do it. I know what you're saying is true; they'll find out sooner or later," he said, his voice little more than a warble. "And I would like them to know my side of it, but I can't face them. I can't look any of them in the eye. I can't do it."

"Tony," I said, keeping my voice level. "Go get your camera."

He started to protest, but I gave him a sharp look and he set the pizza boxes down and scurried out.

My cell phone, still in my hand, rang and I saw that it was Esme. I let it go to voice mail.

"You can tell your story to the camera," I said to Johnny, trying for a sympathetic tone, though I wasn't sure I felt much sympathy for him. "That'll make it easier. We'll show the footage to Olivia, Daniel, and Beth, then they can decide whether they want to see you. I suspect they will because I'm sure they'll have questions. I know I sure do." I hardened my tone. "Either we do it that way, or yeah, I'll head over there now and tell them myself."

Again my cell phone rang, the insistent ring filling the small room. It was Esme again. She knew we were doing this interview, so for her to interrupt—twice—it had to be important. When I answered she blurted out. "She didn't mean it wasn't right morally," she said. "She meant it was inaccurate. She meant it really didn't happen the way they thought for all those years. She meant what she *wrote* wasn't right. Sophreena, I'm not sure Johnny Hargett died when he went off that railroad trestle."

"He didn't," I said.

"How do you know?" she asked.

"Because I'm looking right at him."

I was ridiculously gratified that, for once, I'd been the one to set Esme's world off-kilter. I promised a sputtering Esme details to follow and clicked off as Tony came back in with his camera already set up on a tripod. He had it ready to go in seconds.

Johnny sat back down, reluctantly. "How'd you figure it out?"

I told him about Celestine's diaries and what she'd written about his supposed death. He shook his head slowly from side to side, his shoulders shaking as he began to sob.

"It must have eaten Riley alive," he said, once he'd gotten hold of himself. "I'd planned to go back. I knew he probably thought the fall had killed me. And it nearly did. But then as time passed I thought this way was better."

Tony and I both sat silent, letting him find his way. Johnny confirmed Celestine's assessment of him as a young husband. "I wasn't a man to go through tough times with back then. Fact, for Renny especially, I was the one that made times tough, real tough. I knew full well I didn't deserve her when I married her. There's not a day that's gone by in the last sixty years I didn't wish I could go back and fix things and make it all right. That night Riley told me I had to leave before I hurt her bad. I didn't want to hear that, him telling me how to be with my wife."

"So you and Riley did fight about it?"

"Yeah, just like Celestine wrote," he said. "Riley hauled me off with my arms twisted behind my back down to the trestle. We used to go there when we were kids and talk our big talk about how our lives were gonna go. So he took me out there so he had me trapped and I had to listen, but that just made it worse on my end. I felt like a caged animal or something."

"And you two fought?" Tony asked. "Like physically? Was that part like she wrote?"

Johnny nodded. "Best I remember, Riley was telling me I had to leave and never come back, never see Renny again, nor the baby. That I was never to see him or Celestine again.

The blood rushed to my head and I felt like I was going to catch on fire I was so mad. I hit him in the gut hard. I was stronger and younger than him, but I was also drunk as Cooter Brown. He came at me like a freight train, and next thing I knew there wasn't nothing between me and that river but night air."

"Man," Tony said breathlessly. "How in hell did you survive that fall?"

"The river was deeper back then," Johnny said. "In spots anyway. A lot of the rocks were brought from the quarry at a later time to stop the river from eating away the farmland on the north side. I hit a deep pool when I went in. I got the breath knocked out of me good and broke some ribs and I got beat to hell on the rocks. But somewheres way on downstream a fella from one of the camps jumped in and tried to save me, least that's what I thought he was doing. He pulled me out but then he took my clothes and my boots and just left me there."

He recounted how he'd lain there for maybe a full day, then somehow got himself overland to his buddy Hershel Tillett's family farm. Hershel hid him in the barn for three weeks, sneaking food out to him and tending to his wounds.

"I had a long time to study on it when I was hiding out at the Tilletts'. I came to it that Riley was right. I needed to just get gone. He told me if he had to stop me from hurting Renny again it would be for good and I knew he meant it. He would have killed me and he would have been right to do it. He said he wouldn't stand by and see his brother turn into what I'd become. I didn't understand myself why I acted like I did with Renny; it was like a devil got inside me. So after

I thought on it for a while, I figured he must already think I was dead and this way he'd at least be able to chalk it up as sort of accidental whereas if I stayed and he killed me cold he'd never be able to live with that. And 'course, neither would I," he said, a pained smile twisting his lips.

"Where did you go?" I asked.

"When I was mended enough, me and Hershel set out together. We had in mind to go to California for some reason or other, and the only way we had to get there was to ride the rails."

"So you didn't buy a ticket and board a train carrying a knapsack?"

"Well, I had a rucksack all right, but I didn't have jack to buy a ticket with. Me and Hershel hopped the train out of the Crawford stop."

"Did you make it to California?" Tony asked.

Johnny nodded. "Yep. It wasn't what everybody made it out to be. And whatever I was mad about didn't get left behind, neither. It didn't take nothing at all for me to get in a fight when we was tramping. I was all the time getting my ass whupped or whupping somebody else's. Or getting beat upside the head by the railroad bulls before we caught on good about how to hop the train."

"When and why did you become Charlie Martin?" I asked.

"Hershel got the fire in his belly about enlisting in the army and by then I didn't care much what happened to me, so I said I'd go with him. But that fella that took my clothes got my billfold, too, and anyways, I didn't want anybody to come looking for me, ever. I was leaving the old life behind and I didn't want to be Johnny Hargett anymore. Hershel got the bright idea to go back home and take his brother's papers. There was nothing to 'em back then," Johnny said. "None of this picture ID business. I was pretty close to his brother's age. Nobody thought to check against death certificates. So I became Charlie Martin, and he's a better man than Johnny Hargett ever was."

"And that's the name you signed up under?" I asked.

Johnny nodded. "We went to the war and I had some of the devil knocked out of me. I did Charlie Martin proud during the war. There was times I was even brave. I looked after the other boys and held up my end of things. But when I came back home I turned right back into a coward. I couldn't face folks back home, not Renny and not Riley or Celestine. And I knew I was never going to be fit to live around people 'cause I didn't trust myself. I didn't trust that Johnny Hargett wouldn't come back. So I joined back up and spent my life in the army until I retired."

"And came back here?" I prompted.

Johnny nodded. "I just wanted to see what had become of Renny. I figured she'd remarry and have a good life with some good man who'd take care of her and the baby, but I found out she never did marry again. But she seemed happy from what I could tell in the few days I skulked around Crawford. There for a while I came back every couple of years to check on them. After Renny passed and Olivia was living over here, I decided I'd just stay around. There wasn't anybody here who'd recognize anything about me."

"And you ended up becoming friends with Beth," I said.

"That was pure accidental and I tried to hold her off, but

after a while I couldn't help myself. I liked talking to her so much. She puts me in mind of Renny when she was young."

"She was like Renny in a lot of ways, wasn't she?" I asked. "Are you going to tell the rest?" I was operating on a hunch now and I was a long way from having the pieces put together, but I figured I'd risk the bluff.

Johnny held my gaze, his faded blue eyes filled with anger and hurt. "Turn that thing off," he said to Tony.

Tony still looked dazed, but he turned off the camera and gave me a sidelong glance, widening his eyes and lifting his eyebrows.

"How did it happen?" I asked.

Johnny looked out the small window with a view of the parking lot. A breeze bothered the leaves on a Japanese maple and it reminded me of one of Olivia's sculptures. Time passed and I wasn't sure Johnny was going to answer, but finally he gave a heavy sigh and began.

"I knew what he was, Beth's husband. He had the devil in him, too. I could see it. And I knew sooner or later he'd do something really bad to her. And he did."

"How did you happen to be there that day?" I asked.

"It was near dark," Johnny said. "I'd finished putting in some hostas at a house near Beth's and I went by to return something Beth had lent me."

"That shovel?" I said, nodding toward the tools propped in the corner.

Johnny raised an eyebrow. "You don't let no moss grow on you, do you? I came up the driveway on my rig and I could hear him cussing at her. I got the shovel out of my cart and started for the backyard. Then when I come around the corner I saw him haul off and belt her on the side of her head. It was like I was reliving a nightmare. I hated him and myself both at the same time and all of a sudden I had the notion I could redeem myself if I could stop him. I could finally atone for every bad thing I did to Renny. I pulled out the gun I carry for protection and fired it. I wasn't aiming at him, just wanting to stop him. But that boiled him over and he come at me like he was gonna tear my head off. The gun jammed and I couldn't get off another shot. I'd dropped the shovel with all that was going on and I grabbed for it. He kept on coming so I swung it with everything I had left in me and it connected. He was dead before he hit the ground."

"And you left Beth lying there while you got rid of his body?" I asked, more accusation than question.

Johnny nodded, just once. "I checked her and she seemed to be breathing okay so I figured she's just got knocked out. I thought it would be easier for her if he just disappeared, like I did, or at the very least if she could believe he died somewhere else. I wrapped him up in the tarp and put him in my cart. I got him down to the lake and rolled him in. It was full dark by then and nobody saw me. I left my rig at the lake and went back to see after Beth, but she was gone. Then you," he said, flipping a hand in Tony's direction, "came roaring up on that bike of yours and I figured she must've called you and she was okay."

"What did you do then?" I prompted.

"Well, I had to figure out how to get rid of that tarpaulin. It had blood all over it and I didn't want it pointing the way back to Beth's house. I remembered a young fella I know with a landscaping business. I think you know him. I'd seen his crews at work and knew how they did things so I folded the tarp and later that night I slipped it in with the others at his greenhouse."

"I'm no lawyer," Tony said, "but that sounds like self-defense to me."

"You don't understand, boy," Johnny said harshly. "I don't give a rip what they call it. I don't care about going to jail, or burning in hell, for that matter. And anyhow the way these things draw out I'll be dead and gone before I see the inside of a courthouse. I just don't want my last days to be about all that. And I don't want Beth thinking I'm a murderer. Last I heard she couldn't remember anything about that night and I'm hoping it'll stay that way."

"She's remembered enough," I said. "She knows someone was there and it's only a matter of time before she remembers the rest."

Johnny nodded. "All right, then. There it is. It's all over for me. You can call the cops on me."

"I'll call Detective Carlson and you can tell him your story, but we need to make a stop along the way. I don't want Olivia, Beth, or Daniel hearing this from the news."

I dropped Tony at my house so he could fill Esme in and also because he still didn't want Beth to realize he knew about the abuse. I drove on to Olivia's and, by some convivial trick of fate, found Olivia, Beth, and Daniel all there. I had Johnny wait in the car while I told them everything. I asked if they wanted to see him, but they were all too much in shock to even formulate a question—much to Johnny's relief.

*   *   *

The morning newspaper carried the story, or *a* story—the one he and I had settled on as we drove to meet Denny. The essentials were:

> *Charlie Martin, an elderly World War II veteran, suffering from dementia and a previously undiagnosed case of post-traumatic stress syndrome, had misinterpreted something Blaine Branch said that fateful evening when they'd encountered one another as night was falling. Martin had believed himself under threat. He had no memory of the altercation or what had transpired until recent days when the details started to come back to him. Martin turned himself in to the police and is now at the regional Veterans' Hospital undergoing testing and evaluation. A sad end to a tragic story. Branch's widow could not be reached for comment.*

twenty-four

A FEW WEEKS LATER ESME AND I ATTENDED THE WEIRDEST, most awkward, most poignant, most painful, most mind-bending family reunion imaginable. Olivia, Johnny, Beth, and Daniel hashed through many things that had happened over the past sixty-plus years.

Both Beth and Johnny had asked Esme and me to be there, probably to buffer the friction of raw emotions. But we were woefully inadequate to the task. Sitting on a plastic chair in the small, antiseptic hospital room, with all of us gathered around Johnny's bed, was like being inside a pinball machine gone berserk. Thoughts and feelings came pinging from all directions and the impulse was to duck and cover.

If this had been a made-for-TV movie there would have been a gush of sentimentality and forgiveness all around and everyone would have dissolved into a sappy puddle of tears and smiles. This gathering was sapless. No old family recipe exchanges or reminiscences about Easter egg hunts at Grandma's house or trips to the beach. They don't make a greeting card for *thanks for leaving before you killed my mother*. And as apologists go, Johnny Hargett was a sorry specimen, no pun intended.

"I said I'd tell you anything you want to know; I owe you that," Johnny said to Olivia, rubbing at a two-day growth of gray stubble on his cheek. "And I want you to know I'll tell the whole truth, nothing but. You won't likely thank me for it 'cause none of it's pretty. The first thing I want you to understand is I know your mama was special. And I loved her, I did," he said, giving one slow nod. "She saw something in me that made me want to be a good man." He waved a blue-veined hand. "But it was too late. I was broke and I didn't know how to fix myself and she trusted me too much. And the better she was to me the more of a danger I was to her. I saw plain I had to get away from her to save her."

Olivia let out a deep sigh. "You know you caused a lot of hurt and a lot of pain and guilt by the way you left. I've read Aunt Celestine's diaries. Uncle Riley lived out his days thinking he'd killed you."

Johnny's lips set into a thin line. The air seemed to grow thicker as we all waited. "Well," he said finally, "I hate that Riley and Celestine suffered and I'm not pleased about all of you being shamed by what people had to say about why I left, neither. But the truth of it was worse. And I'll say it right out, I'd do it the same way again if that's how it had to be. Renny stayed safe and that was what mattered. And Riley would tell you the same if he could."

"That's true," Esme whispered, her head tilted over close to mine. "That's what Riley says."

I looked her a question, rolling my eyes toward the ceiling. She gave a nod.

"Where were you all those years?" Olivia asked.

"All over," Johnny said, shrugging a bony shoulder. "Me and Hershel rode the rails for a while and that was all right, but it didn't suit me. I was always getting into scrapes with the other hobos and without anything to live for I got reckless. Then Hershel talked me into joining the army and that got me straightened out. After a few trips to the brig I finally learned some discipline. Then the war taught me some more lessons. I re-upped when I got back stateside. The army was a good place for me; it kept me away from regular people. But I'd take leave every few years to come back and check on you and Renny and see how you were getting on. I was hoping Renny would find a good man and remarry, but I guess I ruined that idea for her for good and all."

"So you were spying on us during all that time?" Olivia asked.

Johnny frowned. "I wouldn't call it spying. I just wanted to know you were okay."

Silence fell and everyone began examining their shoes, the tree outside the small window, or the medical equipment. I searched my mind for something to say that would help move things along, but nothing came to me. The silence went on for what seemed an interminable time, then finally Beth blurted, "You killed my husband."

It wasn't an accusation, just a statement. Johnny responded in kind. "I did," he said, "and given the circumstances facing us that day I'd do the same thing again. He would have killed you. If not that day, then some other day when something in his brain misfired. Now, I don't doubt he loved you, but it was a crooked love, all twisted and tangled and mean. I know about that. 'Course, there's them that would say that's no kind of love at all, and maybe it's not. I'm not the one to say. Anyhow, I said I'd tell the truth so I can't say I'm sorry I killed him, 'cause I'm not. You're here, alive and healthy and young. Not unscarred, I know that, but you can start again and have a good life; you've still got plenty of days ahead of you."

"I loved him, you know," Beth said, her eyes focused on something far away. "In the beginning I really loved him."

"Of course you did, Beth," Olivia said, putting an arm around her. "You did everything you could for him."

"Maybe someday some smart people will figure it all out," Johnny said. "This probably won't make any sense to you and it's a mystery to me, too, but you loving him probably made him ashamed. I expect he knew he wasn't worthy of it. I did. None of this is on you. That's what I wish I could tell Renny. That the sickness was mine and that leaving was the only loving thing I had to give her."

"She knows," Esme whispered again.

Johnny adjusted his position, trying to bring himself into a more upright position. Daniel located the remote and adjusted the bed.

"How about you, boy?" Johnny asked, looking up at him. "You got anything you want to ask?"

Daniel raised his eyebrows. "Nothing to ask," he said after a moment. "But something to say. I don't know how to feel about you or about any of this. On the one hand, I'm grateful to you for saving my sister's life. On the other hand your life isn't exactly a shining example of manhood. In fact I'd say you've caused a lot of people a lot of pain."

Johnny nodded solemnly. "All that's true and I'm not saying I don't have regrets; I've got plenty, but not a one of them is about anything that I've done here in Morningside. I never meant for any of you to know who I was or think of me as anything but an old handyman who was pretty good with flowers, but unfortunately for me, these two are too good at their job." He nodded toward Esme and me. "So it's got complicated."

"Well," Olivia said, "I have to admit that when we started out, I didn't have this view of my family history in mind, but despite everything I'm glad to know the truth. And maybe this is a way-out-there thought, but I'd like to believe that Mama, Uncle Riley, and Aunt Celestine are all resting easier now that I know the whole story."

"Um-hm, they are," Esme whispered. "Well, Celestine's still a little huffy, but she's getting there."

twenty-five

We all dressed in glittery finery for the gala event that was to take place in our glammed-up living room at eight o'clock in the evening on the first day of the new year, a day filled with the promise of better days ahead.

Tony Barrett, Morningside's own auteur, was our guest of honor for the pre-premiere of his Morningside documentary. The club had taken care of food and decorations and Olivia, Daniel, and Beth had joined us for the evening. Denny would also be along soon.

Everyone present now knew *almost* the whole story of how Blaine's death had come about, and though the abuse hadn't been spelled out, I was sure they'd all figured it out. But after all these months it hadn't leaked. I didn't think it would—ever—without Beth's okay.

It was over.

Jennifer Jeffers had been so happy to close the case, she'd accepted everything at face value and shut the file tight before anyone could muck it up for her with wonky details.

Out of deference to Denny's career, we hadn't told him everything. I had absolutely no doubt he was aware there was plenty that people weren't telling, but he trusts us all enough to know this way is better.

I hope Esme appreciated that. She and Denny had been drawing steadily closer. I had a feeling there would be an announcement of something more permanent soon—assuming Esme didn't throw it all away. She still maintained she'd have to give Denny up rather than tell him about her gift. But I had my own intuition on this one. Denny was smart and observant and I was willing to bet he already knew more than he let on. And I'd made up my mind that if she cut him loose I was going to tell him why and I'd told her so. She says blackmail; I say sharing.

Esme blusters a lot, but she's developed quite a soft spot for Tony. She's practically adopted him. She'd loved his video scrapbook for Olivia so much she sent a copy to our client in Wilmington and got Tony the gig for that job. And she was already talking about pitching his services alongside our own.

A lot had happened in the past months. Johnny Hargett, true to his prediction, had not lived to face charges, much less a trial. He'd picked up a bronchial infection, which turned into pneumonia, and he passed away two days before Christmas, with Olivia, Beth, and Daniel at his bedside at the VA hospital. They'd jury-rigged some sort of relationship and while it wasn't exactly Hallmark-worthy, it was a good patch job to see Johnny through to the end and to help Olivia, Daniel, and, most of all, Beth find some understanding and forgiveness.

Beth had told me one reason she was so adamant about keeping quiet about the abuse was that Sterling Branch was seriously ill. Not even Peyton and Madison had known about it until after Christmas, when his doctors told him his treatments weren't working.

"There will come a time when I'll talk about this, and I'll use it to try to help other women," she told me now, alone in the kitchen. "But for now I want what's best for Sterling and Madeline. I want them to believe they lost the son they thought they knew, the one they mourned. And if Sterling doesn't make it through this, I want him to go out remembering a son he was proud of."

"What about Peyton?" I asked. "How do things stand with you two? Is he still harassing you?"

Beth chuffed a laugh. "Oh, Sophreena, he was never harassing me, just the opposite." She carefully folded a dish towel and hung it on the oven handle. "He'd been pushing me for months to get help, to go to the authorities and to leave Blaine. He wasn't trying to keep me quiet; he was trying to get me to tell. But I couldn't. Peyton didn't know about Sterling's illness and I couldn't tell him. Sterling and Madeline had asked me to keep it in strictest confidence, even from their children—especially from their children. The situation with Madison was already volatile and Sterling was afraid Blaine might challenge his competence to handle his own affairs if he learned Sterling was ill. It was all a big mess."

"So you really were in an impossible situation. But what I still don't understand is why Peyton made that false confession."

"To protect me," Beth said with a sigh. "That day when I told you I'd remembered something and that I thought maybe I'd hurt Blaine, or maybe even killed him, Peyton just reacted. He made that very gallant, but extremely *stupid,* gesture to protect me. He knew firsthand how bad it had gotten. He walked into the middle of it once, and Blaine didn't bother to put on his charming act when Peyton was around. I guess he thought his brother would be on his side about everything."

"But he wasn't," I said.

"No, not on this, and not about the situation with Madison. It infuriated Blaine that he couldn't control his younger brother like he'd done when they were growing up. He didn't like it when Peyton stood up to him. Peyton tried to talk to Blaine several times about his demands and his outbursts toward me, but he wouldn't listen. In fact, that's what he and Alan were planning when they drove Blaine to The Sporting Life that morning; they were trying to trap him into an intervention of some kind, make him take a hard look at himself. They'd planned to take him out in the boat so he couldn't walk away, but he caught on. He got angry once he realized what they were up to. He threw a kayak paddle at Alan. It barely missed his head and flew into the lake. Alan could have been seriously hurt."

"So if they were of like mind about that, what was all the tension between Alan and Peyton?"

"Oh, they're all squared up with each other now. But back then Peyton was still pushing me relentlessly to come forward, to tell and get out of the marriage. But I couldn't and I couldn't tell him why. Alan knew because he'd done the legal work for Sterling for Madison's trust. He was trying to get Peyton to let up on me, but, of course, he couldn't tell him the whole story, either. Alan's been a good friend to me."

"Just a friend?" I asked. "Sorry, that's none of my business."

"He's *just* a friend," Beth said smiling. "Alan doesn't feel that way about me. It's Bonnie he's got his eye on, even if she doesn't realize it yet. But I expect she'll know soon. He's planning to move to Morningside to open a law practice within the year."

"How about the store? What's going to happen with it? With Bonnie?"

Beth sighed. "The way it was set up, half ownership reverts to me, and I'm very happy to leave running the place to her. She's always been the smarts of the equation, and the heart, too. I think we'll get on fine. We might even become real friends now. At least I hope so."

"And Peyton?" I asked, sensing there was more there than she was telling. "How do things stand with you two now?"

Beth stared out the kitchen to our backyard, which was shrouded in a mist of cold rain. "Peyton's being very supportive, very tender and caring. It's nice. I definitely married the wrong brother."

"It's not too late," I said.

Beth gave her head a small shake. "It's too complicated," she said. "Despite everything, Peyton and I are both still grieving. Blaine was my husband and I said for better or worse. I never dreamed what the worst would be, but still, I made the vow and I tried with everything I had to honor it. Peyton grew up idolizing Blaine and at one time they were close as brothers could be. I think he lost him twice: once when he found out what Blaine was doing to me, and again when he was killed. We've both got a long way to go before we can come to terms with it all. But for now it's nice to have a friend who knows everything and who supports me in my decisions. And now that he and Madison know about Sterling's condition, he gets why I don't want it to come out just now and he's in total agreement."

As we carried the plates of cookies and cakes to the dessert table, I glimpsed Winston and Marydale out in the yard with Sprocket and Gadget. They were sharing an umbrella, talking animatedly as they waited for the dogs to do their business. I still hadn't figured out what was going on with them, and I was getting heartsick about it. Even Jack had finally noticed that they seemed distant somehow.

Jennifer Jeffers, in a rare fit of altruism, had come on duty early to spell Denny so he could join us. As soon as he arrived we lined up to serve our plates and took them to the living room, where Esme and I had set up every tray table and end table we could beg or borrow. It was our humble version of dinner theater.

After we were all gathered, Daniel tapped his glass to get our attention. "I have an announcement and I wanted you all to be the first to know," he said, lifting his water glass. "If all goes well, next New Year's Day I hope you will all be my guests at my new restaurant, which I intend to call"—he paused for effect, then lifted his glass toward his mother—"*Olivia's.*" We toasted and promised to be regular customers, then launched a salvo of questions about the menu, locale, and décor. We learned that he was working with Madison

Branch on designs for the interior. That seemed to have a nice symmetry.

My expectations for Tony's Morningside film were high. I'd seen enough of his work to know he was a talented guy, and on a personal level I'd come to think of him as the little brother I never had. But his depiction of my hometown took my breath away. It wasn't a fluff piece or a travelogue. It was a hard but respectful look at community life in this particular small town. It explored the dual themes of how the town shapes the people and how the people shape the town.

When the lights came up there was silence in the room, until Marydale finally broke it. "I am so happy I live in Morningside," she said, swiping at tears. "And I am so happy you are all my friends."

Sprocket, sensing something wrong with his mistress, started jumping up on her legs. She reached down to scoop him up and cradled him in her lap. Marydale turned to Winston. "I can't stand this anymore. I know what I said earlier, but I can't stand it another minute."

Winston gave her a smile. "Well, good then. Go right on ahead."

Marydale looked around the room. "I feel like Winston and me have been cheating on y'all. We've been spending a lot of time together lately, just the two of us, I mean. And we've found out we're sort of—" She seemed to be stuck for words.

"Been bit by the love bug," Winston said, smiling over at Marydale, who actually blushed like a schoolgirl.

"I'm sorry we sneaked around, but we didn't want anybody acting different around us. We haven't even told our kids yet," Marydale said. "We wanted to take it slow to make sure."

"But not too slow," Winston said. "I'm not gettin' any younger and life is short. When you find a good thing you need to latch on to it."

The room erupted into laughter and congratulations. Marydale and Winston were besieged with hugs. I looked across the room and found Jack staring at me. He raised his eyebrows and tilted his head. It was a questioning look.

I dared hope I was interpreting the question correctly. Because if it meant what I thought it did, I had the answer ready.